KT-570-141

USBORNE INTERNET-LINKED

GERMAN DICTIONARY FOR BEGINNERS

Helen Davies
Illustrated by John Shackell
Designed by Brian Robertson
Edited by Nicole Irving

Language c e Kornmüller
Additional desig and Sarah Cronin
Editor Daynes

KT-0667868-8
WITHDRAWN

Contents

3 Usborne Quicklinks
4 Meeting people
6 Families
8 Appearance and personality
10 Your body
12 Houses and homes
14 Dining room and living room
15 In the kitchen
16 In the garden
18 Pets
20 Getting up
22 Clothes
24 Going to bed
26 Eating and drinking
28 Buying food
32 Pastimes
36 Going out
38 At the zoo and in the park
40 In the city
42 Shopping
46 At the post office and bank
48 Phonecalls and letters
50 Out and about
52 Driving
54 Travelling by train
56 Travelling by plane and boat
58 Holidays
62 In the countryside
64 On the farm
66 At work
68 Illness and health
70 School and education
74 Shapes and sizes
75 Numbers
76 Sport
78 Celebrations
80 Days and dates
82 Time
84 Weather and seasons
86 World and universe
88 Politics
90 Describing things
92 Colours
93 In, on, under...
94 Action words
96 Grammar hints
106 Phrase explainer
109 English-German word list

About nouns

German nouns are either masculine, feminine or neuter (this is called their gender). "The" is **der** for a masculine word, **die** for a feminine word and **das** for a neuter word. In the plural, the word for "the" is **die**, whatever the gender of the noun. The following abbreviations are sometimes used to make the gender and number clear: **(f)** feminine, **(m)** masculine, **(n)** neuter, **(s)** singular, **(pl)** plural. In German, nouns that describe what people do or are (e.g. dancer) often have a masculine and a feminine form. Both forms are given in the word list at the back of this book. Look out for letters in brackets after a noun. You add these letters to make the plural form. Sometimes, you also add an umlaut (¨) over the vowel.

About adjectives

German adjectives take different endings depending on the noun they are describing and the job it does in the sentence. You can find out more about this on page 98 of the grammar section. It is best to learn the simple form of the adjective without any ending, so this is the form given in the picture labels and word boxes.

About verbs

Verbs in this book appear in the infinitive (e.g. "to hide" in English). In German, the infinitive always ends in **en**. There are two kinds of German verbs, weak verbs and strong verbs. These verbs have different patterns, which you can read about on page 100 of the grammar section.

Usborne Quicklinks

This book has its own Usborne Quicklinks Web site where you can listen to all the words and phrases read by a native German speaker.

To visit the Quicklinks Web site for this book, go to **www.usborne-quicklinks.com** and enter the keywords "german dictionary for beginners".

Listening to the words

To hear the words and phrases in this book, you will need your Web browser (e.g. Internet Explorer or Netscape Navigator) and a programme such as RealPlayer® or Windows® Media Player. These programmes are free and, if you don't already have one of them, you can download them from Usborne Quicklinks. Your computer also needs a sound card but most computers already have one.

Picture puzzles and useful Web sites

In Usborne Quicklinks you will also find German picture puzzles that you can print out for free, and links to lots of other useful Web sites where you can listen to German radio, brush up on your German grammar and find out more about the country and culture.

Disclaimer

The Usborne Quicklinks Web site contains links to external Web sites that do not belong to Usborne Publishing. The links are regularly reviewed and updated, but Usborne Publishing is not responsible for the content on any Web site other than its own. We recommend that children are supervised while on the Internet, that they do not use Internet Chat Rooms, and that you use Internet filtering software to block unsuitable material. Please ensure that children read and follow the safety guidelines displayed in Usborne Quicklinks. For more information, see the **Net Help** area on the Usborne Quicklinks Web site.

Windows® is a trademark of Microsoft Corporation, registered in the US and other countries.
RealPlayer® is a trademark of RealNetworks, Inc., registered in the US and other countries.

Meeting people

Hallo

Auf Wiedersehen

Bis bald.

küssen

der Mann

die Frau

die Hand schütteln

das Baby

der Junge

das Mädchen

Hallo	Hello	**der Mann(¨er)**	man
Auf Wiedersehen*	Goodbye	**die Frau(en)**	woman
Bis bald.	See you later.	**das Baby(s)**	baby
die Hand schütteln	to shake hands with	**der Junge(n)**	boy
		das Mädchen(-)	girl
küssen	to kiss		

vorstellen

treffen

Wie geht's?

Danke, gut.

die Freundin

der Freund

vorstellen	to introduce	**Wie geht's?**	How are you?
die Freundin(nen)	friend (f)	**Danke, gut.**	Very well, thank you.
der Freund(e)	friend (m)		
treffen	to meet		

* You can find the literal meaning of phrases and expressions in the Phrase explainer section on pages 106-9.

sich unterhalten	to chat
Ja	Yes
Nein	No
Das meine ich auch.	I agree.
sagen	to say
in Gelächter ausbrechen	to burst out laughing

der Name(n)	name
der Vorname(n)	first name
der Nachname(n)	surname
Wie heißt du?*	What's your name?
Ich heiße...	My name is...
Er heißt...	His name is...

das Alter(-)	age	**alt**	old
Wie alt bist du?	How old are you?	**älter als**	older than
Ich bin neunzehn.	I'm nineteen	**jünger als**	younger than
jung	young	**genauso alt wie**	the same age as

* ß is a German letter which stands for ss.

Families

die Familie(n)	family	**die Großmutter(¨)**	grandmother
der Vater(¨)	father	**die Tante(n)**	aunt
die Mutter(¨)	mother	**der Onkel(-)**	uncle
der Bruder(¨)	brother	**die Kusine(n)**	cousin (f)
die Schwester(n)	sister	**der Vetter(n)**	cousin (m)
der Großvater(¨)	grandfather		

verwandt sein mit	to be related to	**die Enkelin(nen)**	granddaughter
der Sohn(¨e)	son	**lieb haben**	to be fond of
die Tochter(¨)	daughter	**der Neffe(n)**	nephew
aufziehen	to bring up	**die Nichte(n)**	niece
der Enkel(-)	grandson		

die Ehefrau(en)	wife
der Ehemann(¨er)	husband
die Eltern (pl)	parents
lieben	to love
die Kinder (s: das Kind)*	children
die Zwillinge (s: der Zwilling)*	twins
der einzige Sohn	only son

das Leben	life	**die Hochzeit(en)**	wedding
die Geburt(en)	birth	**arbeiten**	to work
geboren werden	to be born	**das Alter**	old age
die Kindheit	childhood	**der Tod**	death
die Ehe(n)	marriage	**sterben**	to die
heiraten	to get married	**die Beerdigung(en)**	funeral

* **Das Kind** and **der Zwilling** are the singular forms.

Appearance and personality

hübsch	pretty
gutaussehend	handsome
stark	strong
schwach	weak
dünn	thin
schlank	slim
dick	fat

blondes Haar haben	to have blond hair	**Locken**	curly hair
braunes Haar	brown hair	**der Pony(s)**	a fringe
rotes Haar	red hair	**die Zöpfe (pl)**	plaits
glattes Haar	straight hair	**eine Glatze haben**	to be bald

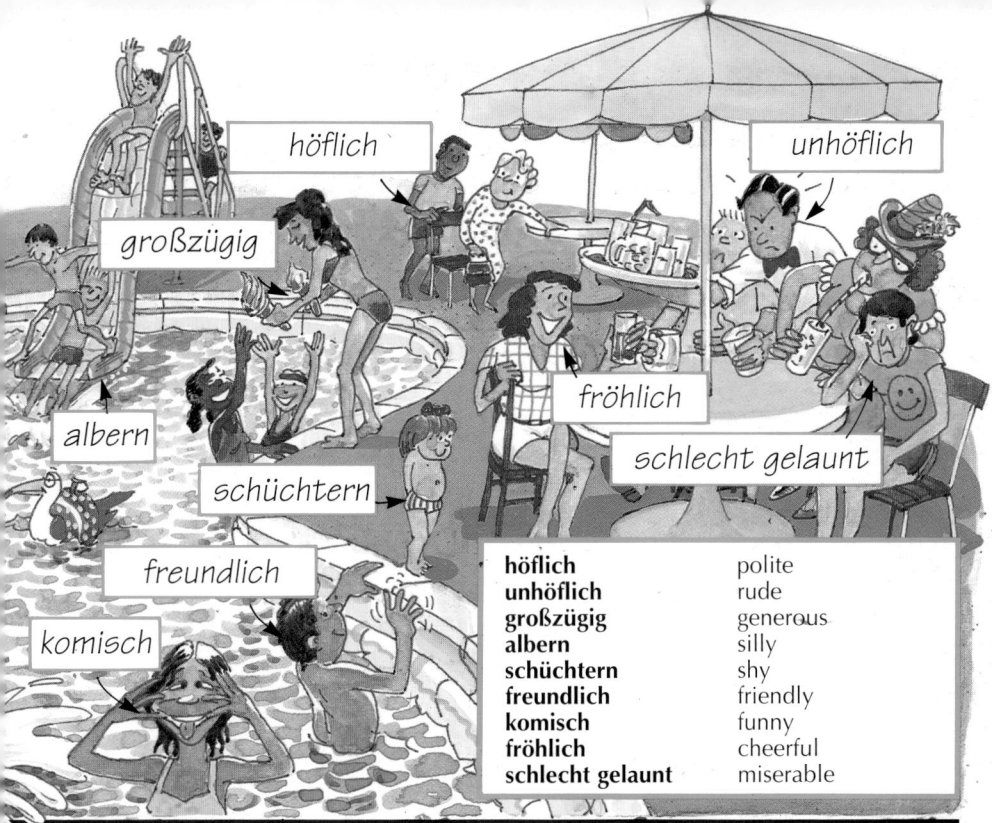

höflich	polite
unhöflich	rude
großzügig	generous
albern	silly
schüchtern	shy
freundlich	friendly
komisch	funny
fröhlich	cheerful
schlecht gelaunt	miserable

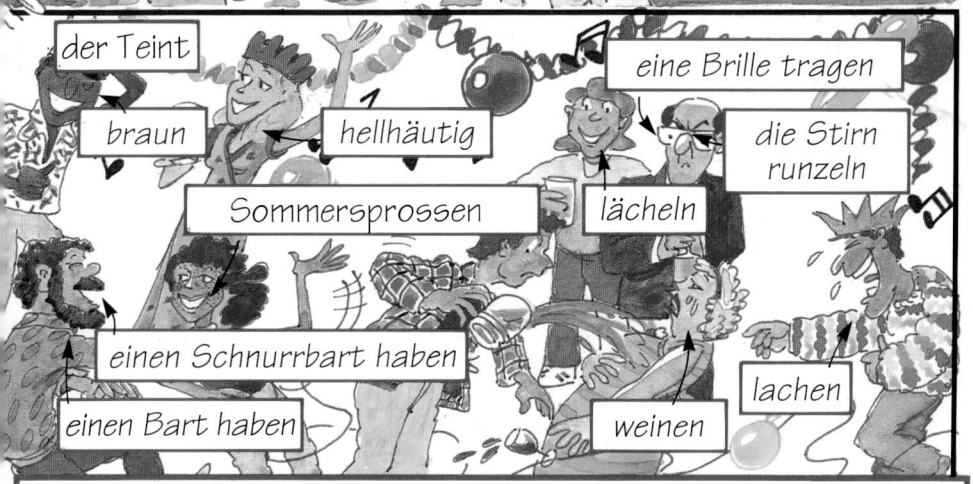

der Teint	complexion	**einen Bart haben**	to have a beard
braun	dark	**eine Brille tragen**	to wear glasses
hellhäutig	fair	**die Stirn runzeln**	to frown
Sommersprossen (pl)	freckles	**lächeln**	to smile
einen Schnurrbart haben	to have a moustache	**lachen**	to laugh
		weinen	to cry

Your body

der Kopf(¨e)	head
das Haar(e)	hair
das Gesicht(er)	face
die Haut	skin
das Auge(n)	eye
die Backe(n)	cheek
die Nase(n)	nose
das Ohr(en)	ear
der Mund(¨er)	mouth
der Zahn(¨e)	tooth
die Zunge(n)	tongue
die Lippe(n)	lip
der Hals(¨e)	neck
das Kinn(e)	chin

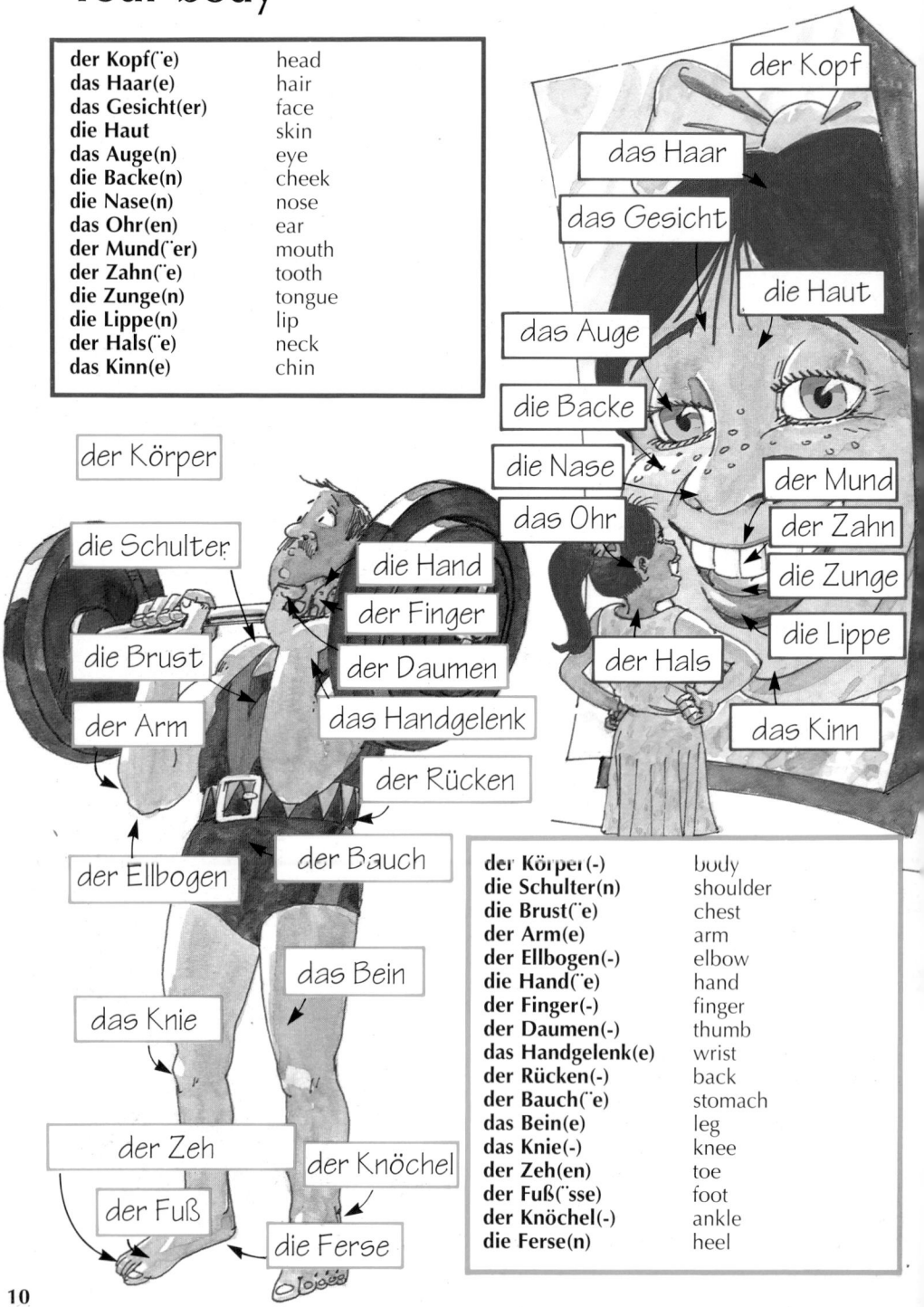

der Körper(-)	body
die Schulter(n)	shoulder
die Brust(¨e)	chest
der Arm(e)	arm
der Ellbogen(-)	elbow
die Hand(¨e)	hand
der Finger(-)	finger
der Daumen(-)	thumb
das Handgelenk(e)	wrist
der Rücken(-)	back
der Bauch(¨e)	stomach
das Bein(e)	leg
das Knie(-)	knee
der Zeh(en)	toe
der Fuß(¨sse)	foot
der Knöchel(-)	ankle
die Ferse(n)	heel

groß sein	to be tall
klein sein	to be short
sich wiegen	to weigh yourself
leicht sein	to be light
schwer sein	to be heavy

die linke Seite	left side
die rechte Seite	right side

barfuß gehen	to walk barefoot
aufstehen	to stand up
stehen	to be standing
sich hinknien	to kneel down
knien	to be kneeling
sich hinlegen	to lie down
liegen	to be lying down
sich setzen	to sit down
sitzen	to be sitting down

Houses and homes

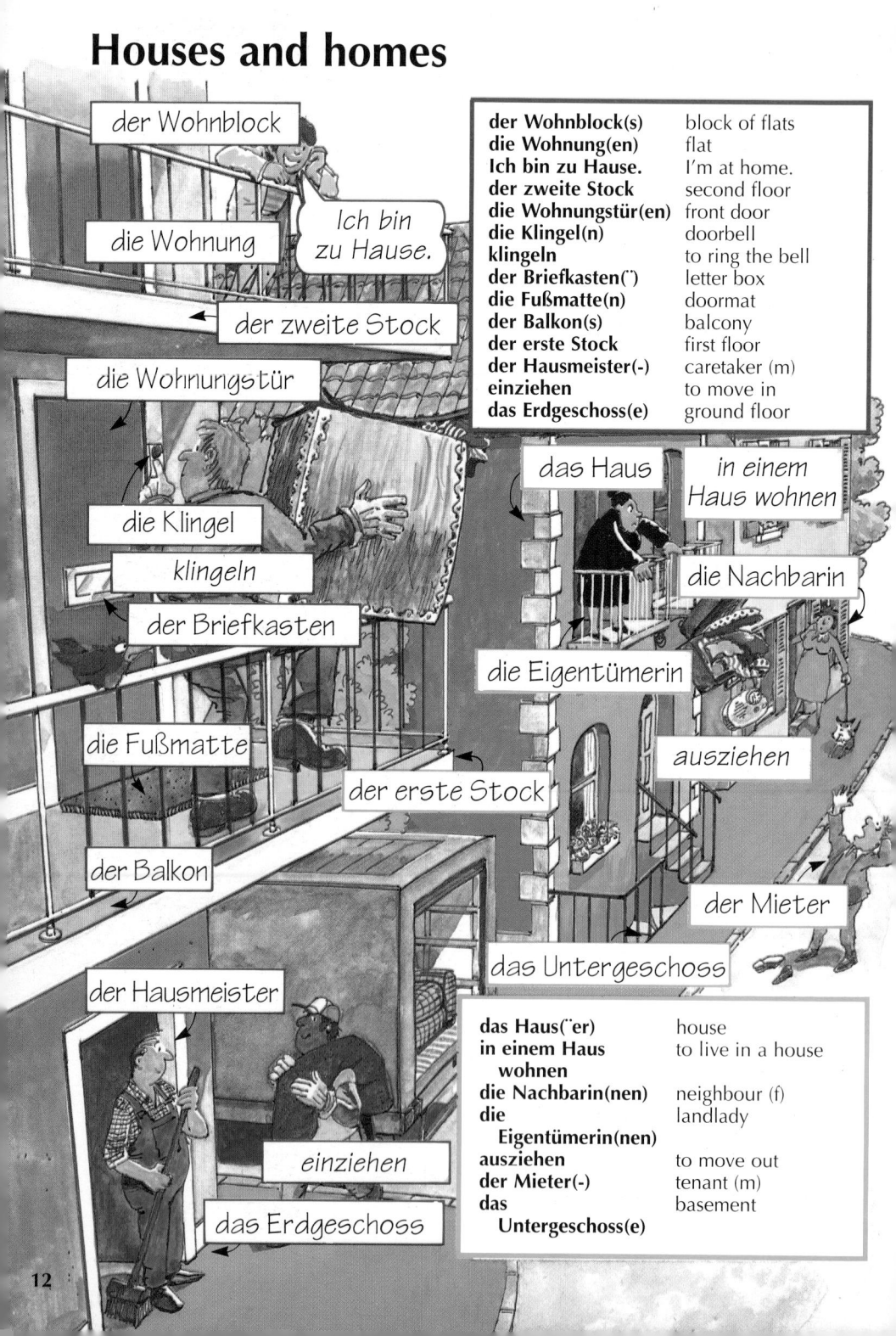

der Wohnblock(s)	block of flats
die Wohnung(en)	flat
Ich bin zu Hause.	I'm at home.
der zweite Stock	second floor
die Wohnungstür(en)	front door
die Klingel(n)	doorbell
klingeln	to ring the bell
der Briefkasten(¨)	letter box
die Fußmatte(n)	doormat
der Balkon(s)	balcony
der erste Stock	first floor
der Hausmeister(-)	caretaker (m)
einziehen	to move in
das Erdgeschoss(e)	ground floor

das Haus(¨er)	house
in einem Haus wohnen	to live in a house
die Nachbarin(nen)	neighbour (f)
die Eigentümerin(nen)	landlady
ausziehen	to move out
der Mieter(-)	tenant (m)
das Untergeschoss(e)	basement

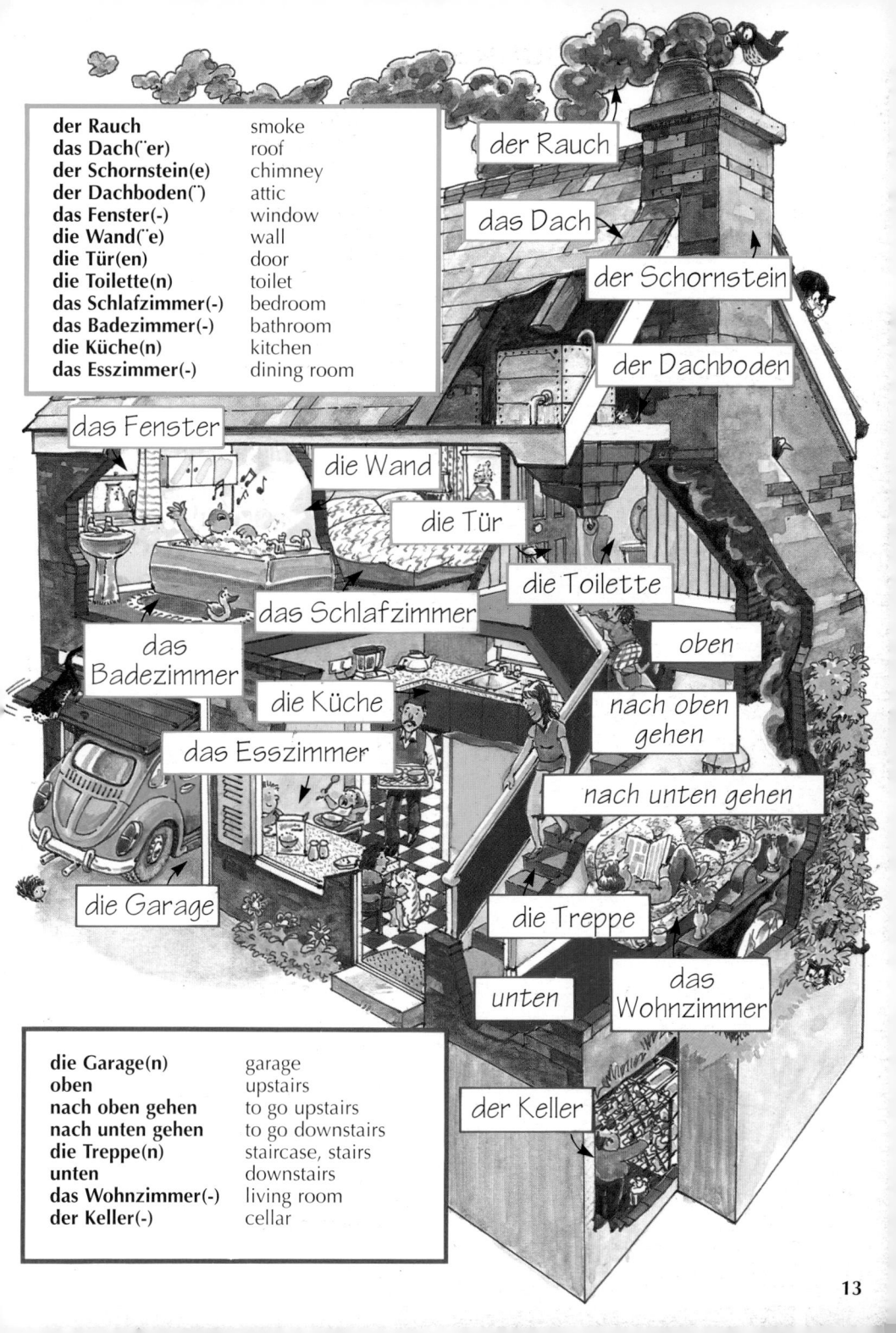

der Rauch	smoke
das Dach(¨er)	roof
der Schornstein(e)	chimney
der Dachboden(¨)	attic
das Fenster(-)	window
die Wand(¨e)	wall
die Tür(en)	door
die Toilette(n)	toilet
das Schlafzimmer(-)	bedroom
das Badezimmer(-)	bathroom
die Küche(n)	kitchen
das Esszimmer(-)	dining room

die Garage(n)	garage
oben	upstairs
nach oben gehen	to go upstairs
nach unten gehen	to go downstairs
die Treppe(n)	staircase, stairs
unten	downstairs
das Wohnzimmer(-)	living room
der Keller(-)	cellar

Dining room and living room

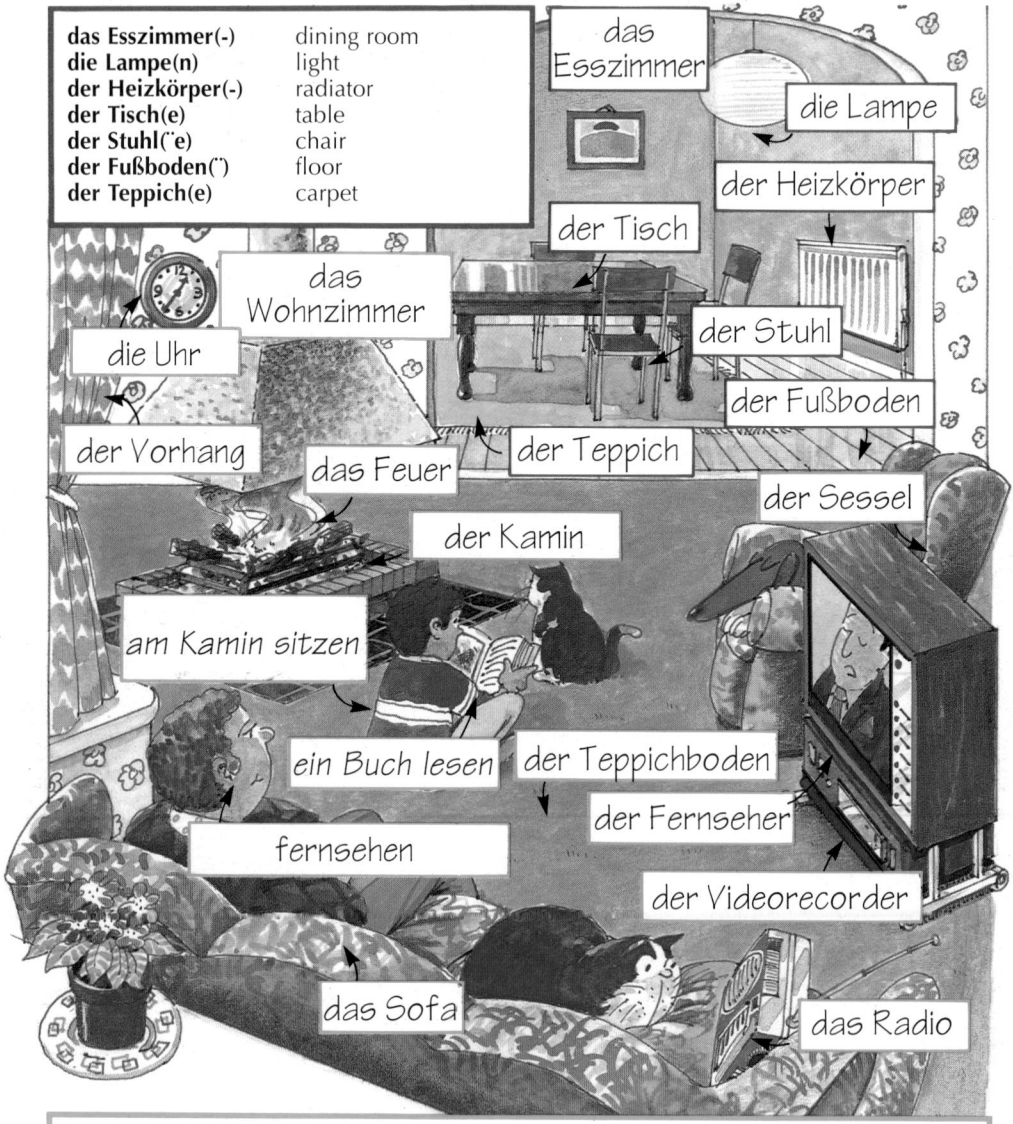

das Esszimmer(-)	dining room
die Lampe(n)	light
der Heizkörper(-)	radiator
der Tisch(e)	table
der Stuhl(¨e)	chair
der Fußboden(¨)	floor
der Teppich(e)	carpet

das Wohnzimmer(-)	living room
die Uhr(en)	clock
der Vorhang(¨e)	curtain
das Feuer(-)	fire
der Kamin(e)	fireplace
der Sessel(-)	armchair
am Kamin sitzen	to sit by the fire
ein Buch lesen	to read a book
das Sofa(s)	sofa
fernsehen	to watch television
der Teppichboden(¨)	fitted carpet
der Fernseher(-)	television
der Videorecorder(-)	video
das Radio(s)	radio

In the kitchen

die Küche(n)	kitchen
der Küchenschrank(¨e)	cupboard
die Waschmaschine(n)	washing machine
waschen	to do the washing
der Kühlschrank(¨e)	fridge

der Backofen(¨)	oven	**staubsaugen**	to vacuum
kochen	to cook	**abwaschen**	to wash up
der Kochtopf(¨e)	saucepan	**schmutzig**	dirty
das Gas	gas	**die Spüle(n)**	sink
der Mülleimer(-)	bin	**abtrocknen**	to dry, to wipe
bügeln	to iron	**das Geschirrtuch(¨er)**	tea towel
der Stecker(-)	plug	**sauber**	clean
der Strom	electricity		

In the garden

im Garten arbeiten	to do the gardening
der Rasen(-)	lawn
der Weg(e)	path
das Blumenbeet(e)	flowerbed
der Gärtner(-)	gardener (m)
der Rasenmäher(-)	lawnmower
den Rasen mähen	to mow the lawn
das Gemüsebeet(e)	vegetable patch
die Erde	soil
das Gras	grass

das Gewächshaus(¨er)	greenhouse
die Wäscheleine(n)	washing line
die Wäscheklammer(n)	clothes peg
der Baum(¨e)	tree
der Vogel(¨)	bird
das Nest(er)	nest
der Strauch(¨er)	bush
der Schatten(-)	shade

die Biene
der Schmetterling
die Rose
duftend
bunt
die Wespe
stechen
die Dahlie
die Geranie
die Tulpe
die Osterglocke
das Vergissmeinnicht
der Blumensamen
das Unkraut
pflanzen
die Blumenzwiebel
Unkraut jäten

die Biene(n)	bee	**die Tulpe(n)**	tulip
der Schmetterling(e)	butterfly	**das Vergissmeinnicht(-)**	forget-me-not
die Wespe(n)	wasp	**die Osterglocke(n)**	daffodil
stechen	to sting	**der Blumensamen(-)**	seed
die Rose(n)	rose	**pflanzen**	to plant
duftend	sweet-smelling	**die Blumenzwiebel(n)**	bulb
bunt	colourful	**Unkraut jäten**	to weed
die Dahlie(n)	dahlia	**das Unkraut(¨er)**	weed
die Geranie(n)	geranium		

das Gartenhäuschen(-)	garden shed
die Schubkarre(n)	wheelbarrow
die Schaufel(n)	trowel
die Harke(n)	rake
der Spaten(-)	spade
die Gabel(n)	fork
die Gießkanne(n)	watering can

Pets

der Hund(e)	dog
die Hundehütte(n)	kennel
der junge Hund	puppy
das Fell	fur
die Pfote(n)	paw
verspielt	playful
bellen	to bark
VORSICHT BISSIGER HUND!	BEWARE OF THE DOG!
jagen	to chase
bringen	to fetch
der Schwanz(¨e)	tail
mit dem Schwanz wedeln	to wag its tail
knurren	to growl
den Hund ausführen	to take the dog for a walk

die Katze(n)	cat
der Korb(¨e)	basket
schnurren	to purr
das Kätzchen(-)	kitten
miauen	to mew
sich strecken	to stretch
die Kralle(n)	claw
weich	soft
süß	sweet

der Wellensittich(e)	budgie	**das Kaninchen(-)**	rabbit
hocken	to perch	**die Schildkröte(n)**	tortoise
der Flügel(-)	wing	**der Käfig(e)**	cage
der Schnabel(¨)	beak	**füttern**	to feed
die Feder(n)	feather	**der Goldfisch(e)**	goldfish
der Hamster(-)	hamster	**die Maus(¨e)**	mouse
der Igel(-)	hedgehog	**das Goldfischglas(¨er)**	goldfish bowl
das Meerschweinchen(-)	guinea pig		

Getting up

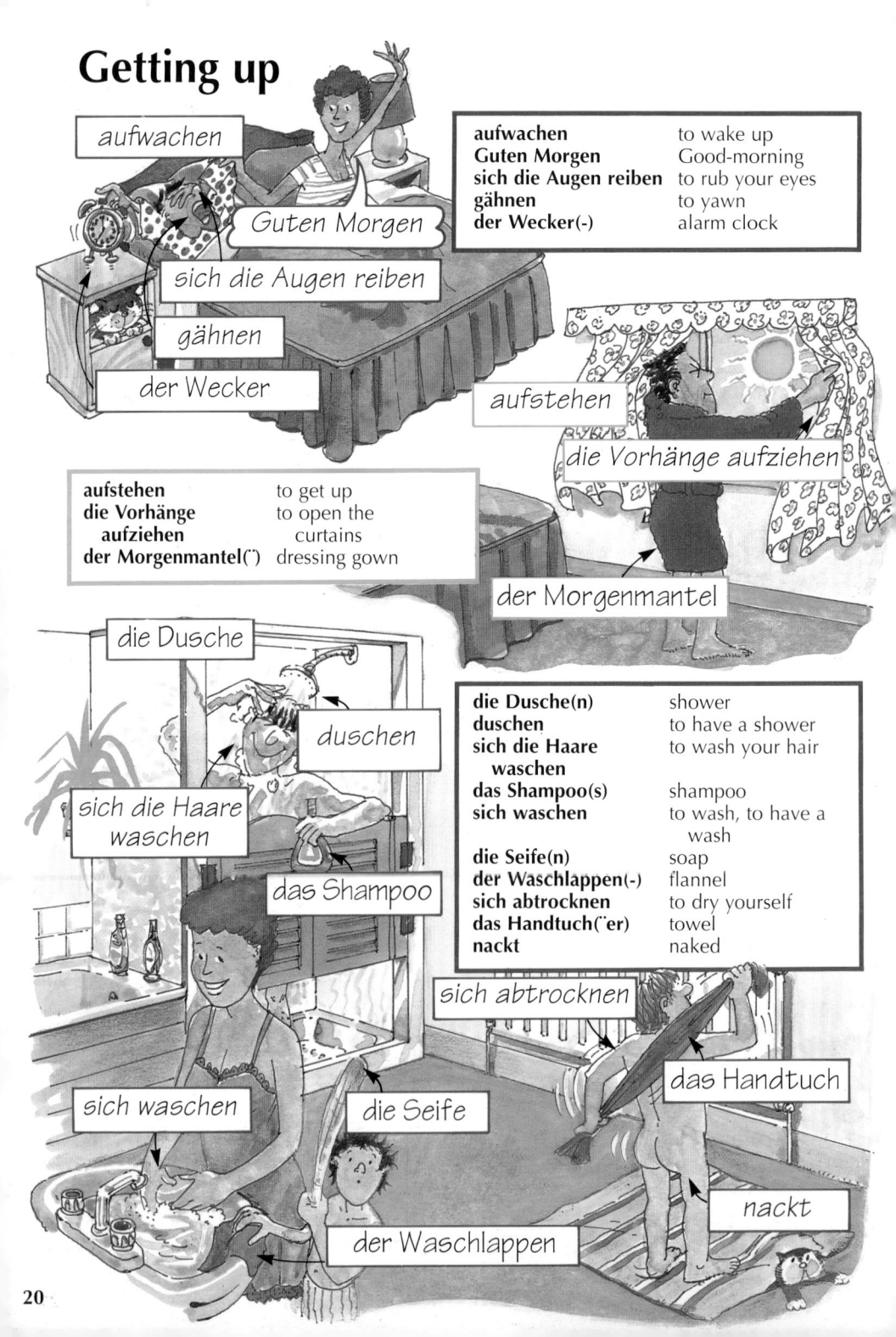

aufwachen	to wake up
Guten Morgen	Good-morning
sich die Augen reiben	to rub your eyes
gähnen	to yawn
der Wecker(-)	alarm clock

aufstehen	to get up
die Vorhänge aufziehen	to open the curtains
der Morgenmantel(¨)	dressing gown

die Dusche(n)	shower
duschen	to have a shower
sich die Haare waschen	to wash your hair
das Shampoo(s)	shampoo
sich waschen	to wash, to have a wash
die Seife(n)	soap
der Waschlappen(-)	flannel
sich abtrocknen	to dry yourself
das Handtuch(¨er)	towel
nackt	naked

sich rasieren	to shave
der Spiegel(-)	mirror
der elektrische Rasierapparat(e)	electric shaver
der Rasierapparat(e)	razor
der Rasierschaum	shaving foam

der Wasserhahn(¨e)	tap
heißes Wasser	hot water
kaltes Wasser	cold water
die Zahnpasta	toothpaste
die Zahnbürste(n)	toothbrush
sich die Zähne putzen	to clean your teeth

sich die Haare fönen	to dry your hair
der Fön(s)	hairdrier
die Haarbürste(n)	brush
der Kamm(¨e)	comb
sich die Haare kämmen	to comb your hair
sich die Haare bürsten	to brush your hair

sich schminken	to put on make-up
die Wimperntusche(n)	mascara
das Make-up(s)	foundation cream
der Lippenstift(e)	lipstick
das Parfüm(s)	perfume

Clothes

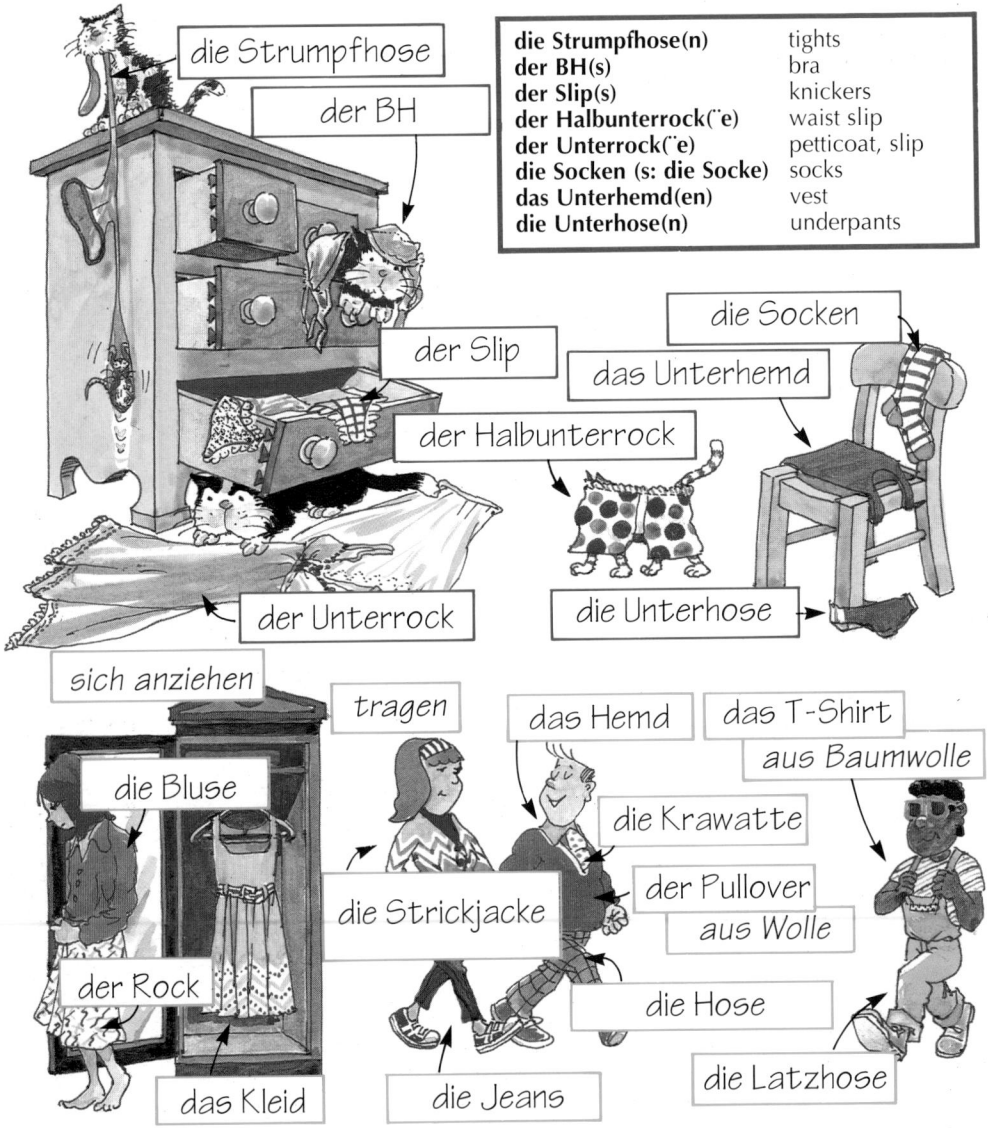

die Strumpfhose(n)	tights
der BH(s)	bra
der Slip(s)	knickers
der Halbunterrock(¨e)	waist slip
der Unterrock(¨e)	petticoat, slip
die Socken (s: die Socke)	socks
das Unterhemd(en)	vest
die Unterhose(n)	underpants

sich anziehen	to get dressed	**die Krawatte(n)**	tie
die Bluse(n)	blouse	**der Pullover(-)**	jumper
der Rock(¨e)	skirt	**aus Wolle**	woollen
das Kleid(er)	dress	**die Hose(n)**	trousers
tragen	to wear	**das T-Shirt(s)**	T-shirt
die Strickjacke(n)	cardigan	**aus Baumwolle**	cotton, made of cotton
die Jeans (pl)	jeans		
das Hemd(en)	shirt	**die Latzhose(n)**	dungarees

der Schmuck	jewellery
die Ohrringe (s: der Ohrring)	earrings
die Brosche(n)	brooch
das Armband(¨er)	bracelet
die Armbanduhr(en)	watch
der Ring(e)	ring
der Ehering(e)	wedding ring
die Halskette(n)	necklace

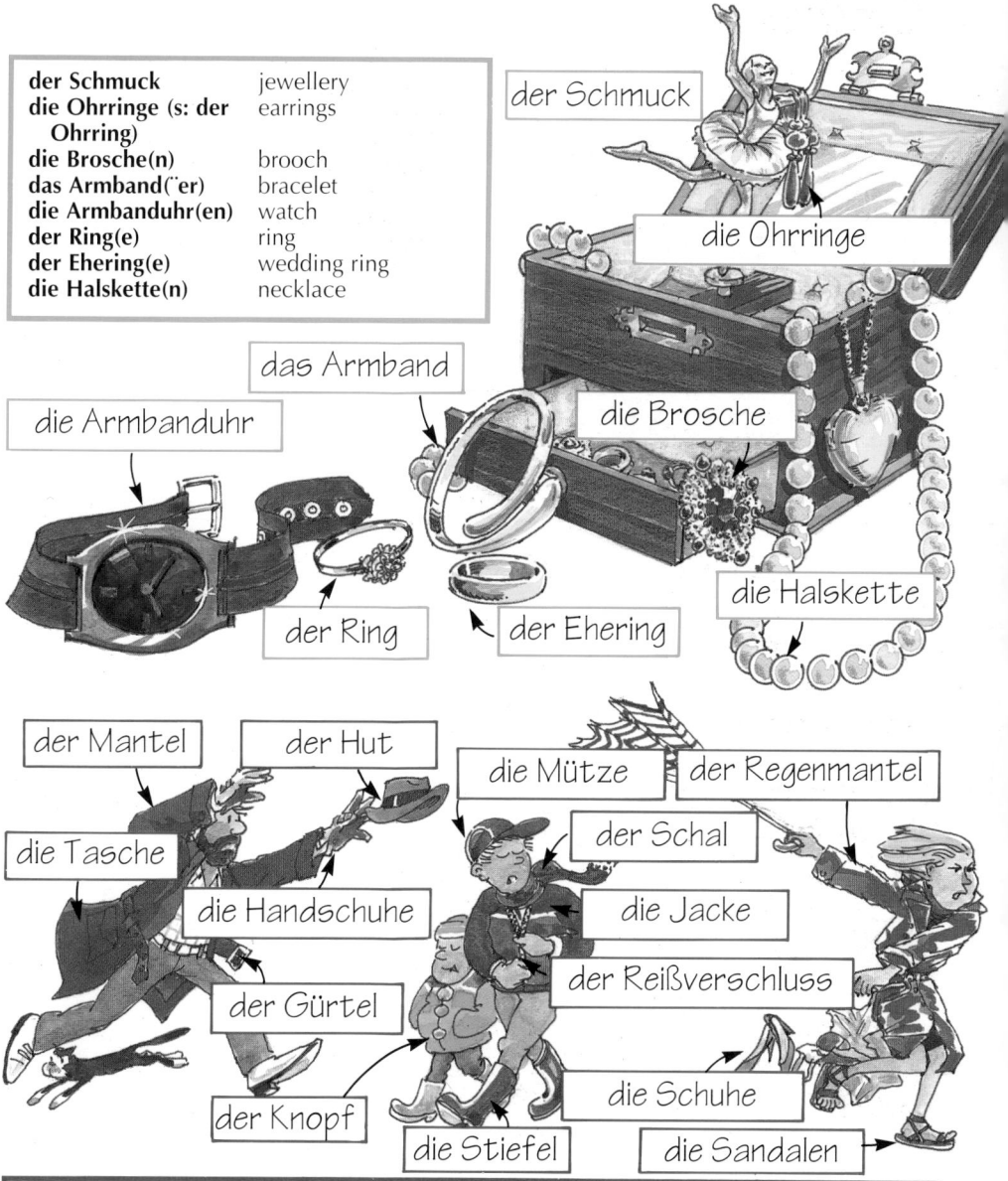

der Mantel(¨)	coat	**die Mütze(n)**	cap
der Hut(¨e)	hat	**der Regenmantel(¨)**	raincoat
die Tasche(n)	pocket	**der Schal(s)**	scarf
die Handschuhe (s: der Handschuh)	gloves	**die Jacke(n)**	jacket
		der Reißverschluss(e)	zip
der Gürtel(-)	belt	**die Schuhe (s: der Schuh)**	shoes
der Knopf(¨e)	button	**die Sandalen (s: die Sandale)**	sandals
die Stiefel (s: der Stiefel)	boots		

Going to bed

die Schlafenszeit	bedtime
das Licht anmachen	to switch the light on
schläfrig sein	to be sleepy
aufräumen	to tidy up
sich ausziehen	to get undressed

das Badewasser einlaufen lassen	to run a bath
ein Bad nehmen	to have a bath
die Badewanne(n)	bath
der Stöpsel(-)	plug
der Bademantel(¨)	bathrobe
spritzen	to splash
die Badematte(n)	bathmat
die Waage(n)	scales

ins Bett gehen	to go to bed
der Schlafanzug(¨e)	pyjamas
das Nachthemd(en)	nightdress
die Hausschuhe (s: der Hausschuh)	slippers

das Schlaflied(er)	lullaby
eine Geschichte vorlesen	to read a story
das Kinderbett(en)	cot
einschlafen	to fall asleep

Gute Nacht.	Good-night.	**das Federbett(en)**	duvet
Schlaf gut.	Sleep well.	**das Bett(en)**	bed
träumen	to dream	**schnarchen**	to snore
schlafen	to sleep	**das Kopfkissen(-)**	pillow
ausschalten	to switch off	**das Bettlaken(-)**	sheet
die Lampe(n)	lamp	**die Tagesdecke(n)**	bedspread
der Nachttisch(e)	bedside table		

Eating and drinking

den Tisch decken	to lay the table
Das Essen ist fertig.	It's ready.
die Kaffeekanne(n)	coffee-pot
die Teekanne(n)	teapot
die Serviette(n)	napkin
das Glas(¨er)	glass
die Suppentasse(n)	bowl
der Teller(-)	plate
die Tasse(n)	cup
die Untertasse(n)	saucer
die Tischdecke(n)	tablecloth
der Krug(¨e)	jug
der Löffel(-)	spoon
das Messer(-)	knife
die Gabel(n)	fork

Greif zu.	Help yourself.
Guten Appetit.	Enjoy your meal.
Durst haben	to be thirsty
trinken	to drink
Hunger haben	to be hungry
essen	to eat
Das schmeckt gut.	It tastes good.
gut gegessen haben	to have eaten well

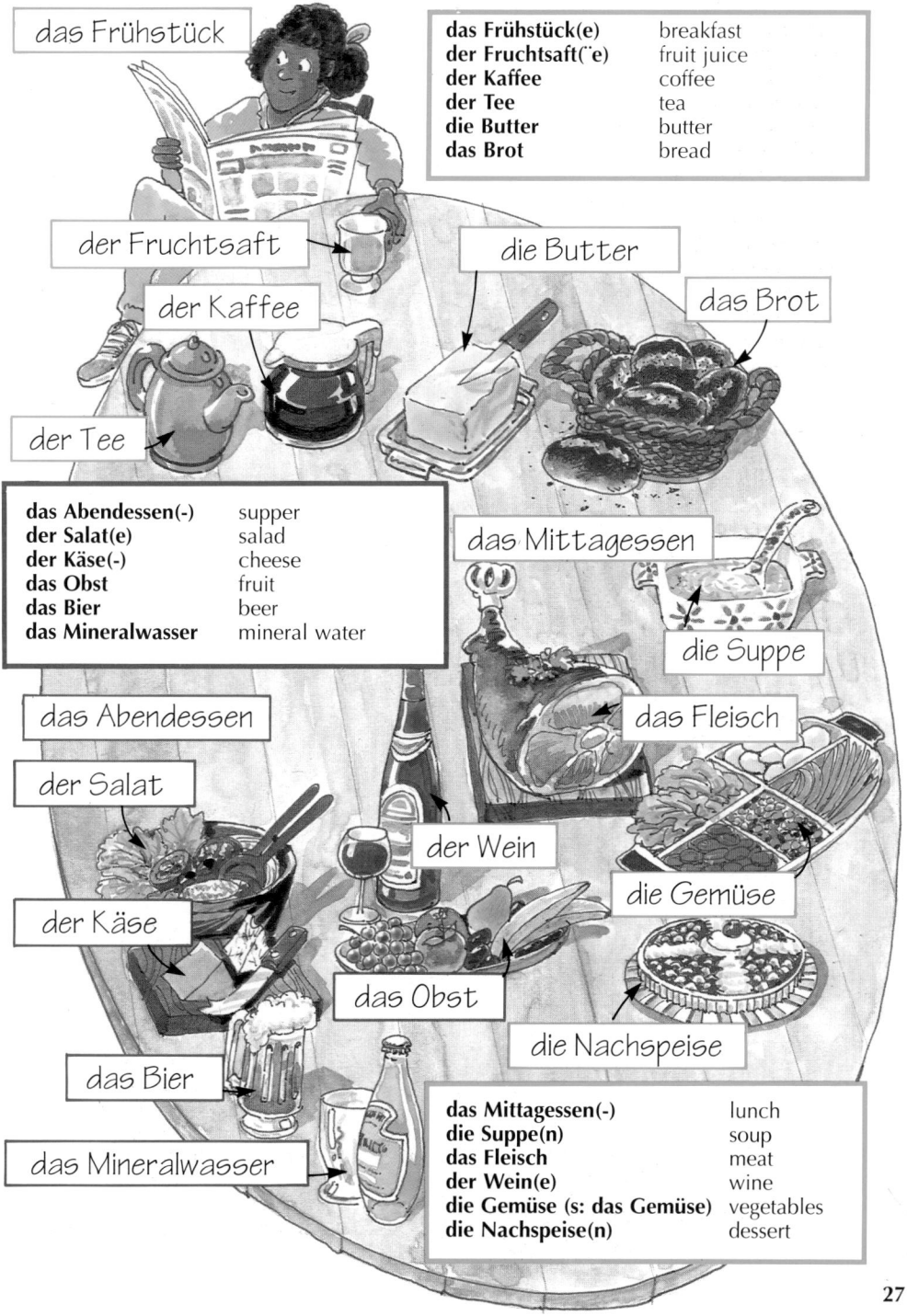

das Frühstück(e)	breakfast
der Fruchtsaft(¨e)	fruit juice
der Kaffee	coffee
der Tee	tea
die Butter	butter
das Brot	bread

das Abendessen(-)	supper
der Salat(e)	salad
der Käse(-)	cheese
das Obst	fruit
das Bier	beer
das Mineralwasser	mineral water

das Mittagessen(-)	lunch
die Suppe(n)	soup
das Fleisch	meat
der Wein(e)	wine
die Gemüse (s: das Gemüse)	vegetables
die Nachspeise(n)	dessert

Buying food

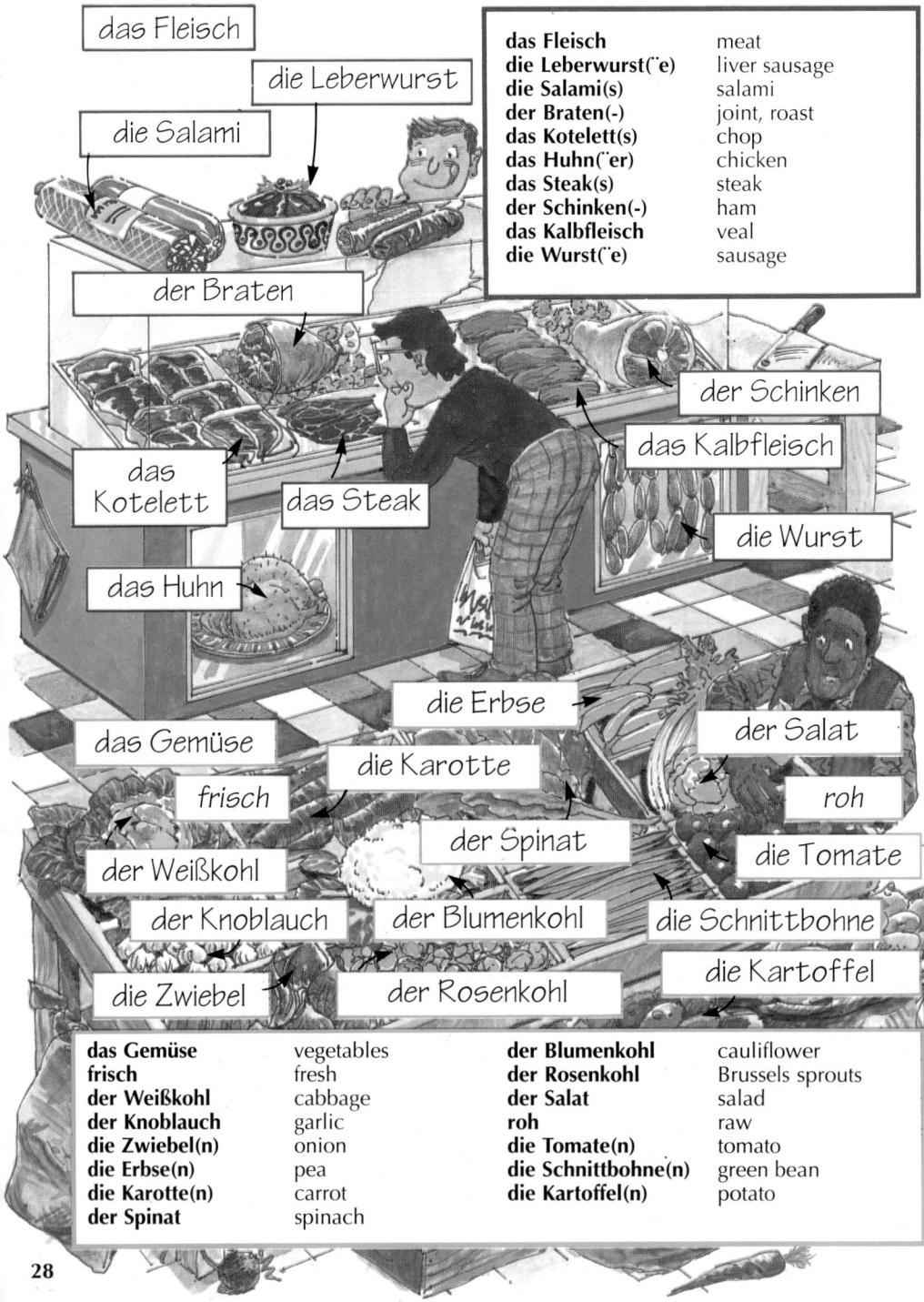

das Fleisch	meat
die Leberwurst(¨e)	liver sausage
die Salami(s)	salami
der Braten(-)	joint, roast
das Kotelett(s)	chop
das Huhn(¨er)	chicken
das Steak(s)	steak
der Schinken(-)	ham
das Kalbfleisch	veal
die Wurst(¨e)	sausage

das Gemüse	vegetables
frisch	fresh
der Weißkohl	cabbage
der Knoblauch	garlic
die Zwiebel(n)	onion
die Erbse(n)	pea
die Karotte(n)	carrot
der Spinat	spinach
der Blumenkohl	cauliflower
der Rosenkohl	Brussels sprouts
der Salat	salad
roh	raw
die Tomate(n)	tomato
die Schnittbohne(n)	green bean
die Kartoffel(n)	potato

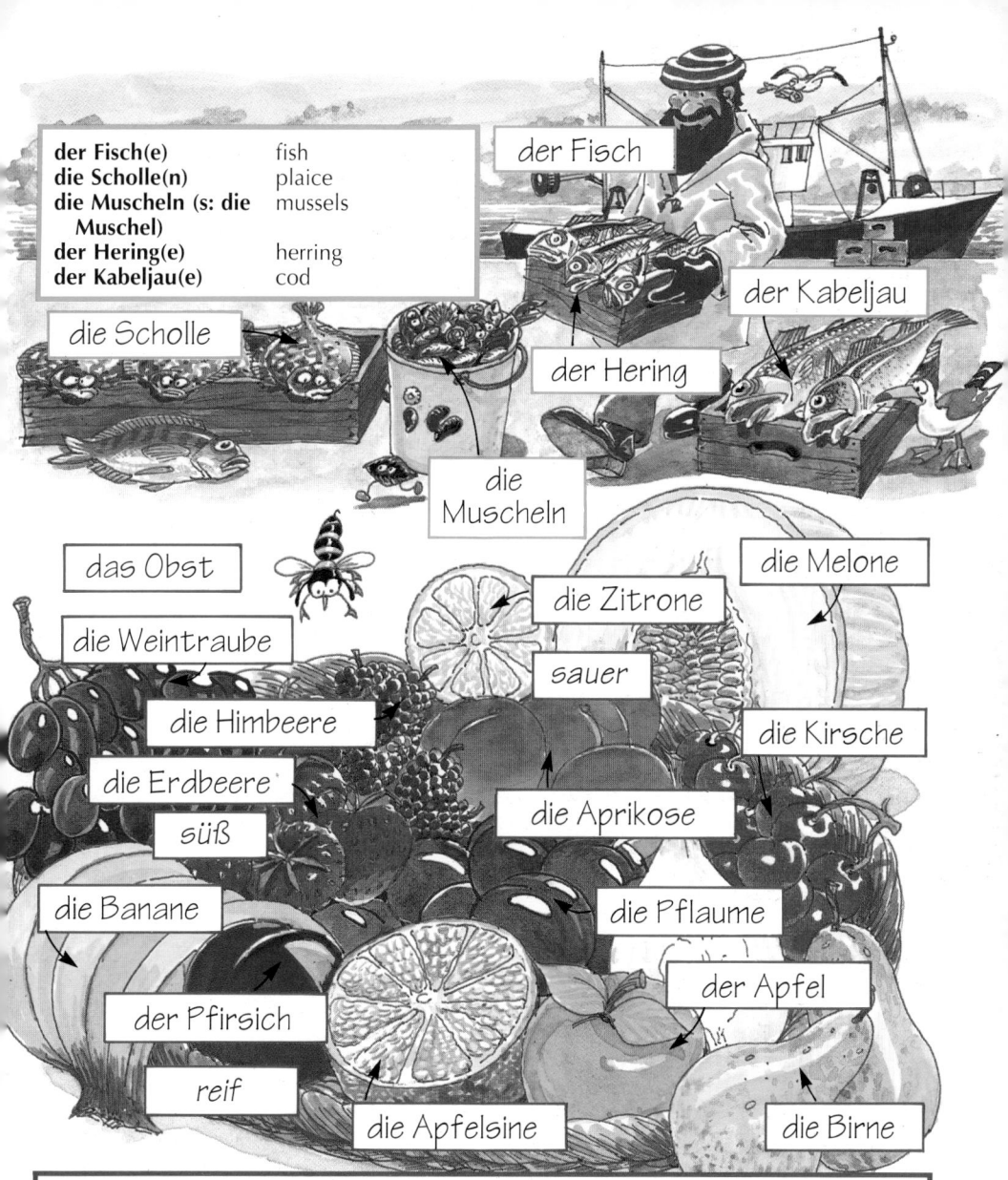

der Fisch(e)	fish
die Scholle(n)	plaice
die Muscheln (s: die Muschel)	mussels
der Hering(e)	herring
der Kabeljau(e)	cod

das Obst	fruit	**sauer**	sour, sharp
die Weintraube(n)	grapes	**die Melone(n)**	melon
die Himbeere(n)	raspberry	**die Kirsche(n)**	cherry
die Erdbeere(n)	strawberry	**die Aprikose(n)**	apricot
süß	sweet	**die Pflaume(n)**	plum
die Banane(n)	banana	**der Apfel(¨)**	apple
der Pfirsich(e)	peach	**die Birne(n)**	pear
reif	ripe	**die Apfelsine(n)**	orange
die Zitrone(n)	lemon		

Buying food

die Nudeln (pl)	noodles
die Linsen (pl)	lentils
die Bohnen (pl)	beans
die Sahne	cream
die Milch	milk
die Margarine	margarine
das Joghurt(s)	yoghurt
der Honig	honey
die Eier (s: das Ei)	eggs
die Marmelade(n)	jam
der Zucker	sugar
das Mehl	flour

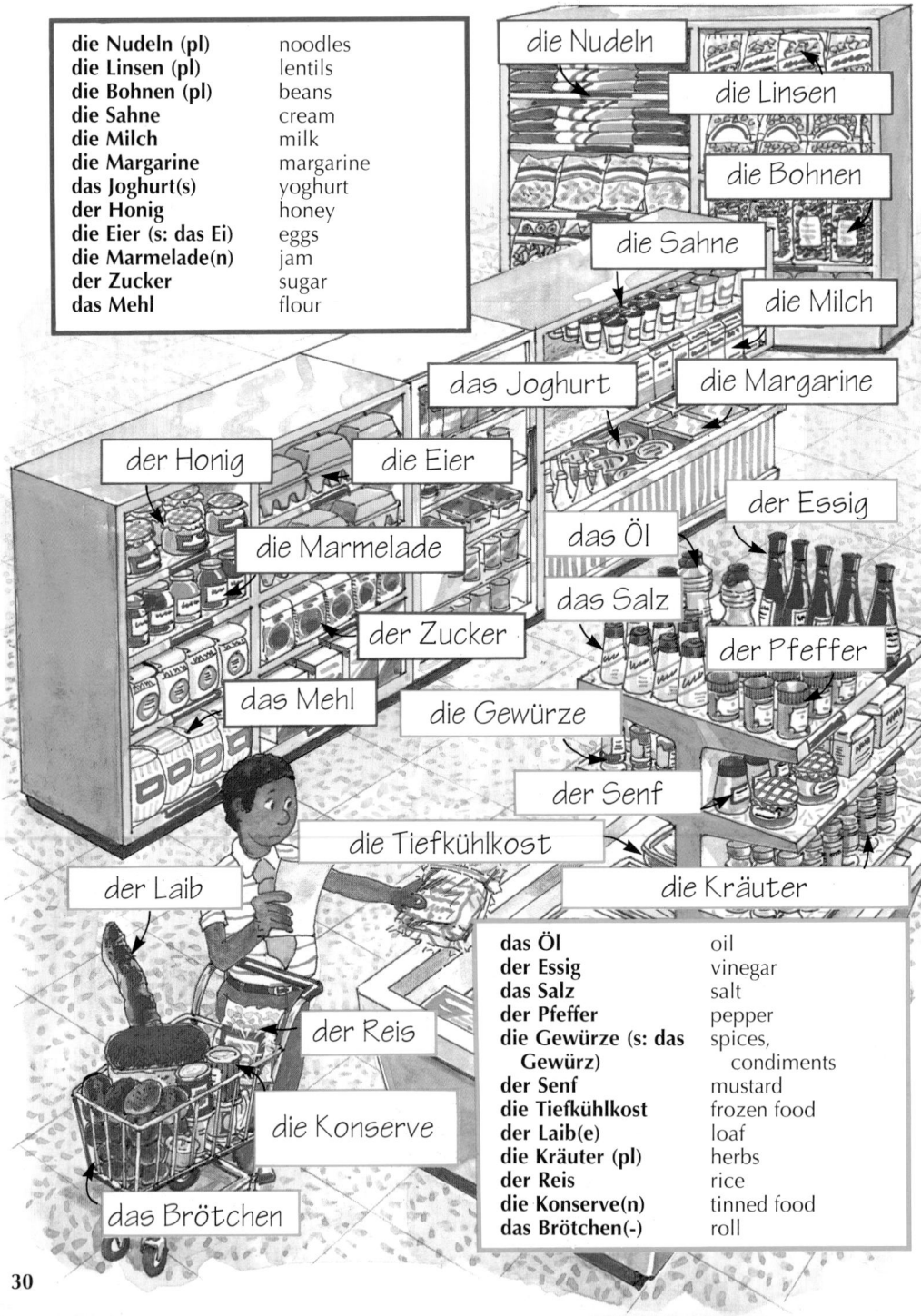

das Öl	oil
der Essig	vinegar
das Salz	salt
der Pfeffer	pepper
die Gewürze (s: das Gewürz)	spices, condiments
der Senf	mustard
die Tiefkühlkost	frozen food
der Laib(e)	loaf
die Kräuter (pl)	herbs
der Reis	rice
die Konserve(n)	tinned food
das Brötchen(-)	roll

die Schokolade	chocolate
der Keks(-)	biscuit
das Obsttörtchen(-)	small tart
der Berliner Pfannkuchen(-)	doughnut
die Sahnetorte(n)	cream cake
das Eis	ice-cream
das Hefeteilchen(-)	Danish pastry

kochen	to cook
das Rezept(e)	recipe
die Zutat(en)	ingredients
rühren	to mix
probieren	to taste
der Geschmack	flavour
Lecker!	Delicious!

Pastimes

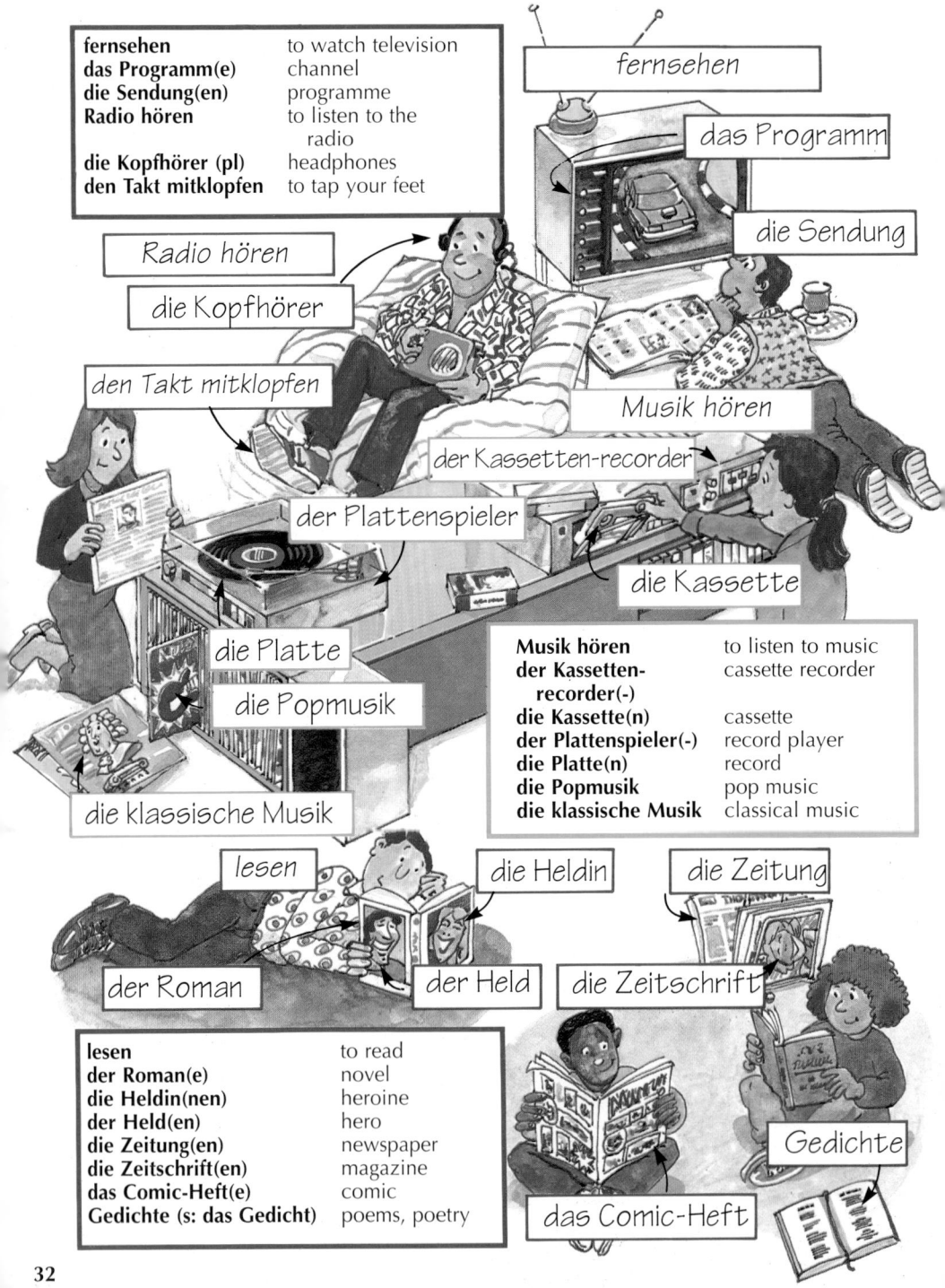

fernsehen	to watch television
das Programm(e)	channel
die Sendung(en)	programme
Radio hören	to listen to the radio
die Kopfhörer (pl)	headphones
den Takt mitklopfen	to tap your feet

Musik hören	to listen to music
der Kassetten-recorder(-)	cassette recorder
die Kassette(n)	cassette
der Plattenspieler(-)	record player
die Platte(n)	record
die Popmusik	pop music
die klassische Musik	classical music

lesen	to read
der Roman(e)	novel
die Heldin(nen)	heroine
der Held(en)	hero
die Zeitung(en)	newspaper
die Zeitschrift(en)	magazine
das Comic-Heft(e)	comic
Gedichte (s: das Gedicht)	poems, poetry

stricken	to knit
die Stricknadeln (pl)	knitting needles
das Muster(-)	pattern
die Wolle	wool

nähen	to sew
der Stoff(e)	fabric
die Schere(n)	scissors
der Faden(¨)	thread
die Stecknadel(n)	pin
die Nadel(n)	needle
machen	to make

das Tischlern	woodwork
das Heimwerken	odd jobs
die Säge(n)	saw
bauen	to make, to build
der Hammer(¨)	hammer
geschickt	skilful, good with your hands
reparieren	to mend
der Schraubenzieher(-)	screwdriver

Pastimes

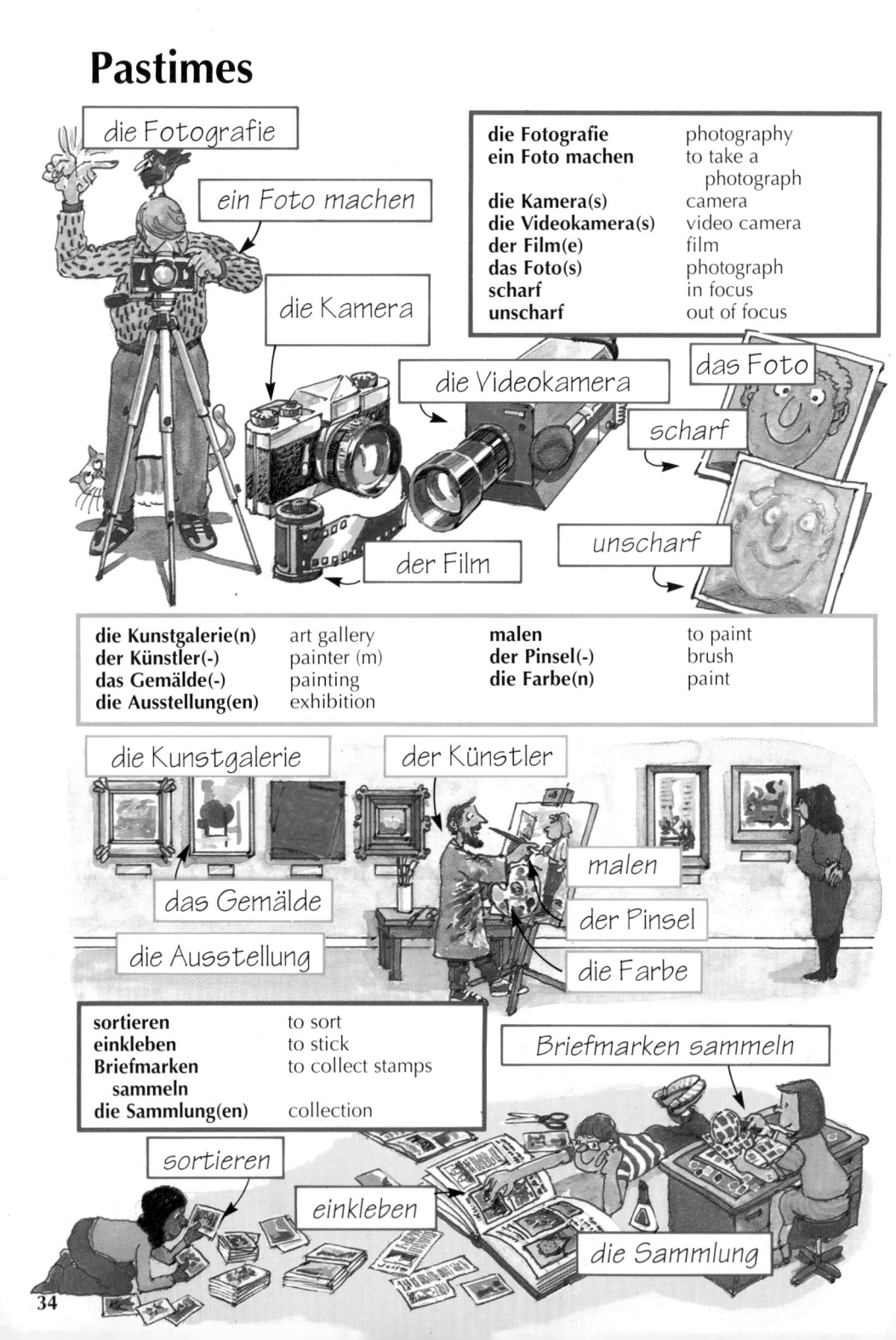

die Fotografie	photography
ein Foto machen	to take a photograph
die Kamera(s)	camera
die Videokamera(s)	video camera
der Film(e)	film
das Foto(s)	photograph
scharf	in focus
unscharf	out of focus

die Kunstgalerie(n)	art gallery	**malen**	to paint
der Künstler(-)	painter (m)	**der Pinsel(-)**	brush
das Gemälde(-)	painting	**die Farbe(n)**	paint
die Ausstellung(en)	exhibition		

sortieren	to sort
einkleben	to stick
Briefmarken sammeln	to collect stamps
die Sammlung(en)	collection

die Musikerin(nen)	musician (f)	**Schlagzeug spielen**	to play the drums
das Instrument(e)	instrument	**Trompete spielen**	to play the trumpet
Geige spielen	to play the violin	**Cello spielen**	to play the cello
Klavier spielen	to play the piano	**das Orchester(-)**	orchestra
Gitarre spielen	to play the guitar	**der Dirigent(en)**	conductor (m)

singen	to sing
die Melodie(n)	tune
der Chor(¨e)	choir
falsch singen	to sing out of tune

falsch singen

die Spiele

die Spiele (s: das Spiel)	games
Karten spielen	to play cards
Dame spielen	to play draughts
Schach spielen	to play chess
das Brettspiel(e)	board game

Going out

das Kino(s)	cinema
ins Kino gehen	to go to the cinema
der Film(e)	film
der Platz(¨e)	seat
die Platzanweiserin(nen)	usherette
die Kasse(n)	box-office

das Kino

ins Kino gehen

der Film

die Platzanweiserin

der Platz

die Kasse

in die Disko gehen

der Diskjockey

in die Disko gehen	to go to a discothèque
der Diskjockey(s)	disc jockey
tanzen	to dance
die Tanzfläche(n)	dance floor

tanzen

die Tanzfläche

das Theater

das Stück

das Bühnenbild

Zugabe!

die Schauspielerin

der Scheinwerfer

der Schauspieler

die Bühne

das Publikum

klatschen

sich gut unterhalten

das Theater(-)	theatre
das Stück(e)	play
das Bühnenbild(er)	scenery
der Scheinwerfer(-)	spotlight
die Schauspielerin(nen)	actress
der Schauspieler(-)	actor
die Bühne(n)	stage
das Publikum	audience
klatschen	to clap
sich gut unterhalten	to enjoy yourself
Zugabe!	Encore!

das Ballett	ballet	**die Oper(n)**	opera
der Balletttänzer(-)	ballet dancer (m)	**der Sänger(-)**	singer (m)
auftreten	to perform, to appear on stage	**berühmt**	famous

das Restaurant(s)	restaurant	**das Dessert(s)**	dessert, pudding
der Ober(-)	waiter	**die Rechnung(en)**	bill
die Speisekarte(n)	menu	**Mit Bedienung?**	Is service included?
Was hätten Sie gerne?	What would you like?	**Ohne Bedienung!**	Service not included!
bestellen	to order	**das Trinkgeld(er)**	tip
servieren	to serve	**das Tablett(s)**	tray
die Vorspeise(n)	starter		
das Hauptgericht(e)	main course		

At the zoo

der Zoo(s)	zoo
das Tier(e)	animal
das Zebra(s)	zebra
die Giraffe(n)	giraffe
der Eisbär(en)	polar bear
der Elefant(en)	elephant
der Rüssel(-)	trunk
der Stoßzahn(¨e)	tusk
der Gorilla(s)	gorilla
wild	wild
zahm	tame
füttern	to feed
der Wärter(-)	keeper (m)

der Zoo
das Tier
das Zebra
die Giraffe
der Eisbär
der Elefant
der Rüssel
der Gorilla
füttern
wild
der Stoßzahn
zahm
der Wärter

In the park

der Park(s)	park
der Teich(e)	pond
das Ruderboot(e)	rowing boat
rudern	to row
das Ruder(-)	oar
das Picknick(e)	picnic
die Bank(¨e)	bench
sich ausruhen	to rest

der Park
der Teich
das Ruder
das Ruderboot
rudern
sich ausruhen
das Picknick
die Bank

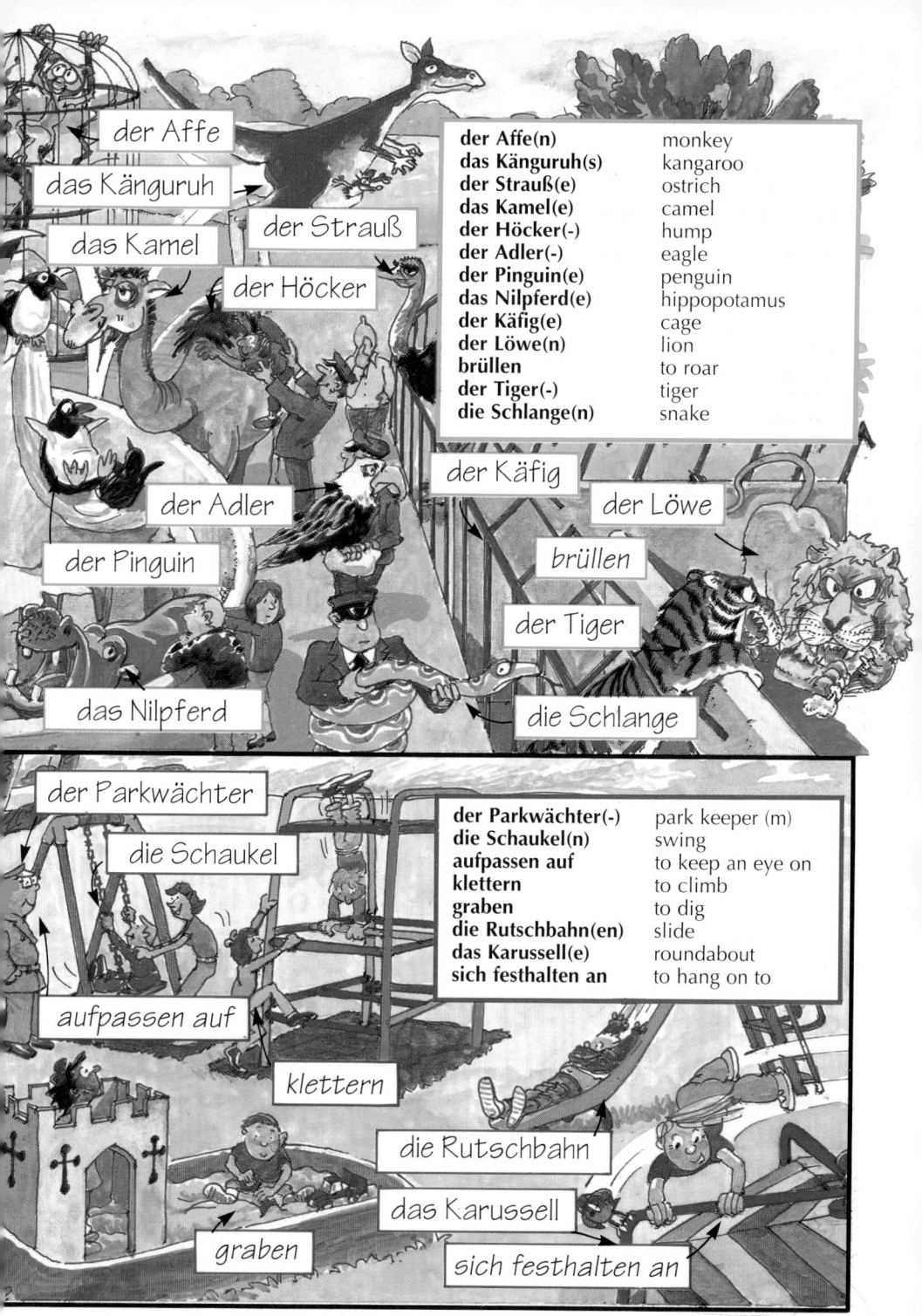

der Affe(n)	monkey
das Känguruh(s)	kangaroo
der Strauß(e)	ostrich
das Kamel(e)	camel
der Höcker(-)	hump
der Adler(-)	eagle
der Pinguin(e)	penguin
das Nilpferd(e)	hippopotamus
der Käfig(e)	cage
der Löwe(n)	lion
brüllen	to roar
der Tiger(-)	tiger
die Schlange(n)	snake

der Parkwächter(-)	park keeper (m)
die Schaukel(n)	swing
aufpassen auf	to keep an eye on
klettern	to climb
graben	to dig
die Rutschbahn(en)	slide
das Karussell(e)	roundabout
sich festhalten an	to hang on to

In the city

die Großstadt(¨e)	city
die Vorort(e)	suburb
die Stadt(¨e)	town
der Wolkenkratzer(-)	skyscraper
der Dom(e)	cathedral
der Fluss(¨e)	river
die Brücke(n)	bridge
der Stadtteil(e)	district
das Gebäude(-)	building
die Kirche(n)	church
der Friedhof(¨e)	cemetery

die Feuerwache(n)	fire station
das Feuerwehrauto(s)	fire engine
die Fabrik(en)	factory
das Rathaus(¨er)	town hall
das Bürogebäude(-)	office block
die Polizeiwache(n)	police station
das Polizeiauto(s)	police car
die Bücherei(en)	library

die Innenstadt(¨e)	town centre
die Straße(n)	street
schmal	narrow
breit	broad
die Ecke(n)	corner
die Straße überqueren	to cross the street
der Zebrastreifen(-)	pedestrian crossing
der Fußgänger(-)	pedestrian (m)
der Platz(¨e)	square
die Statue(n)	statue
die Straßenlaterne(n)	street light
der Marktplatz(¨e)	market place
die Unterführung(en)	subway

der Kiosk(e)	newspaper stand
die Taube(n)	pigeon
die Menge(n)	crowd
belebt	bustling
der Papierkorb(¨e)	litter bin
der Bürgersteig(e)	pavement
sich beeilen	to hurry
die Reklame(n)	advertisement

Shopping

eine Liste machen	to make a list
die Einkaufstasche(n)	shopping bag

die Geschäfte (pl)	shops	**die Drogerie(n)**	chemist
einkaufen gehen	to go shopping	**der Buchladen(¨)**	bookshop
der Fleischer	butcher	**das Hand-arbeitsgeschäft(e)**	needlework and woolshop
das Feinkostgeschäft(e)	delicatessen	**das Blumengeschäft(e)**	florist
das Lebens-mittelgeschäft(e)	grocery shop	**der Friseur(e)**	hairdresser
der Bäcker	bakery	**das Schall-plattengeschäft(e)**	record shop
die Konditorei(en)	cake shop	**die Boutique(n)**	boutique
der Fischhändler	fishmonger		

auf dem Markt einkaufen	to shop at the market
der Marktstand(¨e)	stall
anstehen	to queue

Wie viel macht das?	How much is that?
Das macht…	That will be…
wiegen	to weigh
Ein Kilo…	A kilo of…
Ein Pfund…	Half a kilo of…

in den Supermarkt gehen	to go to the supermarket
der Einkaufskorb(¨e)	basket
der Einkaufswagen(-)	trolley
der Lautsprecher(-)	loudspeaker
die Theke(n)	counter
der Gang(¨e)	aisle
die Dose(n)	tin
das Päckchen(-)	packet
die Flasche(n)	bottle
der Eingang(¨e)	entrance
der Ausgang(¨e)	exit
die Kasse(n)	checkout
die Tragetasche(n)	carrier-bag
die Kassiererin(nen)	cashier (f)

Shopping

einen Schaufensterbummel machen	to go window-shopping	**das Sonderangebot(e)**	bargain
das Schaufenster(-)	shop window	**die Kundin(nen)**	customer (f)
Das ist preiswert.	It's good value.	**kaufen**	to buy
Das ist teuer.	It's expensive.	**die Verkäuferin(nen)**	shop assistant (f)
SCHLUSSVERKAUF (m)	sale	**verkaufen**	to sell

Geld ausgeben	to spend money	**Welche Größe ist es?**	What size is this?
der Preis(e)	price	**klein**	small
die Quittung(en)	receipt	**mittel**	medium
Womit kann ich dienen?	Can I help you?	**groß**	large
Ich hätte gern...	I'd like...	**Was kostet...?**	How much is...?
		Das kostet...	It costs...

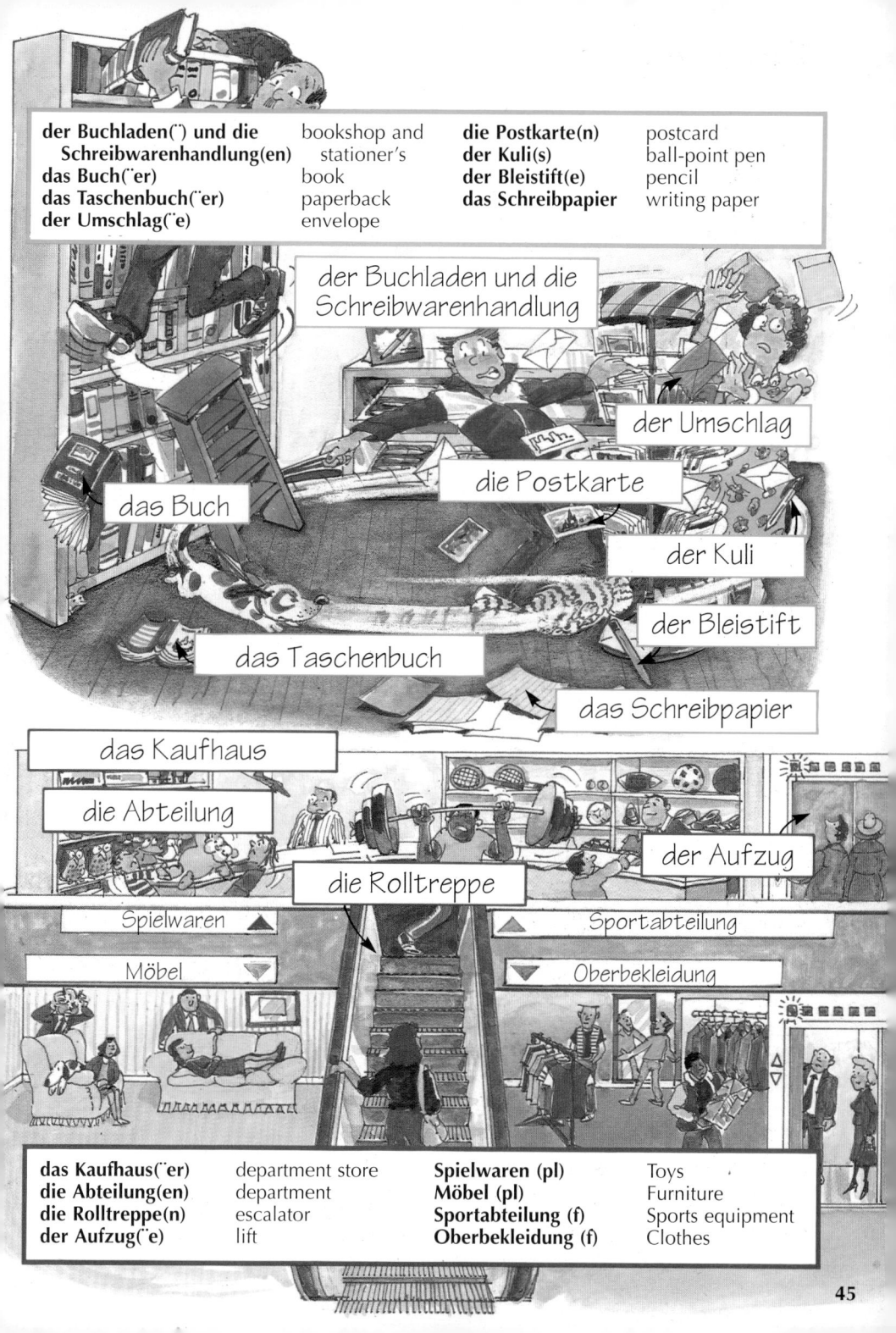

der Buchladen(¨) und die Schreibwarenhandlung(en)	bookshop and stationer's	**die Postkarte(n)**	postcard
das Buch(¨er)	book	**der Kuli(s)**	ball-point pen
das Taschenbuch(¨er)	paperback	**der Bleistift(e)**	pencil
der Umschlag(¨e)	envelope	**das Schreibpapier**	writing paper

das Kaufhaus(¨er)	department store	**Spielwaren (pl)**	Toys
die Abteilung(en)	department	**Möbel (pl)**	Furniture
die Rolltreppe(n)	escalator	**Sportabteilung (f)**	Sports equipment
der Aufzug(¨e)	lift	**Oberbekleidung (f)**	Clothes

At the post office and bank

das Postamt(¨er)	post office	**schicken**	to send
der Briefkasten(¨)	post-box	**das Telegramm(e)**	telegram
einwerfen	to post	**das Formular(e)**	form
der Brief(e)	letter	**die Briefmarke(n)**	stamp
das Paket(e)	parcel	**Luftpost**	airmail
die Leerung(en)	collection, collection time	**die Adresse(n)**	address
		die Postleitzahl(en)	postal code

der Briefträger(-)	postman (m)
die Post	mail
austeilen	to deliver

die Bank(en)	bank	**die Banknote(n)**	note
das Geld	money	**die Kreditkarte(n)**	credit card
Geld wechseln	to change money	**Geld einzahlen**	to put money in
der Umtauschkurs(e)	exchange rate	**Geld abheben**	to take money out
der Geschäftsführer(-) der Bank	bank manager	**das Scheckbuch(¨er)**	cheque-book
der Kassierer(-)	cashier (m)	**einen Scheck ausstellen**	to write a cheque
Haben Sie Kleingeld?	Have you any small change?	**die Brieftasche(n)**	wallet
die Münze(n)	coin	**die Geldbörse(n)**	purse
		die Handtasche(n)	handbag

Phonecalls and letters

telefonieren
das Telefon
der Telefonhörer
läuten
ans Telefon gehen
Wolfgang
Glöckler*
Hier ist Anke.
den Telefonhörer abnehmen
wählen
Ich rufe dich zurück.
die Vorwahl
die Telefon-nummer
Wiederhören
das Telefonbuch
auflegen

telefonieren	to make a phonecall	**das Telefonbuch(¨er)**	telephone directory
das Telefon(e)	telephone	**läuten**	to ring
der Telefonhörer(-)	receiver	**ans Telefon gehen**	to answer the phone
den Telefonhörer abnehmen	to pick up the receiver	**Hier ist Anke.**	It's Anke.
wählen	to dial	**Ich rufe dich zurück.**	I'll call you back.
die Telefonnummer(n)	telephone number	**Wiederhören**	Goodbye
die Vorwahl	area code	**auflegen**	to hang up

die Telefonzelle(n)	telephone box
der Notfall(¨e)	emergency
der Notruf	999 call

* When speaking German, the most usual way of answering the phone is to say your name.

einen Brief schreiben

Sehr geehrte Damen und Herren,
25.10.02
Vielen Dank für Ihren Brief vom...
Beigefügt finden Sie...
...postwendend.
Mit freundlichen Grüßen...

einen Brief schreiben	to write a letter	**Beigefügt finden Sie...**	I enclose...
Sehr geehrte Damen und Herren,	Dear Sir/Madam,	**postwendend**	by return of post
Vielen Dank für Ihren Brief vom...	Thank you for your letter of...	**Mit freundlichen Grüßen...**	Yours faithfully,

einen Brief öffnen

Liebe Anke,
9.1.2002
Schön, mal wieder von dir zu hören. Mit getrennter Post erhältst du...
Alles Gute...

einen Brief öffnen	to open a letter	**Mit getrennter Post erhältst du...**	I am sending... separately.
Liebe Anke,	Dear Anke,	**Alles Gute...**	Love from...
Schön, mal wieder von dir zu hören.	It was lovely to hear from you.		

eine Ansichtskarte schicken

Es ist ganz toll hier.
Schade, dass du nicht hier bist.

ein Telegramm schicken

Dringend stop
sofort zu Hause
anrufen stop

eine Ansichtskarte schicken	to send a postcard	**ein Telegramm schicken**	to send a telegram
Es ist ganz toll hier.	Having a lovely time.	**Dringend stop sofort zu Hause anrufen stop**	Urgent message stop phone home stop
Schade, dass du nicht hier bist.	Wish you were here.		

Out and about

gehen
laufen
der Sportwagen
In welcher Richtung ist...?
nach dem Weg fragen
die Karte
das Hinweisschild
Wie weit ist...?

gehen	to walk	**nach dem Weg fragen**	to ask the way
laufen	to run		
der Sportwagen(-)	push-chair	**die Karte(n)**	map
In welcher Richtung ist...?	Which way is...?	**das Hinweisschild(er)**	signpost
		Wie weit ist...?	How far is...?

mit dem Bus fahren
der Passagier
aussteigen
die U-Bahnstation
die U-Bahn
einsteigen
die Fahrkarte
der Bus
die Bushaltestelle

mit dem Bus fahren	to take the bus	**der Bus(se)**	bus
der Passagier(e)	passenger (m/f)	**die Bushaltestelle(n)**	bus stop
aussteigen	to get off	**die U-Bahnstation(en)**	underground station
einsteigen	to get on		
die Fahrkarte(n)	ticket	**die U-Bahn(en)**	underground

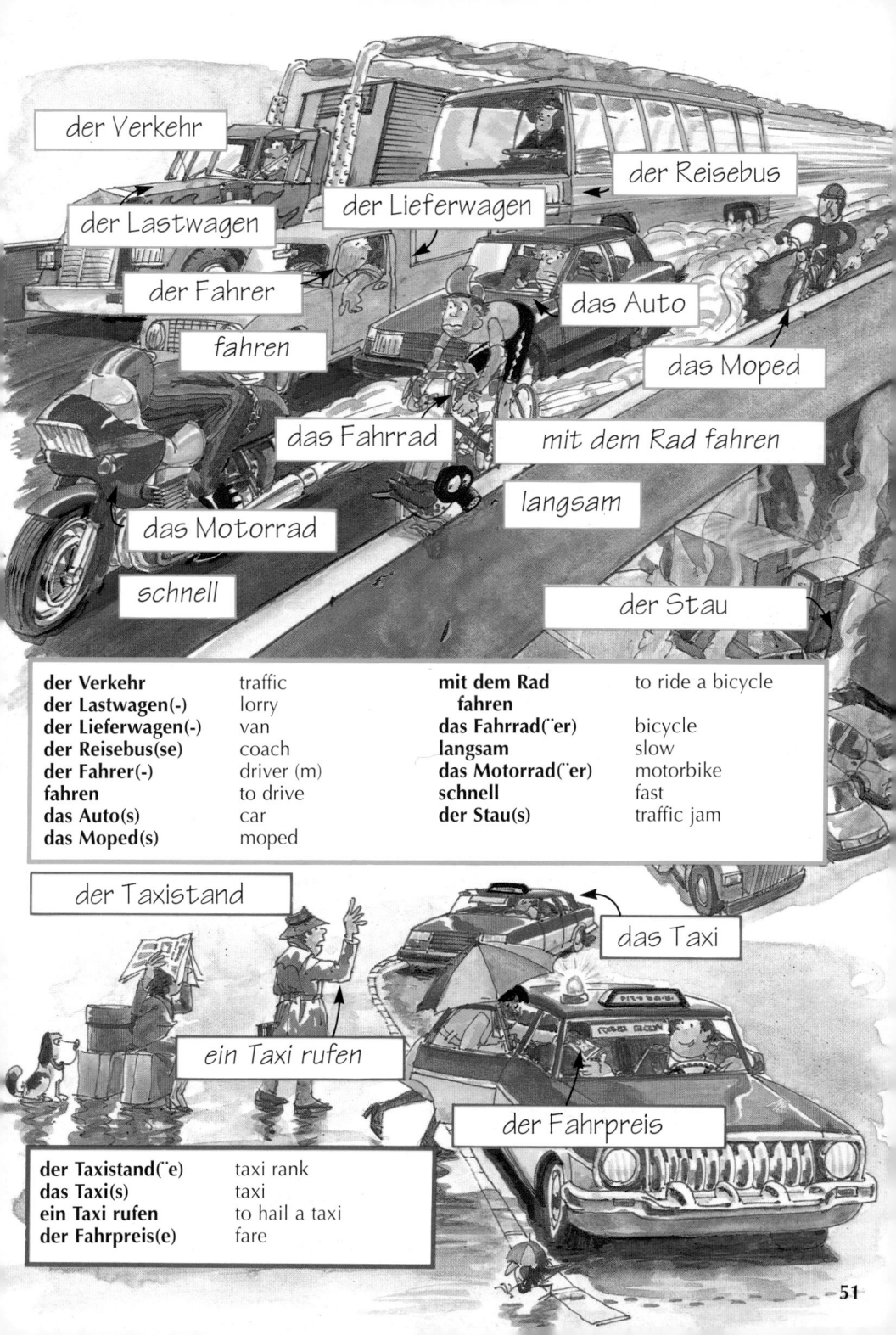

der Verkehr	traffic
der Lastwagen(-)	lorry
der Lieferwagen(-)	van
der Reisebus(se)	coach
der Fahrer(-)	driver (m)
fahren	to drive
das Auto(s)	car
das Moped(s)	moped
mit dem Rad fahren	to ride a bicycle
das Fahrrad(¨er)	bicycle
langsam	slow
das Motorrad(¨er)	motorbike
schnell	fast
der Stau(s)	traffic jam

der Taxistand(¨e)	taxi rank
das Taxi(s)	taxi
ein Taxi rufen	to hail a taxi
der Fahrpreis(e)	fare

Driving

losfahren	to start off
schneller werden	to gather speed
überholen	to overtake
bremsen	to brake
die Autobahn(en)	motorway
die Ampel(n)	traffic lights
die Hauptstraße(n)	main road
links abbiegen	to turn left
rechts abbiegen	to turn right
geradeaus weiterfahren	to go straight on
die Seitenstraße(n)	side street
die Einbahnstraße(n)	one way street
keine Einfahrt	no entry

Parkverbot!	No parking!	**rückwärts**	backwards
der Parkplatz(¨e)	car-park	**vorwärts**	forwards
parken	to park		

der Unfall(¨e)	accident
das Lenkrad(¨er)	steering wheel
die Windschutzscheibe(n)	windscreen
der Sicherheitsgurt(e)	safety belt
der Blinker(-)	indicator
der Scheinwerfer(-)	headlight
die Motorhaube(n)	bonnet
der Kofferraum(¨e)	boot
das Nummernschild(er)	number plate
das Rad(¨er)	wheel
der Reifen(-)	tyre
die Hupe(n)	horn

einen Platten haben	to have a flat tyre
eine Panne haben	to have a breakdown
der Automechaniker(-)	mechanic (m)
das Öl	oil
die Tankstelle(n)	petrol station
volltanken	to fill up with petrol
das Benzin	petrol

Travelling by train

der Bahnhof(¨e)	station	**Der Zug aus...**	The train from...
der Gepäckträger(-)	porter (m)	**der Fahrkarten-schalter(-)**	ticket office
die Gepäckauf-bewahrung	left luggage office	**die Fahrkarte(n)**	ticket
der Kontrolleur(e)	ticket collector (m)	**die Rückfahrkarte(n)**	return ticket
der Wartesaal (die Wartesäle)	waiting-room	**die Zeitkarte(n)**	season ticket
die Schranke(n)	barrier	**der Fahrkarten-automat(en)**	ticket machine
der Reisende(n)	traveller (m)	**die Bahnsteigkarte(n)**	platform ticket
der Fahrplan(¨e)	timetable	**einen Platz reservieren**	to reserve a seat
Der Zug nach...	The train to...		

die Eisenbahn
die erste Klasse
der Zug
die zweite Klasse
verspätet
pünktlich
der Schlafwagen
der Speisewagen
den Zug erreichen
der Wagen
die Lokomotive
den Zug verpassen
die Gleise
der Bahnsteig
der Schaffner

die Eisenbahn	railway	**der Wagen(-)**	carriage
der Zug(¨e)	train	**den Zug erreichen**	to catch the train
die erste Klasse	first class	**den Zug verpassen**	to miss the train
die zweite Klasse	second class	**die Lokomotive(n)**	engine
verspätet	late	**die Gleise (pl)**	track
pünktlich	on time	**der Bahnsteig(e)**	platform
der Schlafwagen(-)	sleeping-car	**der Schaffner(-)**	guard (m)
der Speisewagen(-)	buffet car		

der Intercity
der Güterzug
der Platz
der reservierte Platz
die Gepäckablage
Nichtrauche

der Intercity	inter-city train
der Güterzug(¨e)	goods train
der Platz(¨e)	seat
der reservierte Platz	reserved seat
die Gepäckablage(n)	luggage-rack
Nichtraucher	No smoking

Travelling by plane and boat

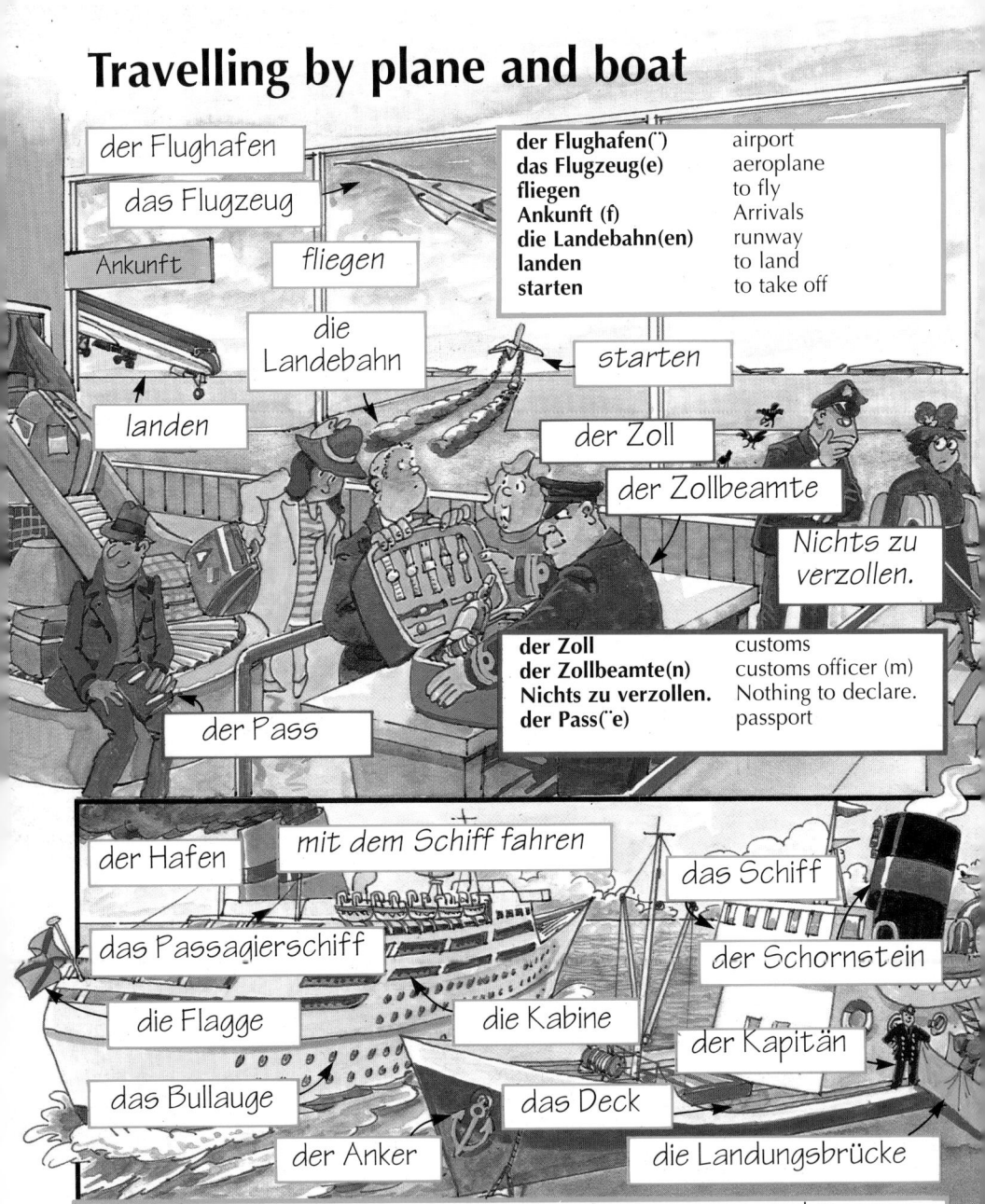

der Flughafen(¨)	airport
das Flugzeug(e)	aeroplane
fliegen	to fly
Ankunft (f)	Arrivals
die Landebahn(en)	runway
landen	to land
starten	to take off

der Zoll	customs
der Zollbeamte(n)	customs officer (m)
Nichts zu verzollen.	Nothing to declare.
der Pass(¨e)	passport

der Hafen(¨)	port
mit dem Schiff fahren	to travel by boat, to sail
das Schiff(e)	ship
das Passagierschiff(e)	liner
die Flagge(n)	flag
das Bullauge(n)	porthole
der Anker(-)	anchor
die Kabine(n)	cabin
das Deck(s)	deck
der Schornstein(e)	funnel
der Kapitän(e)	captain
die Landungsbrücke(n)	gangway

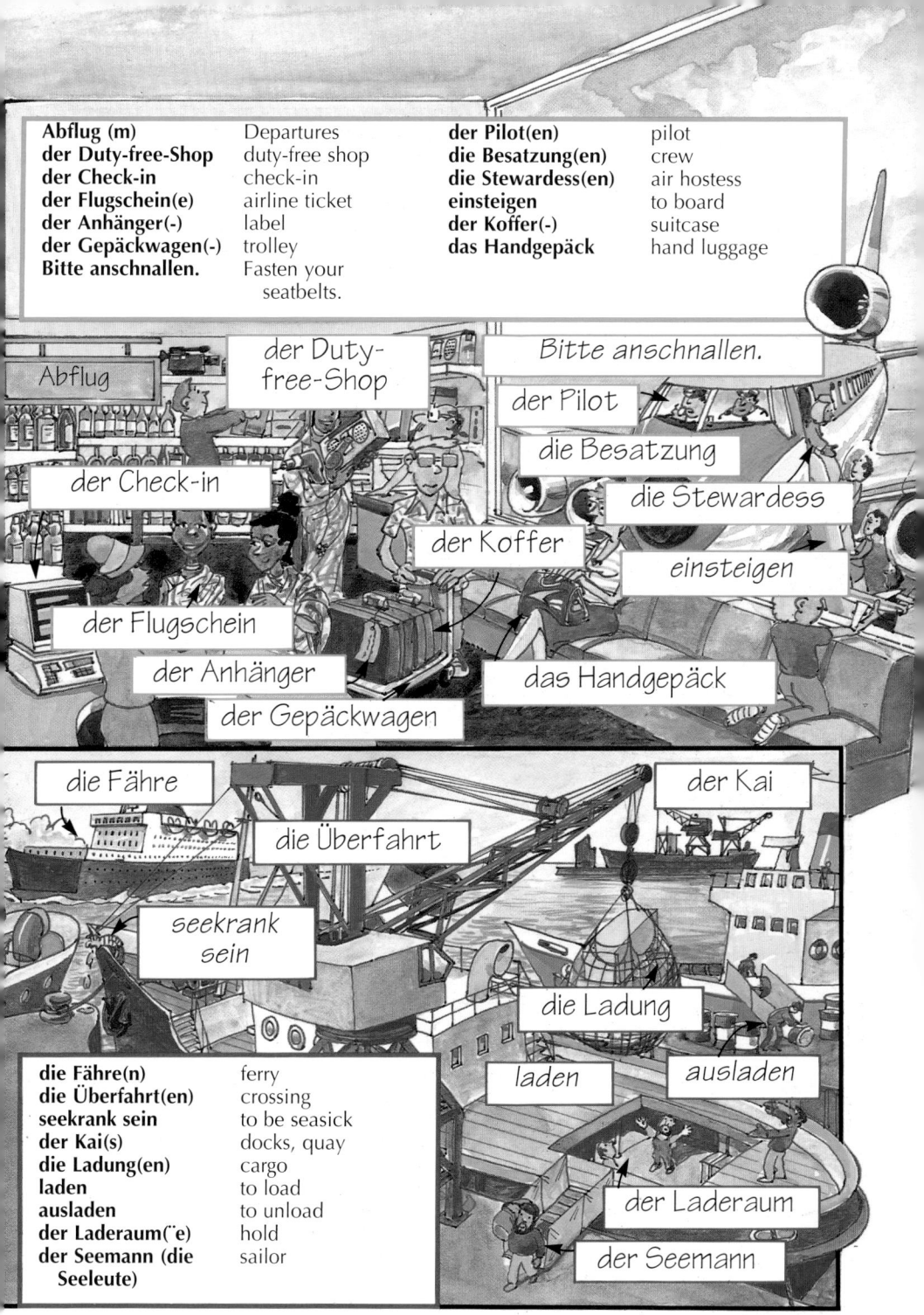

Abflug (m)	Departures
der Duty-free-Shop	duty-free shop
der Check-in	check-in
der Flugschein(e)	airline ticket
der Anhänger(-)	label
der Gepäckwagen(-)	trolley
Bitte anschnallen.	Fasten your seatbelts.
der Pilot(en)	pilot
die Besatzung(en)	crew
die Stewardess(en)	air hostess
einsteigen	to board
der Koffer(-)	suitcase
das Handgepäck	hand luggage

die Fähre(n)	ferry
die Überfahrt(en)	crossing
seekrank sein	to be seasick
der Kai(s)	docks, quay
die Ladung(en)	cargo
laden	to load
ausladen	to unload
der Laderaum(¨e)	hold
der Seemann (die Seeleute)	sailor

Holidays

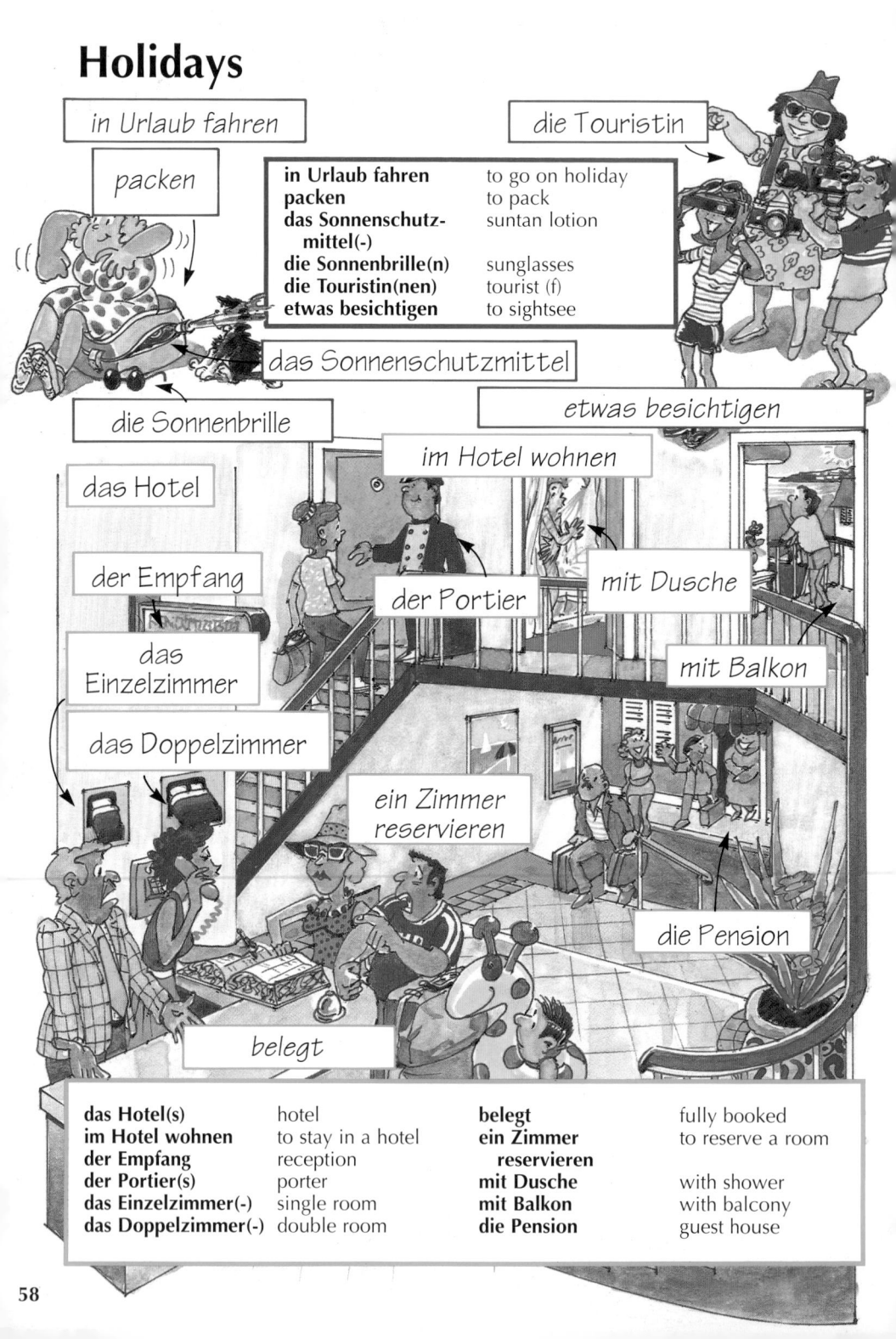

in Urlaub fahren	to go on holiday
packen	to pack
das Sonnenschutzmittel(-)	suntan lotion
die Sonnenbrille(n)	sunglasses
die Touristin(nen)	tourist (f)
etwas besichtigen	to sightsee

das Hotel(s)	hotel
im Hotel wohnen	to stay in a hotel
der Empfang	reception
der Portier(s)	porter
das Einzelzimmer(-)	single room
das Doppelzimmer(-)	double room
belegt	fully booked
ein Zimmer reservieren	to reserve a room
mit Dusche	with shower
mit Balkon	with balcony
die Pension	guest house

am Meer	at the seaside
die Möwe(n)	seagull
der Rettungs-schwimmer(-)	lifeguard
die Welle(n)	wave
das Motorboot(e)	powerboat
Wasserski laufen	to waterski
windsurfen	to windsurf
ins Wasser gehen	to go in, to have a swim
planschen	to paddle
das Meer(e)	sea
der Sand	sand
der Strand(¨e)	beach

sonnenbaden	to sunbathe
braun	tanned
der Sonnenschirm(e)	sunshade
die Sandburg(en)	sandcastle
der Eimer(-)	bucket
die Schaufel(n)	spade

der Felsen(-)	rock
der Seetang	seaweed
der Krebs(e)	crab
die Muschel(n)	shell

Holidays

zum Bergsteigen gehen	to go mountaineering
der Berg(e)	mountain
der Gipfel(-)	summit
die Aussicht	view
steil	steep
klettern	to climb
der Bergsteiger(-)	climber (m)
der Rucksack(¨e)	rucksack, backpack

zum Skilaufen gehen	to go skiing
der Skiort(e)	ski resort
der Sessellift(e)	chairlift
der Skilehrer(-)	ski instructor (m)
der Hang(¨e)	ski slope, ski run
der Schlitten(-)	sledge
der Skistock(¨e)	ski pole
die Skistiefel (pl)	ski boots
die Skier (pl)	skis

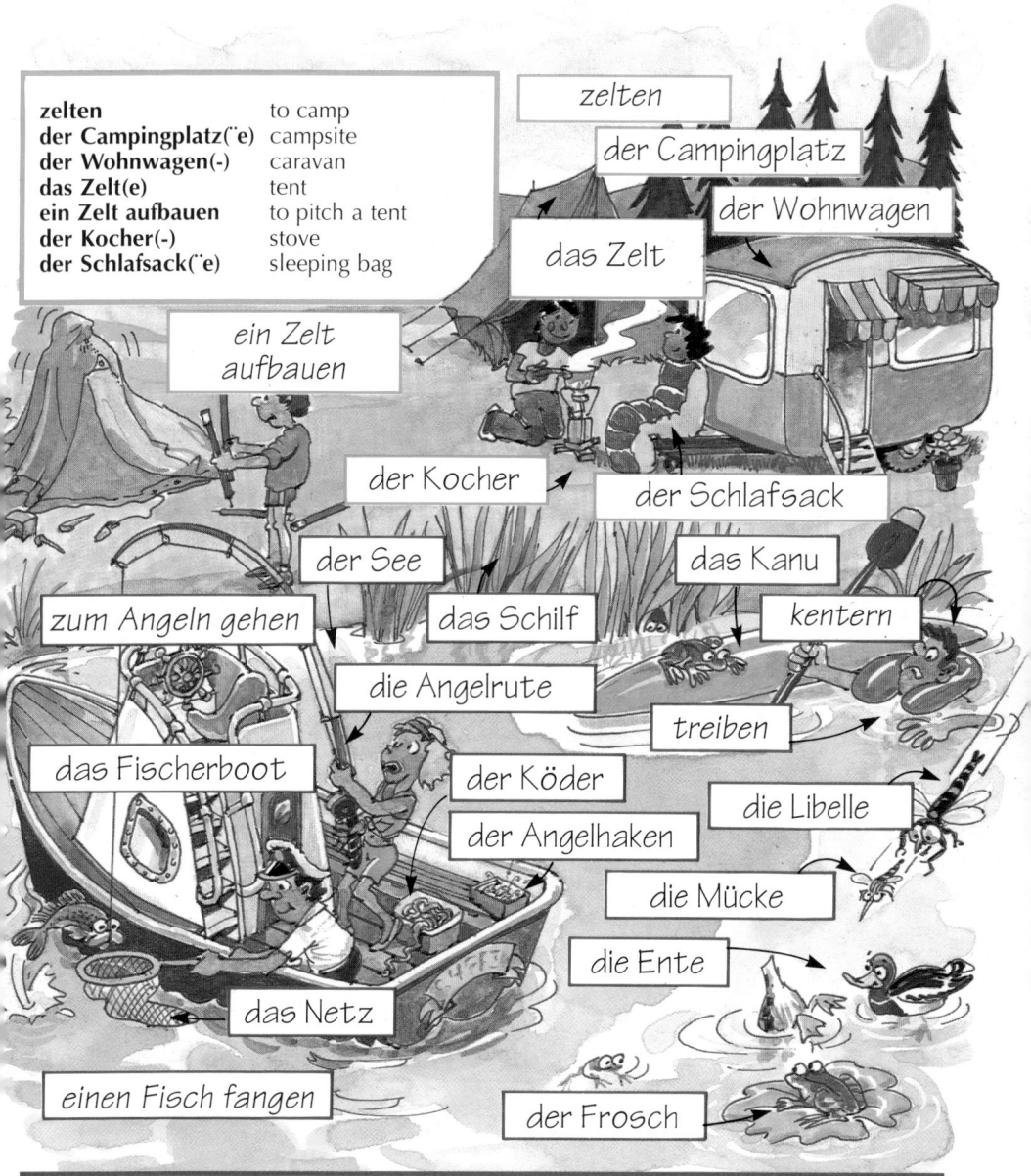

zelten	to camp
der Campingplatz(¨e)	campsite
der Wohnwagen(-)	caravan
das Zelt(e)	tent
ein Zelt aufbauen	to pitch a tent
der Kocher(-)	stove
der Schlafsack(¨e)	sleeping bag

der See(n)	lake
das Schilf	reed
zum Angeln gehen	to go fishing
die Angelrute(n)	fishing rod
das Fischerboot(e)	fishing boat
der Köder(-)	bait
der Angelhaken(-)	hook
das Netz(e)	net
einen Fisch fangen	to catch a fish
das Kanu(s)	canoe
kentern	to capsize
treiben	to float
die Libelle(n)	dragonfly
die Mücke(n)	mosquito
die Ente(n)	duck
der Frosch(¨e)	frog

On the farm

der Bauernhof(¨e)	farm	**die Leiter(n)**	ladder
der Kuhstall(¨e)	cowshed	**das Bauernhaus(¨er)**	farmhouse
der Pferdestall(¨e)	stable	**der Hof(¨e)**	farmyard
das Pferd(e)	horse	**das Huhn(¨er)**	chicken
die Scheune(n)	barn	**der Hahn(¨e)**	cock
das Heu	hay	**der Hühnerstall(¨e)**	henhouse
die Kuh(¨e)	cow	**Eier legen**	to lay eggs
melken	to milk	**die Bäuerin(nen)**	farmer (f), farmer's wife
das Kalb(¨er)	calf		
der Esel(-)	donkey	**die Gans(¨e)**	goose
das Schwein(e)	pig	**die Ziege(n)**	goat

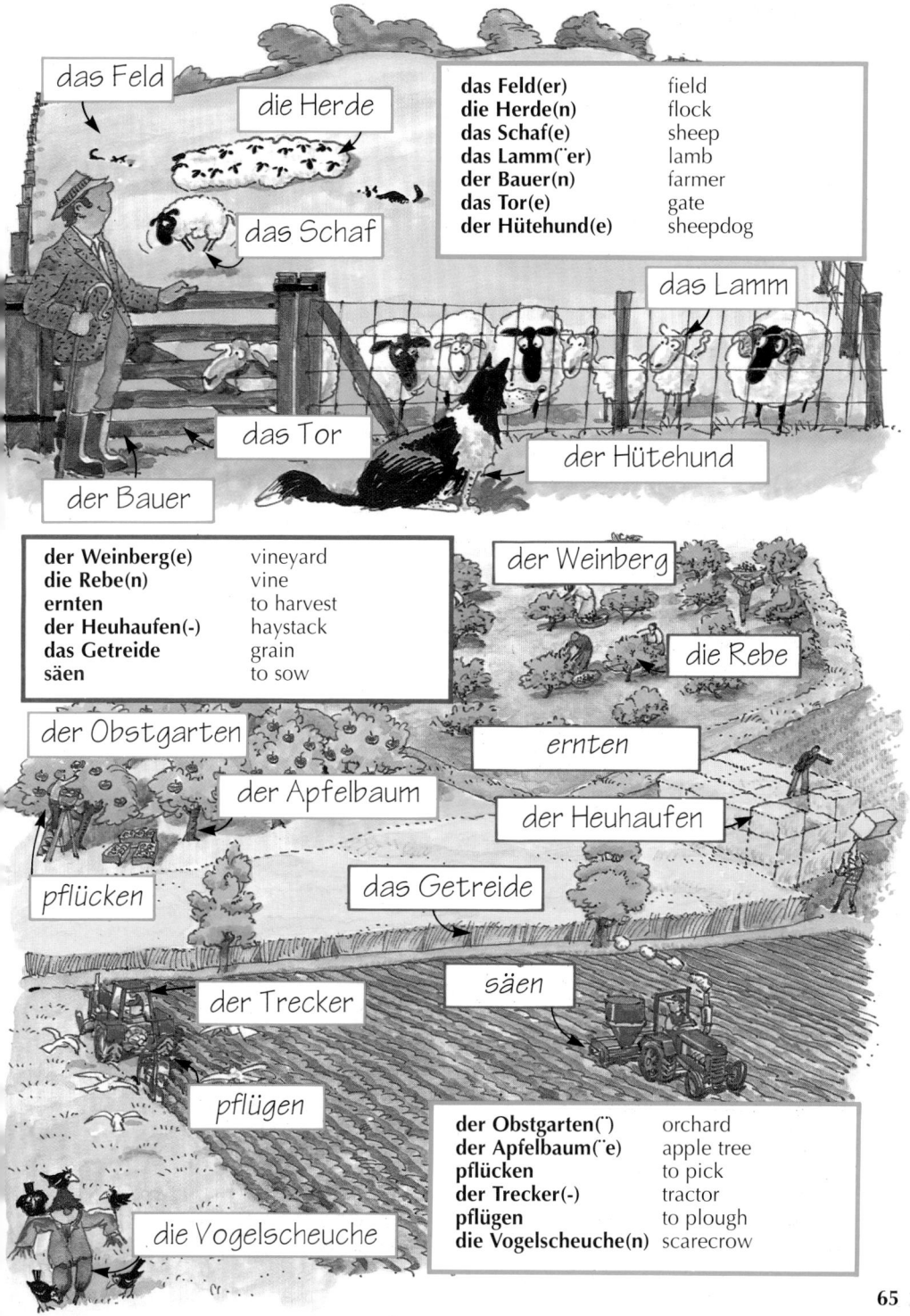

das Feld(er)	field
die Herde(n)	flock
das Schaf(e)	sheep
das Lamm(¨er)	lamb
der Bauer(n)	farmer
das Tor(e)	gate
der Hütehund(e)	sheepdog

der Weinberg(e)	vineyard
die Rebe(n)	vine
ernten	to harvest
der Heuhaufen(-)	haystack
das Getreide	grain
säen	to sow

der Obstgarten(¨)	orchard
der Apfelbaum(¨e)	apple tree
pflücken	to pick
der Trecker(-)	tractor
pflügen	to plough
die Vogelscheuche(n)	scarecrow

At work

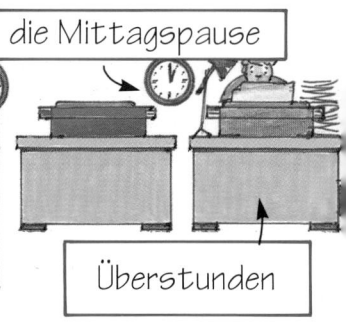

zur Arbeit gehen	to go to work	**die Mittagspause(n)**	lunch hour
zu spät kommen	to be late	**Überstunden (pl)**	overtime
pünktlich sein	to be on time		

das Büro(s)	office	**der Angestellte(n)**	employee (m)
die Chefin(nen)	boss (f)	**fleißig**	hard-working
die Sekretärin(nen)	secretary (f)	**faul**	lazy
jemanden einstellen	to employ someone	**aufhören zu arbeiten**	to retire
		jemanden entlassen	to fire someone

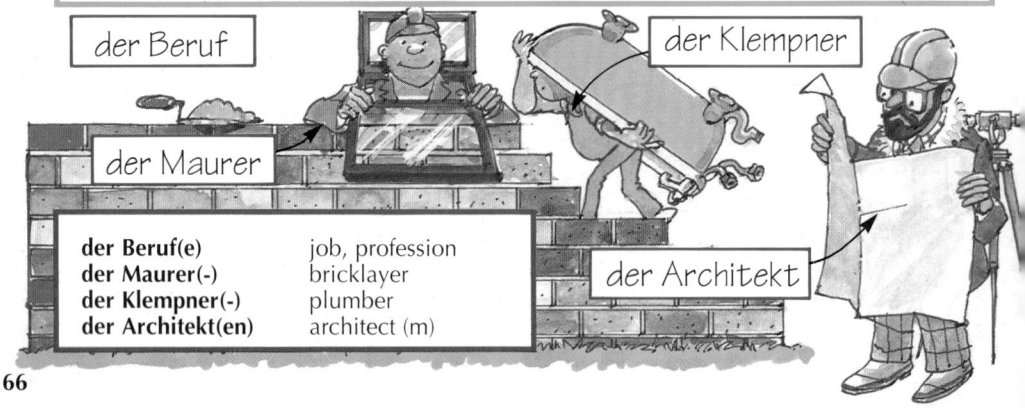

der Beruf(e)	job, profession
der Maurer(-)	bricklayer
der Klempner(-)	plumber
der Architekt(en)	architect (m)

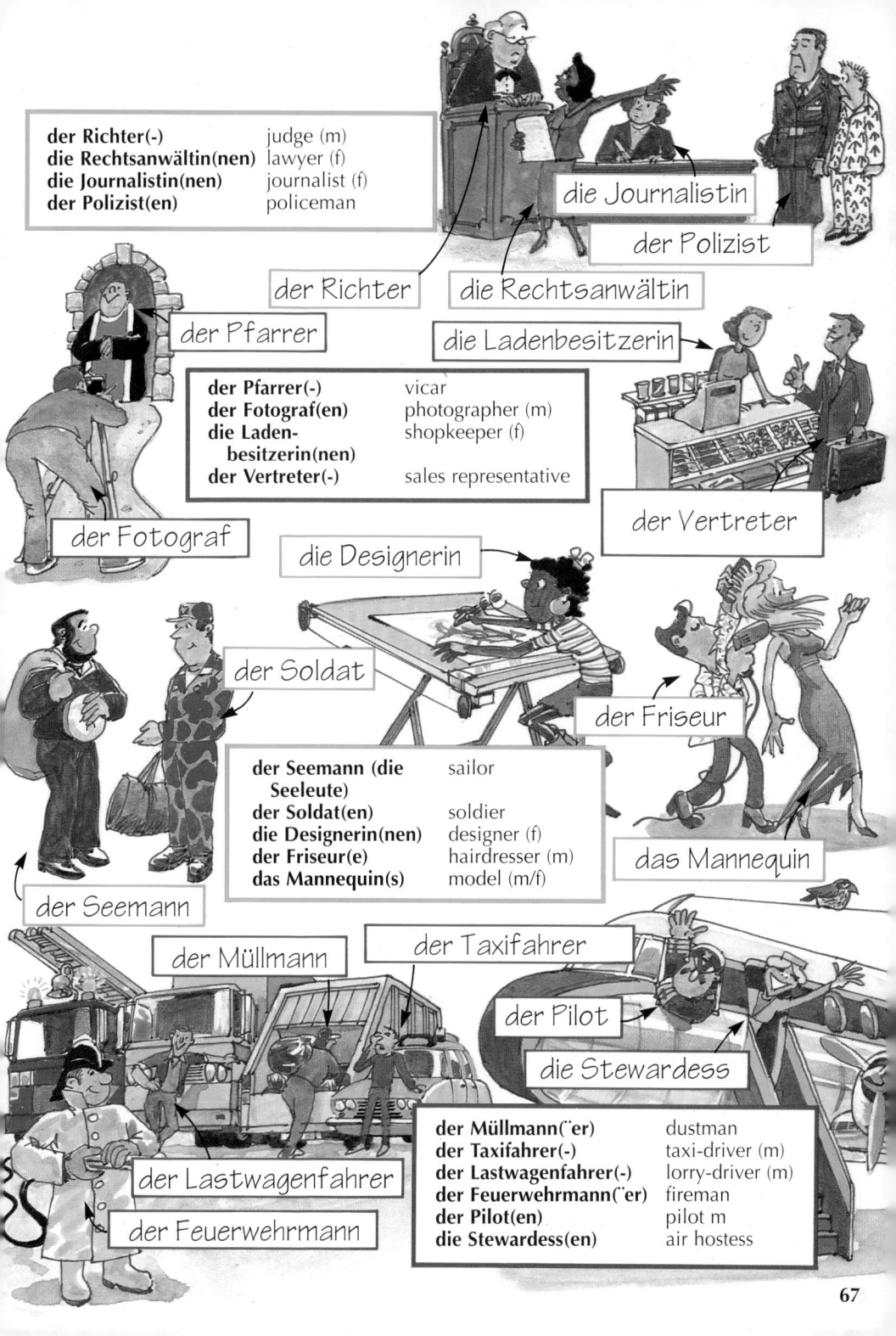

der Richter(-)	judge (m)
die Rechtsanwältin(nen)	lawyer (f)
die Journalistin(nen)	journalist (f)
der Polizist(en)	policeman

der Pfarrer(-)	vicar
der Fotograf(en)	photographer (m)
die Ladenbesitzerin(nen)	shopkeeper (f)
der Vertreter(-)	sales representative

der Seemann (die Seeleute)	sailor
der Soldat(en)	soldier
die Designerin(nen)	designer (f)
der Friseur(e)	hairdresser (m)
das Mannequin(s)	model (m/f)

der Müllmann(¨er)	dustman
der Taxifahrer(-)	taxi-driver (m)
der Lastwagenfahrer(-)	lorry-driver (m)
der Feuerwehrmann(¨er)	fireman
der Pilot(en)	pilot m
die Stewardess(en)	air hostess

Illness and health

sich krank fühlen	to feel ill	**die Ärztin(nen)**	doctor (f)
die Temperatur messen	to take someone's temperature	**das Rezept(e)**	prescription
das Thermometer(-)	thermometer	**heilen**	to cure
Fieber haben	to have a temperature	**die Tablette(n)**	pill
		sich besser fühlen	to feel better
		gesund	healthy

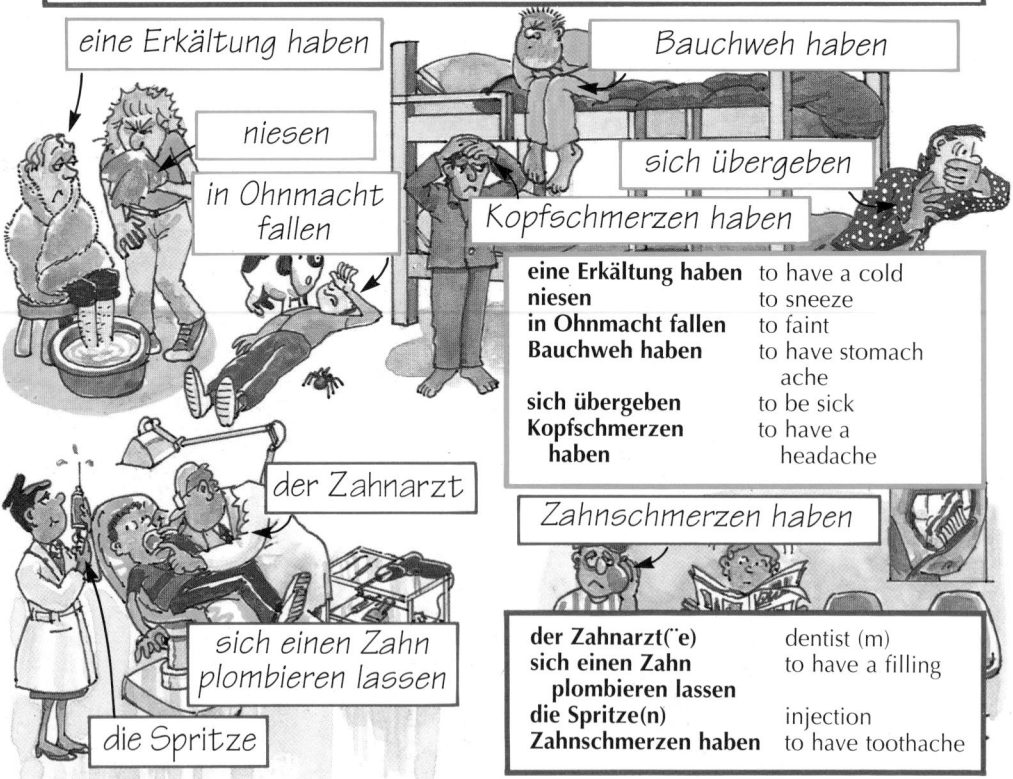

eine Erkältung haben	to have a cold		
niesen	to sneeze		
in Ohnmacht fallen	to faint		
Bauchweh haben	to have stomach ache		
sich übergeben	to be sick		
Kopfschmerzen haben	to have a headache		

der Zahnarzt(¨e)	dentist (m)		
sich einen Zahn plombieren lassen	to have a filling		
die Spritze(n)	injection		
Zahnschmerzen haben	to have toothache		

das Krankenhaus
die Unfallstation
der blaue Fleck
sich das Bein brechen
die Verbrennung
sich die Hand verstauchen
die Schnittwunde
das Heftpflaster
der Verband

das Krankenhaus(¨er)	hospital
die Unfallstation(en)	casualty department
sich das Bein brechen	to break your leg
der blaue Fleck(en)	bruise
die Schnittwunde(n)	cut
die Verbrennung(en)	burn
sich die Hand verstauchen	to sprain your wrist
das Heftpflaster(-)	sticking plaster
der Verband(¨e)	bandage

der Krankenwagen
den Puls fühlen
der Patient
die Bahre

der Krankenwagen(-)	ambulance
den Puls fühlen	to take someone's pulse
die Bahre(n)	stretcher
der Patient(en)	patient (m)

der Operationssaal
die Operation
die Krankenschwester
der Chirurg

der Operationssaal	operating theatre
der Chirurg(en)	surgeon (m)
die Operation(en)	operation
die Krankenschwester(n)	nurse (f)

School and education

der Kindergarten
die Grundschule
der Direktor
das Gymnasium
die Universität
die Direktorin

der Kindergarten(¨)	nursery school	**das Gymnasium (die Gymnasien)**	secondary school
die Grundschule(n)	primary school	**die Direktorin(nen)**	headmistress
der Direktor(en)	headmaster	**die Universität(en)**	university

in der Schule
das Klassenzimmer
die Unterrichtsstunde
der Lehrer
die Karte
lehren
der Schüler
die Tafel
lernen
einfach
schwierig
die Kreide
etwas fragen
lesen
schreiben

in der Schule	at school	**lernen**	to learn
das Klassenzimmer(-)	classroom	**einfach**	easy
die Karte(n)	map	**schwierig**	difficult
die Unterrichts-stunde(n)	lesson	**die Tafel(n)**	blackboard
		die Kreide(n)	chalk
der Lehrer(-)	teacher (m)	**lesen**	to read
lehren	to teach	**schreiben**	to write
der Schüler(-)	pupil (m)	**etwas fragen**	to ask a question

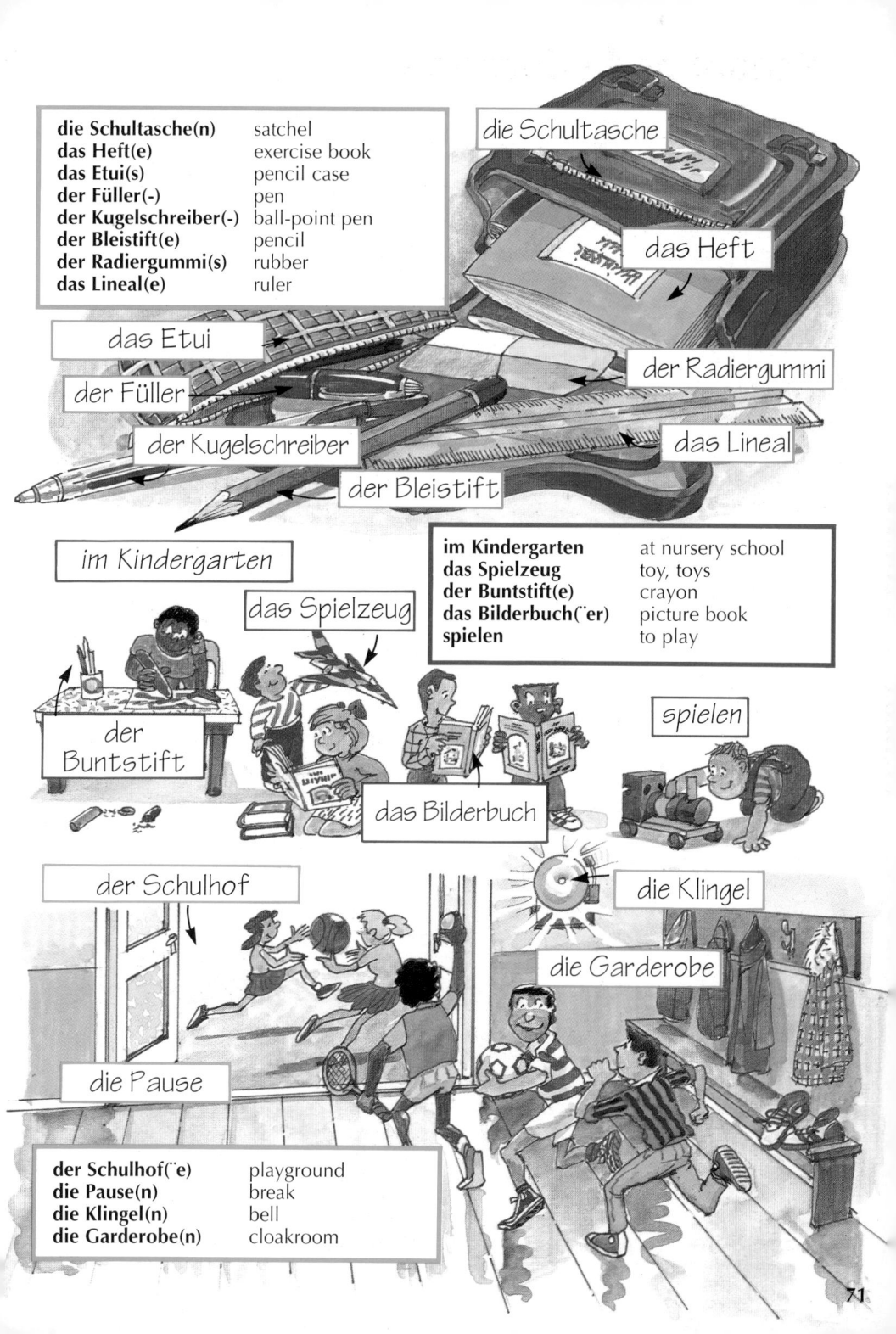

die Schultasche(n)	satchel
das Heft(e)	exercise book
das Etui(s)	pencil case
der Füller(-)	pen
der Kugelschreiber(-)	ball-point pen
der Bleistift(e)	pencil
der Radiergummi(s)	rubber
das Lineal(e)	ruler

im Kindergarten	at nursery school
das Spielzeug	toy, toys
der Buntstift(e)	crayon
das Bilderbuch(¨er)	picture book
spielen	to play

der Schulhof(¨e)	playground
die Pause(n)	break
die Klingel(n)	bell
die Garderobe(n)	cloakroom

School and education

das Schulhalbjahr
der Stundenplan
das Fach
der Anfang des Schulhalbjahres
Deutsch
Mathematik
Physik
Englisch
Chemie
Französisch
Biologie
Spanisch
Geschichte
Erdkunde
Musik
das Ende des Schulhalbjahres
Informatik
Sport

das Schulhalbjahr(e)	term	**Spanisch**	Spanish
der Anfang des Schulhalbjahres	beginning of term	**Mathematik**	maths
		Physik	physics
das Ende des Schulhalbjahres	end of term	**Chemie**	chemistry
		Biologie	biology
der Stundenplan(¨e)	timetable	**Geschichte**	history
das Fach(¨er)	subject	**Erdkunde**	geography
Deutsch	German	**Musik**	music
Englisch	English	**Informatik**	computer studies
Französisch	French	**Sport**	PE

A B C D E F G H I J K L M N O P Q R S T U V W X Y Z

der Buchstabe
das Alphabet
die Grammatik
die Rechtschreibung
der Großbuchstabe
das Wort
der Satz
der Punkt

der Buchstabe(n)	letter
das Alphabet(e)	alphabet
die Grammatik	grammar
die Rechtschreibung	spelling
der Großbuchstabe(n)	capital letter
das Wort(¨er)	word
der Satz(¨e)	sentence
der Punkt(e)	full stop

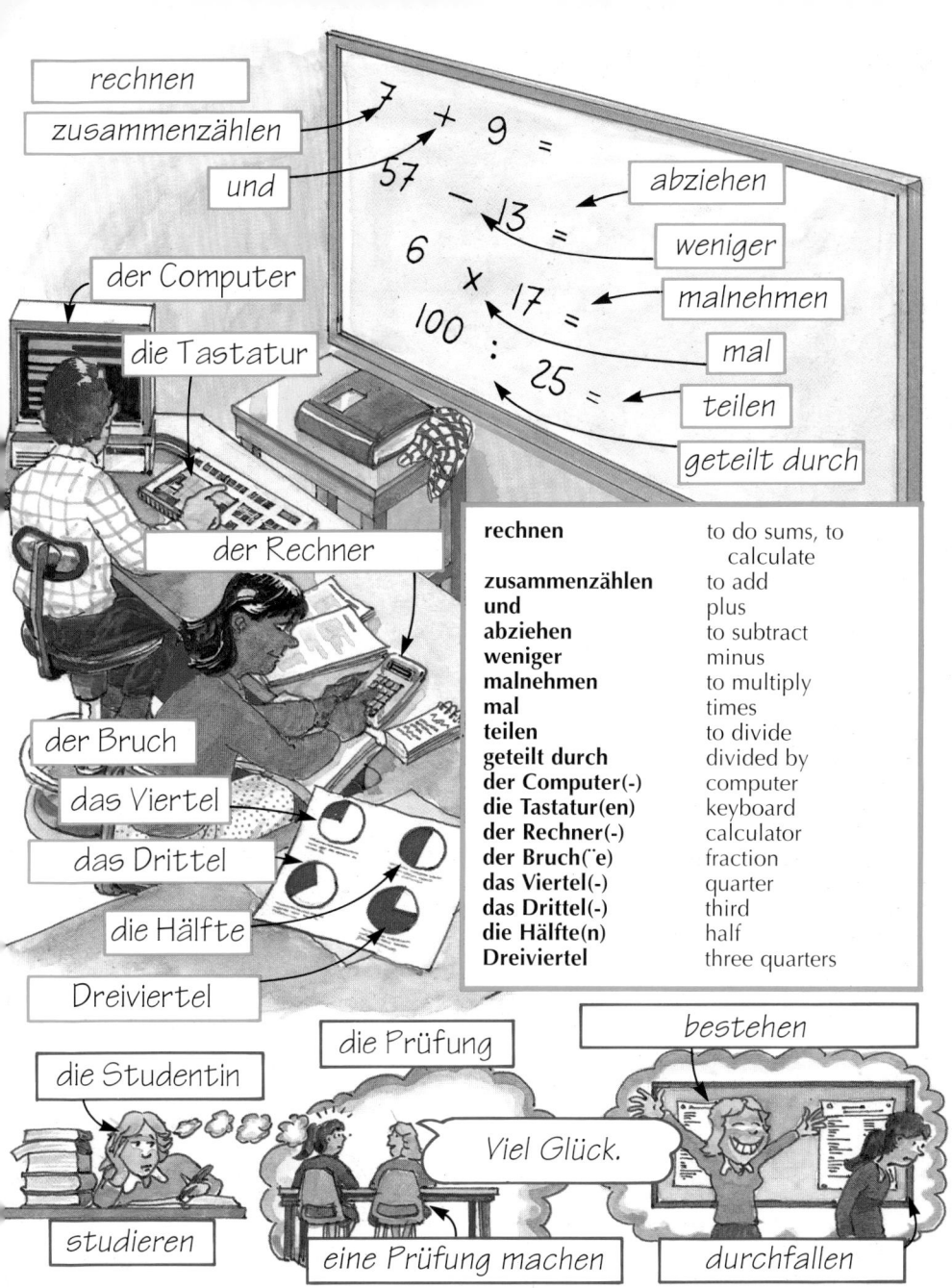

rechnen	to do sums, to calculate
zusammenzählen	to add
und	plus
abziehen	to subtract
weniger	minus
malnehmen	to multiply
mal	times
teilen	to divide
geteilt durch	divided by
der Computer(-)	computer
die Tastatur(en)	keyboard
der Rechner(-)	calculator
der Bruch(¨e)	fraction
das Viertel(-)	quarter
das Drittel(-)	third
die Hälfte(n)	half
Dreiviertel	three quarters

die Studentin(nen)	student (f)	**Viel Glück.**	Good luck.
studieren	to study	**bestehen**	to pass
die Prüfung(en)	exam	**durchfallen**	to fail
eine Prüfung machen	to sit an exam		

Shapes and sizes

die Form(en)	shape
der Kreis(e)	circle
das Quadrat(e)	square
das Dreieck(e)	triangle
der Kegel(-)	cone
das Rechteck(e)	rectangle

riesig	enormous
groß	big
klein	small
winzig	tiny

die Größe(n)	size
messen	to measure
der Meter(-)	metre
der Zentimeter(-)	centimetre
die Länge(n)	length
die Breite(n)	width

der Inhalt(e)	volume	**das Gewicht(e)**	weight
der Liter(-)	litre	**das Kilo(-)**	kilo
ein halber Liter(-)	half a litre	**ein Pfund(e)**	half a kilo

Numbers

100
hundert
tausend
1 000
eine Million
1 000 000
neunzig 90
achtzig 80
siebzig
sechzig 70
fünfzig 60
vierzig 50
dreiunddreißig 40
zweiunddreißig 33
einunddreißig 32
dreißig 31
fünfundzwanzig 30
vierundzwanzig 25
dreiundzwanzig 24
zweiundzwanzig 23
22
21
einundzwanzig
zwanzig 20
neunzehn 19
achtzehn 18
siebzehn 17
sechzehn 16
fünfzehn 15
vierzehn 14
dreizehn 13
zwölf 12
elf 11
zehn 10
neun 9
acht 8
sieben 7
sechs 6
fünf 5
vier 4
drei 3
zwei 2
eins 1
null 0

Sport

fit halten

joggen gehen

das Stirnband

trainieren

die Turnschuhe

der Trainingsanzug

fit halten	to keep fit	**die Turnschuhe** (s: **der Turnschuh**)	gym shoes
trainieren	to exercise		
joggen gehen	to go jogging	**der Trainingsanzug(¨e)**	tracksuit
das Stirnband(¨er)	headband		

Golf spielen

Tennis spielen

der Golfschläger

der Tennisplatz

Squash spielen

der Spieler

Nicht aus.

aufschlagen

Aus.

das Netz

der Ball

der Schläger

Tennis spielen	to play tennis	**das Netz(e)**	net
der Tennisplatz(¨e)	tennis court	**der Ball(¨e)**	ball
der Spieler(-)	player (m)	**der Schläger(-)**	racket
aufschlagen	to serve	**Golf spielen**	to play golf
Nicht aus.	In.	**der Golfschläger(-)**	golf club
Aus.	Out.	**Squash spielen**	to play squash

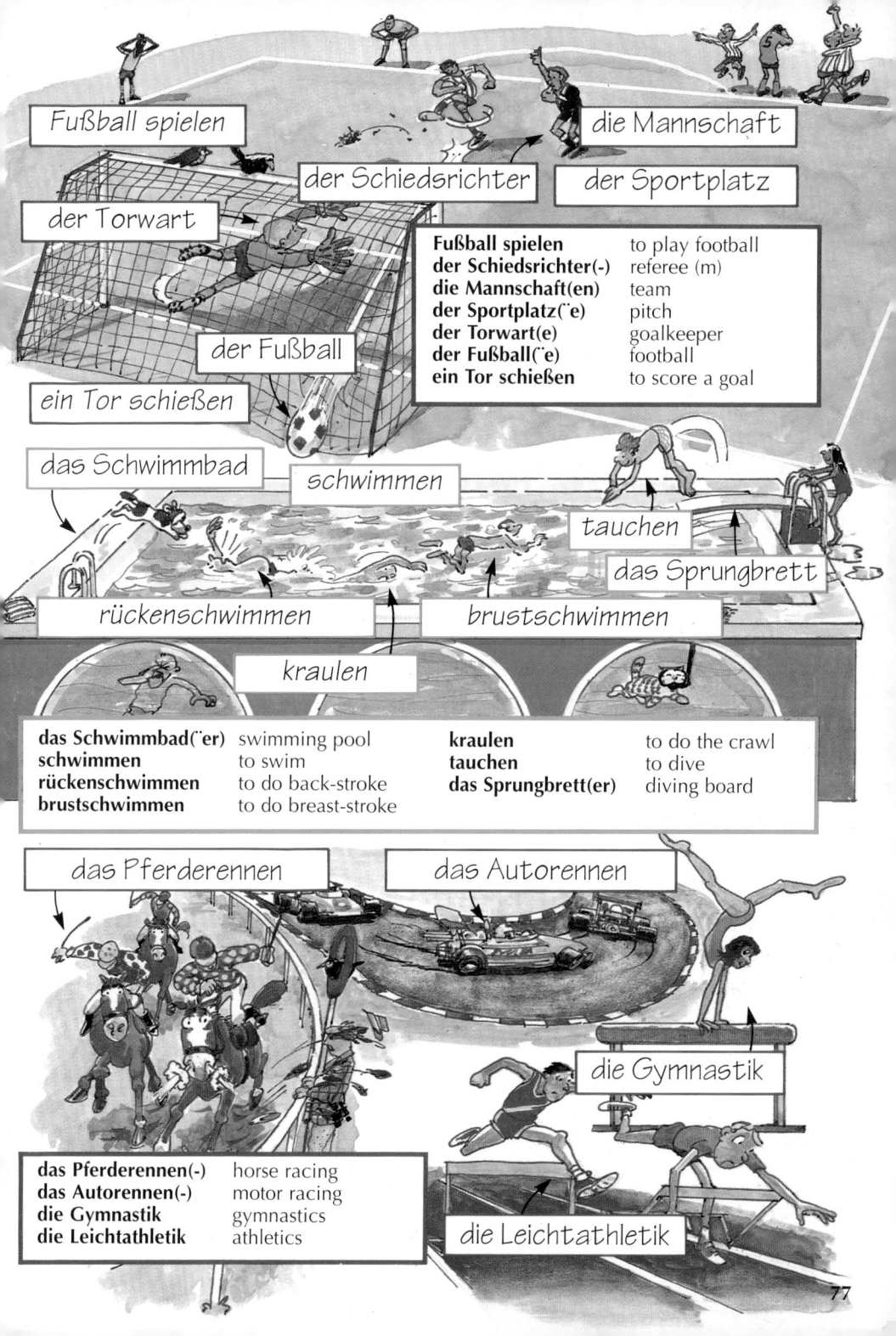

Fußball spielen	to play football
der Schiedsrichter(-)	referee (m)
die Mannschaft(en)	team
der Sportplatz(¨e)	pitch
der Torwart(e)	goalkeeper
der Fußball(¨e)	football
ein Tor schießen	to score a goal

das Schwimmbad(¨er)	swimming pool	**kraulen**	to do the crawl
schwimmen	to swim	**tauchen**	to dive
rückenschwimmen	to do back-stroke	**das Sprungbrett(er)**	diving board
brustschwimmen	to do breast-stroke		

das Pferderennen(-)	horse racing
das Autorennen(-)	motor racing
die Gymnastik	gymnastics
die Leichtathletik	athletics

Celebrations

der Geburtstag(e)	birthday
die Party(s)	party
der Luftballon(s)	balloon
Herzlichen Glückwunsch zum Geburtstag.	Happy Birthday.
einladen	to invite
Spaß haben	to have fun, to enjoy yourself
die Torte(n)	cake
die Kerze(n)	candle
die Karte(n)	card
das Geschenk(e)	present
die Verpackung(en)	wrapping

Ostern	Easter
Weihnachten	Christmas
der Heilige Abend	Christmas Eve
der erste Weihnachstag	Christmas Day
der Weihnachtsbaum(¨e)	Christmas tree

sich verloben	to get engaged
die Hochzeit(en)	wedding
heiraten	to get married
der Bräutigam(e)	bridegroom
die Braut(¨e)	bride
der Gast(¨e)	guest (m)
gratulieren	to congratulate
der Blumenstrauß(¨e)	bouquet
glücklich sein	to be happy
die Flitterwochen (pl)	honeymoon

Frohe Weihnachten.	Happy Christmas.
das Weihnachtslied(er)	Christmas carol
schenken	to give (a present)
bekommen	to receive
Danke schön.	Thank you very much.
sich bedanken	to thank

Silvester	New Year's Eve
Neujahr	New Year's Day
feiern	to celebrate
Glückliches Neues Jahr.	Happy New Year.

Days and dates

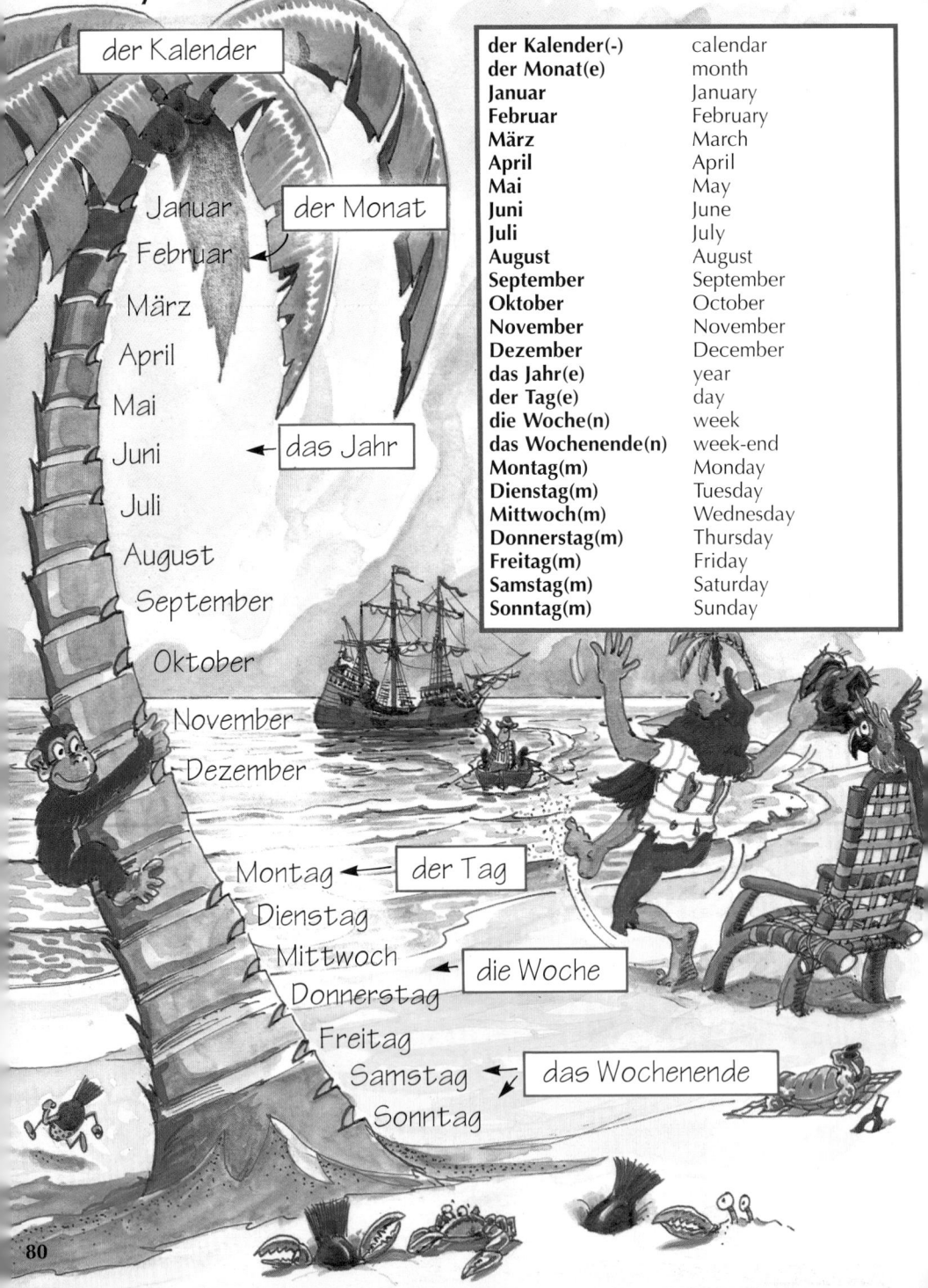

der Kalender(-)	calendar
der Monat(e)	month
Januar	January
Februar	February
März	March
April	April
Mai	May
Juni	June
Juli	July
August	August
September	September
Oktober	October
November	November
Dezember	December
das Jahr(e)	year
der Tag(e)	day
die Woche(n)	week
das Wochenende(n)	week-end
Montag(m)	Monday
Dienstag(m)	Tuesday
Mittwoch(m)	Wednesday
Donnerstag(m)	Thursday
Freitag(m)	Friday
Samstag(m)	Saturday
Sonntag(m)	Sunday

der Kalender(-)	diary
das Datum (pl: Daten)	date
Dienstag, der zweite Juni	Tuesday, the second of June
der erste	the first
der zweite	the second
der dritte	the third
der vierte	the fourth
der fünfte	the fifth

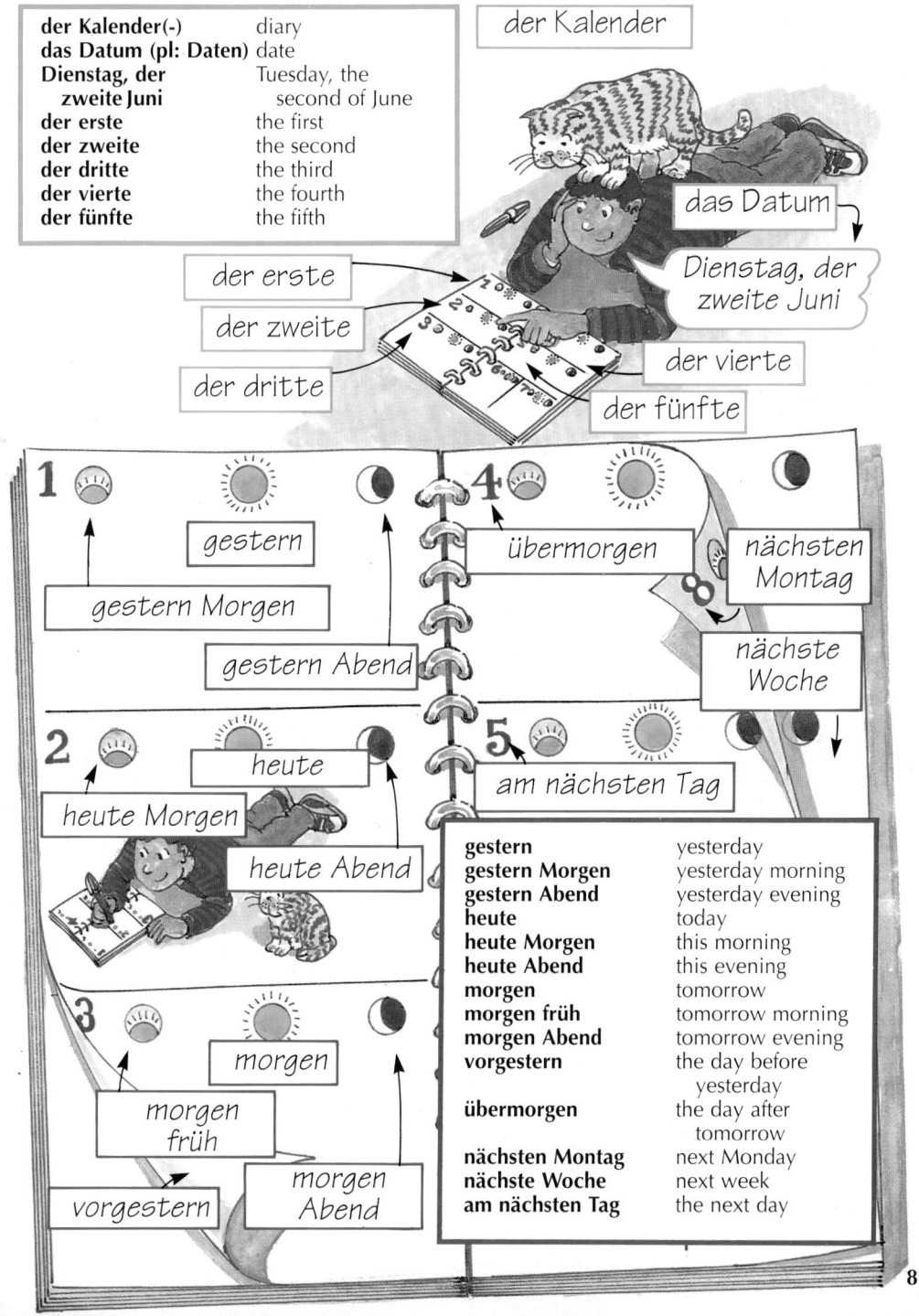

gestern	yesterday
gestern Morgen	yesterday morning
gestern Abend	yesterday evening
heute	today
heute Morgen	this morning
heute Abend	this evening
morgen	tomorrow
morgen früh	tomorrow morning
morgen Abend	tomorrow evening
vorgestern	the day before yesterday
übermorgen	the day after tomorrow
nächsten Montag	next Monday
nächste Woche	next week
am nächsten Tag	the next day

Time

das Morgengrauen(-)	dawn	**die Sonne**	sun
der Sonnenaufgang(¨e)	sunrise	**der Himmel**	sky
Es wird hell.	It is getting light.	**Es ist hell.**	It is light.
der Morgen(-)	morning	**der Tag(e)**	day

der Nachmittag(e)	afternoon	**die Nacht(¨e)**	night
der Abend(e)	evening	**die Sterne (s: der Stern)**	stars
der Sonnenuntergang(¨e)	sunset	**der Mond**	moon
Es wird dunkel.	It is getting dark.	**Es ist dunkel.**	It is dark.

Wie spät ist es?	What time is it?	**Mitternacht**	midnight
die Stunde(n)	hour	**Viertel vor zehn**	a quarter to 10
die Minute(n)	minute	**fünf nach zehn**	five past 10
die Sekunde(n)	second	**Viertel nach zehn**	a quarter past 10
Es ist ein Uhr.	It is 1 o'clock.	**halb elf**	half past 10
Es ist drei Uhr.	It is 3 o'clock.	**acht Uhr morgens**	8 a.m.
Mittag	midday	**acht Uhr abends**	8 p.m.

die Zeit	time	**damals**	in the past
die Vergangenheit	past	**in der Zukunft**	in the future
die Zukunft	future	**jetzt**	now, nowadays
die Gegenwart	present		

Weather and seasons

die Jahreszeit(en)	season
der Frühling	spring
der Sommer	summer
der Herbst	autumn
der Winter	winter

das Wetter	weather
Es regnet.	It's raining.
der Regen	rain
der Sturm(¨e)	storm
die Wolke(n)	cloud
der Blitz(e)	lightning
der Donner	thunder
der Regenschirm(e)	umbrella
der Regenbogen(-)	rainbow
die Gummistiefel (pl)	wellington boots
klatschnass	soaked to the skin
die Pfütze(n)	puddle
der Regentropfen(-)	raindrop
der Hagel	hail
die Überschwemmung(en)	flood

das Klima(s)	climate
die Wettervorhersage(n)	weather forecast
Wie ist das Wetter?	What is the weather like?

Es ist schön.	It's fine.
Die Sonne scheint.	The sun is shining.
schwitzen	to sweat
Mir ist warm.	I'm hot.

der Wind	wind
Es ist windig.	It's windy.
der Nebel	fog
Es ist neblig.	It's foggy.

Es ist kalt.	It's cold.
halb erfroren sein	to be frozen
der Frost	frost
der Eiszapfen(-)	icicle
der Schnee	snow
der Schneemann(¨er)	snowman
Es schneit.	It's snowing.
tauen	to thaw

World and universe

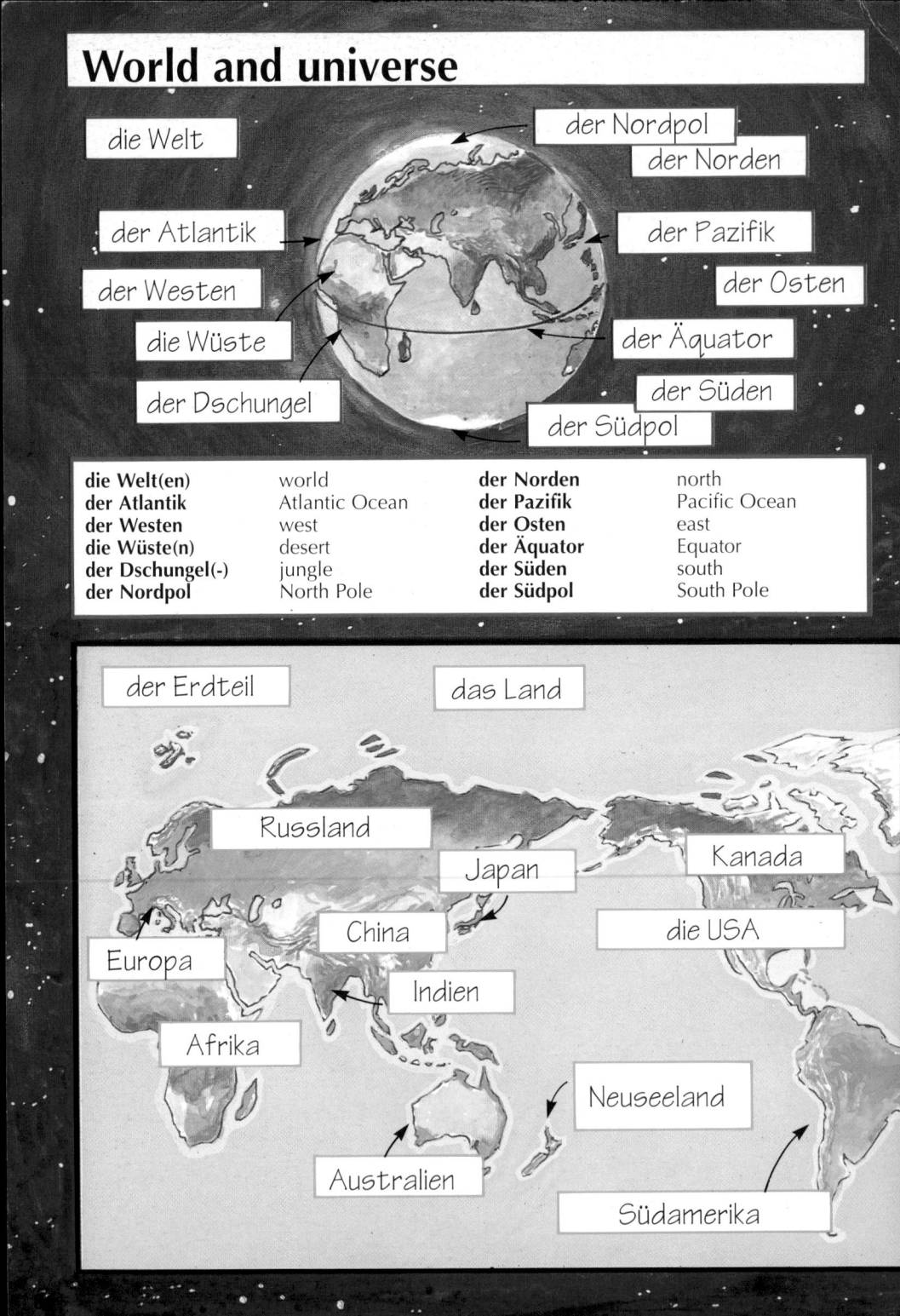

die Welt(en)	world	**der Norden**	north
der Atlantik	Atlantic Ocean	**der Pazifik**	Pacific Ocean
der Westen	west	**der Osten**	east
die Wüste(n)	desert	**der Äquator**	Equator
der Dschungel(-)	jungle	**der Süden**	south
der Nordpol	North Pole	**der Südpol**	South Pole

das Universum
der Weltraum
der Stern
der Planet
das Raumschiff
die Milchstraße
das Fernrohr

das Universum	universe
der Weltraum	space
der Planet(en)	planet
der Stern(e)	star
das Raumschiff(e)	spaceship
die Milchstraße(n)	Milky Way
das Fernrohr(e)	telescope

der Erdteil(e)	continent
das Land(¨er)	country
Russland	Russia
Europa	Europe
Afrika	Africa
Japan	Japan
China	China
Indien	India
Australien	Australia
Neuseeland	New Zealand
Kanada	Canada
die USA (pl)	USA
Südamerika	South America

Skandinavien	Scandinavia
Großbritannien	Great Britain
die Niederlande (pl)	Netherlands
Belgien	Belgium
Deutschland	Germany
Frankreich	France
die Schweiz	Switzerland
Italien	Italy
Spanien	Spain

Skandinavien
Großbritannien
die Niederlande
Belgien
Deutschland
Frankreich
die Schweiz
Italien
Spanien

Politics

der Präsident(en)	president (m)
das Parlament(e)	parliament
die Abgeordnete(n)	member of parliament (f)
der Bundeskanzler(-)*	prime minister (m)
die Regierung(en)	government

die Partei(en)	party
die Vorsitzende(n)	leader (f)
beliebt	popular
das Mitglied(er)	member (m/f)

die Wahl(en)	election	**liberal**	centre
wählen	to vote	**konservativ**	right wing
gewinnen	to win	**Mitglied werden**	to join
verlieren	to loose	**Mitglied sein**	to belong
links	left wing		

* This is the prime minister (or chancellor) of Germany. For prime ministers of other countries, you say **der Premierminister** or **der Ministerpräsident**.

die Medien (pl)	the media
interviewen	to interview
wichtig	important
interessant	interesting
die Zeitung(en)	newspaper
die Nachrichten (pl)	news
die Schlagzeile(n)	headline
der Artikel(-)	article
wahr	true
falsch	false

die Politik	politics
die Gesellschaft	society
demokratisch	democratic
der Lohn(¨e)	wages
die Steuern (s: die Steuer)	taxes
die Gewerkschaft(en)	trade union
die Arbeitslosigkeit	unemployment

Describing things

laut	noisy
ruhig	quiet
gehorsam	obedient
frech	naughty
gleich	same
unterschiedlich	different

beschäftigt	busy
nützlich	useful
zusammen	together
allein	alone
ängstlich	frightened
mutig	brave

unvorsichtig	careless
vorsichtig	careful
böse	cross
zufrieden mit	pleased with
lebhaft	lively
langweilig	boring

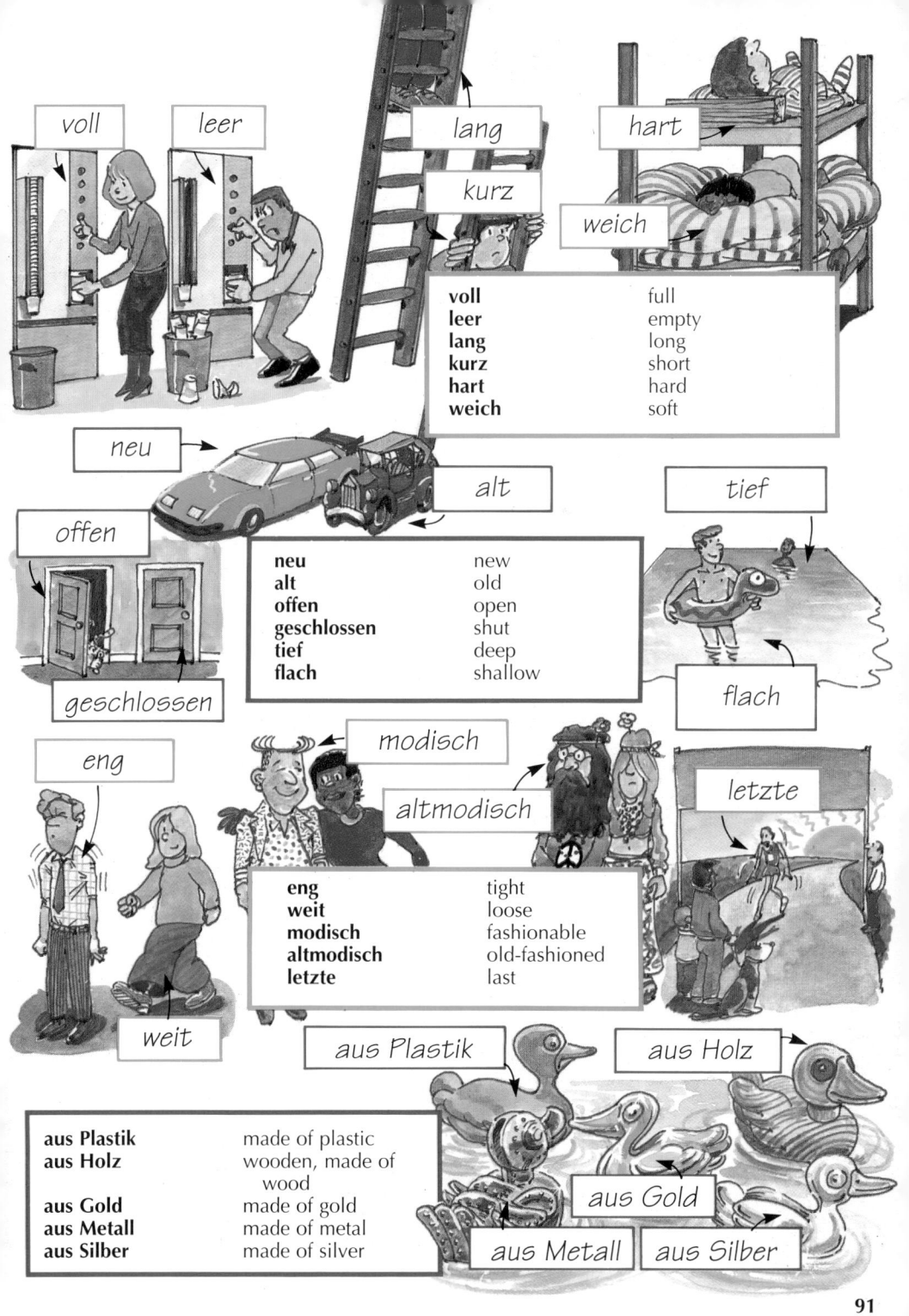

voll	full
leer	empty
lang	long
kurz	short
hart	hard
weich	soft

neu	new
alt	old
offen	open
geschlossen	shut
tief	deep
flach	shallow

eng	tight
weit	loose
modisch	fashionable
altmodisch	old-fashioned
letzte	last

aus Plastik	made of plastic
aus Holz	wooden, made of wood
aus Gold	made of gold
aus Metall	made of metal
aus Silber	made of silver

Colours

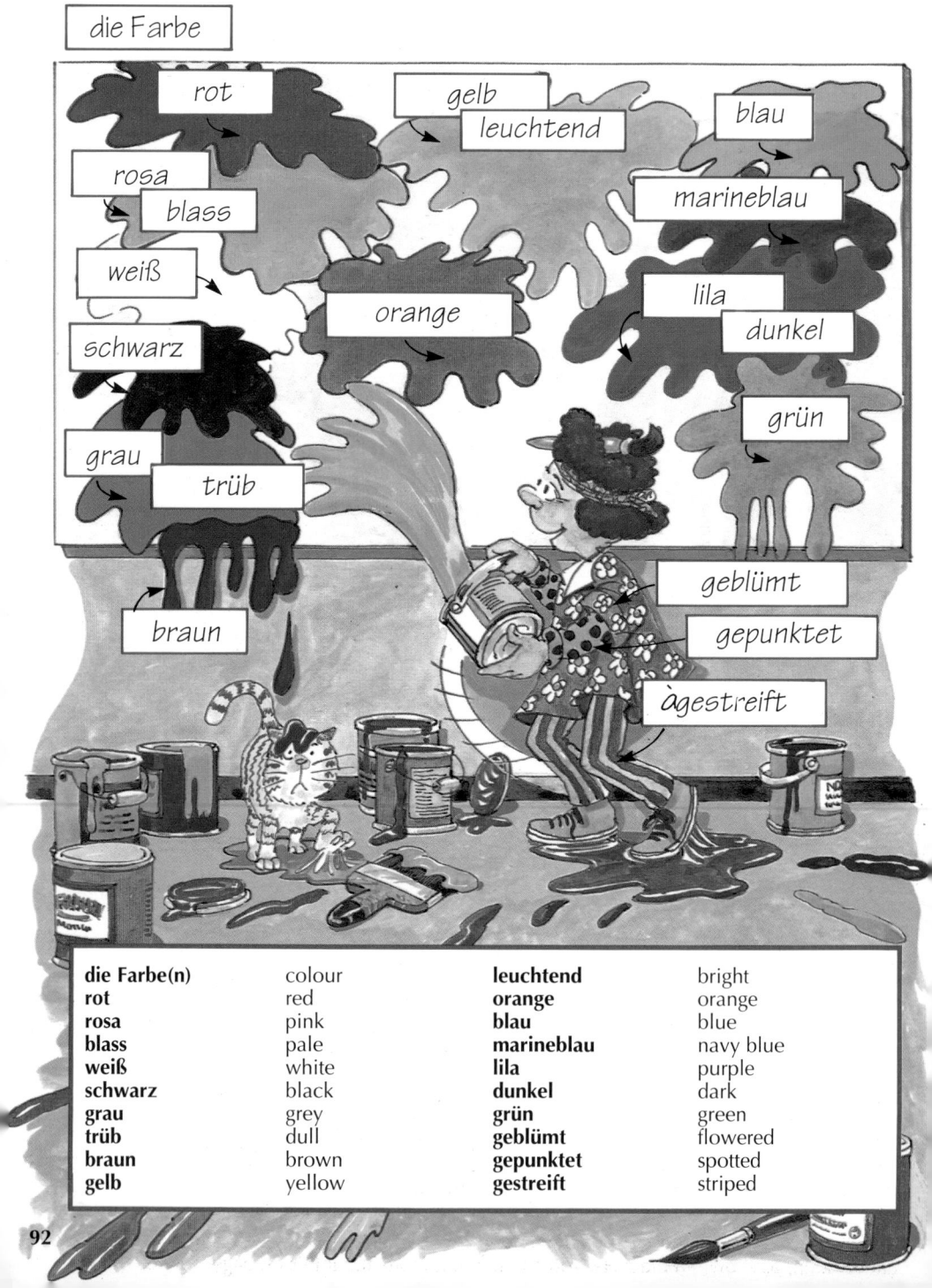

die Farbe(n)	colour	**leuchtend**	bright
rot	red	**orange**	orange
rosa	pink	**blau**	blue
blass	pale	**marineblau**	navy blue
weiß	white	**lila**	purple
schwarz	black	**dunkel**	dark
grau	grey	**grün**	green
trüb	dull	**geblümt**	flowered
braun	brown	**gepunktet**	spotted
gelb	yellow	**gestreift**	striped

In, on, under...

in (dat)*	in	**gegen (acc)**	against
auf (acc or dat)	on	**durch (acc)**	through
unter (acc or dat)	under	**zwischen (acc or dat)**	among
über (acc or dat)	over	**auf (acc)...zu**	to, towards
in (acc)	into	**weg von (dat)**	away from
aus (dat)	out of	**hinauf (acc. Always follows noun)**	up
neben (acc or dat)	beside		
zwischen (acc or dat)	between	**hinunter (acc. Always follows noun)**	down
nahe an (dat)	near		
weit weg von (dat)	far away from	**gegenüber (dat)**	opposite
vor (acc or dat)	in front of	**mit (dat)**	with
hinter (acc or dat)	behind	**ohne (acc)**	without

*Words like "in" are prepositions. In German they are followed by an accusative or dative noun, as shown in brackets. You can find out more about this on pages 96-98.

Action words

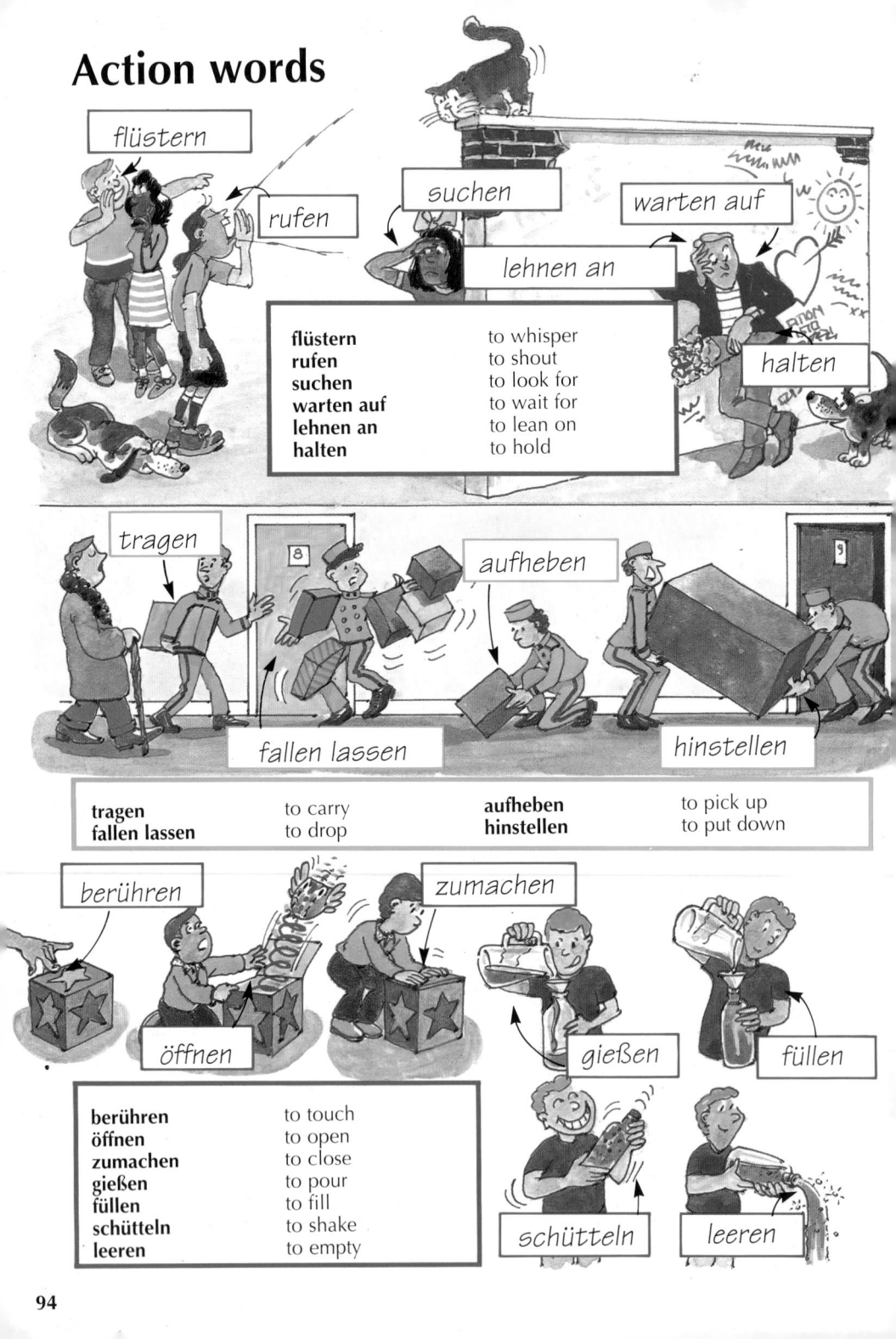

flüstern	to whisper
rufen	to shout
suchen	to look for
warten auf	to wait for
lehnen an	to lean on
halten	to hold

tragen	to carry	**aufheben**	to pick up
fallen lassen	to drop	**hinstellen**	to put down

berühren	to touch
öffnen	to open
zumachen	to close
gießen	to pour
füllen	to fill
schütteln	to shake
leeren	to empty

zerreißen	to tear
flicken	to mend
werfen	to throw
fangen	to catch
umwerfen	to knock over
zerbrechen	to break

ziehen	to pull	**weglaufen**	to run away
drücken	to push	**verfolgen**	to follow
stehlen	to steal	**sich verstecken**	to hide
ausrutschen	to slip		

Grammar hints

In order to speak German well, you need to learn a bit about the grammar, that is, how words fit together and work in sentences. On the next few pages, there are some hints on German grammar. Some of its rules are quite complicated, so don't worry if you cannot remember them all at first. Try to learn a little grammar at a time and then practise using it.

Nouns

In German, all nouns begin with a capital letter and are either masculine, feminine or neuter (this is called their gender). The word you use for "the" shows which gender they are. It is **der** before masculine nouns, **die** before feminine nouns and **das** before neuter nouns:

der Mann	the man (m)
die Frau	the woman (f)
das Kind	the child (n)

Some nouns have a masculine and a feminine form. These are often nouns which describe what people are or what they do:

der Arzt	the doctor (m)
die Ärztin	the doctor (f)
der Journalist	the journalist (m)
die Journalistin	the journalist (f)

When they appear in the illustrated section of this book, only the form which matches the picture is given, but both masculine and feminine forms are given in the word list at the back.

Plurals

When you are talking about more than one thing, the word for "the" is **die**. German nouns often change their endings in the plural and sometimes add an umlaut (¨):

der Mann becomes **die Männer**
die Frau becomes **die Frauen**
das Kind becomes **die Kinder**

It is a good idea when you are learning nouns to learn the plural as well. In this book the plurals are given in brackets after the nouns, e.g. **der Mann(¨er).**

Cases

In German, nouns have four forms, or cases, depending on what job they do in the sentence. The cases are:

Nominative – a noun is nominative when it is the subject of the sentence (when it is the person or thing doing the action).

Accusative – a noun is accusative when it is the direct object of the sentence (when it is the person or thing to whom the action is done).

Genitive – a noun is genitive when it tells you to whom something belongs (in English, it often has an "'s" after it, e.g. The cat's whiskers).

Dative – a noun is dative when it is the indirect object of the sentence (when it is the person or thing to whom or for whom the action is being done).

Nominative: **The dog** bites the boy.
Accusative: The boy hits **the dog**.
Genitive: **The dog's** eyes look sad.
Dative: The boy gives **the dog** a bone.

der, die, das

The word for "the" changes depending on the case of the noun and on whether the noun is masculine, feminine, neuter or plural. It is a good idea to learn all the cases of **der**, **die** and **das** in lists as shown below:

	singular			plural
	m	f	n	
Nom	**der**	**die**	**das**	**die**
Acc	**den**	**die**	**das**	**die**
Gen	**des**	**der**	**des**	**der**
Dat	**dem**	**der**	**dem**	**den**

Occasionally, the noun also changes when it is in a particular case. For example, in the masculine and neuter genitive singular:

der Mann becomes **des Mannes**
das Kind becomes **des Kindes**

ein, eine, ein

The word for "a" or "an" is **ein** before masculine and neuter nouns and **eine** before feminine nouns. **Ein**, **eine** and **ein**, like **der**, **die** and **das**, change depending on the case of the noun. It is best to learn the changes by heart:

	m	f	n
Nom	**ein**	**eine**	**ein**
Acc	**einen**	**eine**	**ein**
Gen	**eines**	**einer**	**eines**
Dat	**einem**	**einer**	**einem**

kein, keine, kein

The word **kein** means "no" or "not a":

Ich habe kein Geld.
I have no money.

In the singular, **kein** changes like **ein**, **eine**, **ein**. The plural is also shown here:

	singular			plural
	m	f	n	
Nom	**kein**	**keine**	**kein**	**keine**
Acc	**keinen**	**keine**	**kein**	**keine**
Gen	**keines**	**keiner**	**keines**	**keiner**
Dat	**keinem**	**keiner**	**keinem**	**keinen**

dieser, diese, dieses

To say "this" in German, you use **dieser**:

dieser Mann this man

Dieser changes like **der, die, das:**

	singular			plural
	m	f	n	
Nom	**dieser**	**diese**	**dieses**	**diese**
Acc	**diesen**	**diese**	**dieses**	**diese**
Gen	**dieses**	**dieser**	**dieses**	**dieser**
Dat	**diesem**	**dieser**	**diesem**	**diesen**

mein, dein, sein

Mein (my), **dein** (your), **sein** (his, her, its) and so on are called possessive adjectives. They have the same endings as **ein** and **kein** (see over).

m	f	n	
mein	**meine**	**mein**	my
dein	**deine**	**dein**	your (s)
sein	**seine**	**sein**	his, its
ihr	**ihre**	**ihr**	her
unser	**unsere**	**unser**	our
euer	**eure**	**euer**	your (pl)
ihr	**ihre**	**ihr**	their
Ihr	**Ihre**	**Ihr**	your (s and pl polite)*

Here are some examples of how to use "my", "your", etc in German:

Ich liebe meinen Hund.
I love my dog.
Sie spielt mit ihrer Katze.
She is playing with her cat.
Wir besuchen unsere Großeltern.
We are visiting our grandparents.
Er fährt auf meinem Rad.
He is riding my bicycle.

Prepositions

Prepositions are words which tell you where things are (e.g. under the table), where things are going (e.g. the train to Hamburg; the card is for you) or when they will happen (e.g. on Friday). In German, prepositions are followed either by an accusative or a dative:

durch (acc) through:
Die Katze springt durch das Fenster.
The cat leaps through the window.

aus (dat) out of:
Die Katze springt aus dem Korb. The cat leaps out of the basket.

A few prepositions can take either case. They take the accusative when a change of place or a movement is involved (e.g. The cat ran under the table), and the dative when there is no change of place or no movement (e.g. The cat is sleeping under the table):

auf (acc) on:
Mein Hut ist auf den Tisch gefallen.
My hat fell onto the table.

auf (dat) on:
Mein Hut liegt auf dem Tisch.
My hat is on the table.

There is a list of prepositions on page 93 which tells you which case each takes. The cases are also shown in the word list at the back.

Adjectives

Adjectives are words which describe a noun. They too have different endings depending on which case the noun is in and whether they are used with **der, die, das** or **ein, eine, ein.**

With **der, die, das:**

singular	m	f
Nom	**der junge**	**die junge**
Acc	**den jungen**	**die junge**
Gen	**des jungen**	**der jungen**
Dat	**dem jungen**	**der jungen**

	n	plural
Nom	**das junge**	**die jungen**
Acc	**das jungen**	**die jungen**
Gen	**des jungen**	**der jungen**
Dat	**dem jungen**	**den jungen**

der junge Mann the young man
die grünen Äpfel the green apples

*See Pronouns on page 99.

With **ein, eine, ein:**

singular	m	f
Nom	**ein junger**	**eine junge**
Acc	**einen jungen**	**eine junge**
Gen	**eines jungen**	**einer jungen**
Dat	**einem jungen**	**einer jungen**

	n	plural
Nom	**ein junges**	**junge**
Acc	**ein junges**	**junge**
Gen	**eines jungen**	**junger**
Dat	**einem jungen**	**jungen**

ein roter Lutballon a red balloon
ein hübsches Mädchen a pretty girl

Adjectives with **kein, mein, dein**, etc have the same endings as they do with **ein** in the singular. In the plural, they end with "en" whatever the case:

mein neues Fahrrad my new bicycle
deine kleine Schwester your little sister
keine roten Schuhe no red shoes

Comparing adjectives

When you compare things in German, the adjectives change in the same way as English ones, adding "er" or "est/st":

frisch	fresh
frischer	fresher
frischest	freshest

Often you also add an umlaut (¨) when the adjective is short and has just one syllable:

jung	young
jünger	younger
jüngst	youngest

These adjectives take the same endings as ordinary ones:

der frischeste Apfel the freshest apple

Some common adjectives change completely as they do in English:

gut	good	**viel**	many
besser	better	**mehr**	more
best	best	**meist**	most

Pronouns

"I", "you", "he", "she" and so on are called subject pronouns. You use them in place of a nominative noun (one which is the subject of a sentence). Here are the nominative pronouns:

ich	I	**wir**	we
du	you (s)	**ihr**	you (pl)
er	he	**sie**	they
sie	she	**Sie**	you (s and pl polite)
es	it		

In German, there are three words for you: **du, ihr** and **Sie**. For people you know well, such as friends and family, you use **du** in the singular and **ihr** in the plural. **Sie** is a polite form that you use with people you do not know very well. When it means you, **Sie** is always spelt with a capital "S".

An object pronoun is one which you put in place of a noun which is the object of the sentence. German pronouns have cases just like nouns: there are accusative ones to replace a direct object, and dative ones to replace an indirect object.

Here are the accusative pronouns:

mich	me
dich	you (s)
ihn	him
sie	her
es	it
uns	us
euch	you (pl)
sie	they
Sie	you (s and pl polite)

The following is a list of the dative pronouns:

mir	to/for me
dir	to/for you (s)
ihm	to/for him
ihr	to/for her
ihm	to/for it·
uns	to/for us
euch	to/for your (pl)
ihnen	to/for them
Ihnen	to/for you (s and pl polite)

Verbs

Verbs are 'doing' or action words. They change their endings depending on who is doing the action. In German most verbs follow a regular pattern. You take the "en" off the infinitive then add the different endings. These are the endings for the present tense:

infinitive: **hören** to hear

ich hör -e	I hear/am hearing
du hör -st	
er/sie/es hör -t	
wir hör -en	
ihr hör -t	
sie hör -en	
Sie hör -en	

Verbs like **hören** are called weak verbs. There are other verbs, like **geben**, which change the vowel in the **du** and **er** forms of the present tense. These belong to a group of verbs called strong verbs:

geben to give

ich geb -e
du gib -st
er/sie/es gib -t
wir geb -en
ihr geb -t
sie geb -en
Sie geb -en

You can find a list of strong verbs on page 105.

Some very common verbs, such as **sein** (to be) and **haben** (to have) do not take the normal pattern of endings. They are known as irregular verbs and it is best to learn them as you come across them. The present tenses of **sein** and **haben** are shown below. You can find the present tenses of other irregular verbs on pages 103-104.

sein to be	**haben** to have
ich bin	**ich habe**
du bist	**du hast**
er/sie/es ist	**er/sie/es hat**
wir sind	**wir haben**
ihr seid	**ihr habt**
sie sind	**sie haben**
Sie sind	**Sie haben**

The future tense is used for things you are going to do. In German you make the future by putting the infinitive with the present tense of the verb **werden**.

Werden means "to become". When it is used to make the future, **werden** is equivalent to "shall" or "will" in English. **Werden** is a strong verb:

ich werde essen	I will eat
du wirst essen	
er/sie/es wird essen	
wir werden essen	
ihr werdet essen	
sie werden essen	
Sie werden essen	

You use the perfect tense for events which have already happened ("I have danced", "I danced", in English). In German the perfect is made by putting **haben** with the past participle of the verb. The past participle is based on the infinitive. For weak verbs you take the "en" off the infinitive, add "ge" at the beginning and "t" or "et" at the end:

	infinitive	past participle
to hear	**hören**	**gehört**
to play	**spielen**	**gespielt**
to wait	**warten**	**gewartet**

Strong verbs keep the "en" ending of the infinitive, add "ge" at the beginning and often change the vowel:

	infinitive	past participle
to give	**geben**	**gegeben**
to find	**finden**	**gefunden**
to see	**sehen**	**gesehen**

The list of strong verbs on page 105 shows their past participles. It is best to try and learn them by heart.

Here is the perfect tense of hören:

ich habe gehört
du hast gehört
er/sie/es hat gehört
wir haben gehört
ihr habt gehört
sie haben gehört
Sie haben gehört

A few German verbs use **sein** rather than **haben** to make the perfect tense:
ich bin gekommen I came
ich bin gefahren I went, I travelled

They are usually verbs which involve movement or change of some kind. There is a list of common verbs which take **sein** on page 104.

Separable verbs

Some German verbs are made up of two parts which are separated in a sentence. For example, **ankommen** (to arrive) is made up of **an** (in, at) and **kommen** (to come). **Kommen** is used like a normal verb, but you usually put **an** (called the prefix) at the end of the sentence:

Der Zug kommt um vier Uhr an.
The train arrives at four o'clock.

In the perfect tense, the "ge" of the past participle comes between the prefix and the main part of the verb:

Der Zug ist um vier Uhr angekommen. The train arrived at four o'clock.

Here is a list of the prefixes of separable verbs. If a verb begins with any of these you know that it separates:

ab	off	**los**	away
an	at, on	**mit**	with
auf	up	**nach**	after
aus	out	**vor**	before
ein	in, into	**weg**	away
her	here	**zu**	to
hin	there, away	**zurück**	back

Reflexive verbs

Reflexive verbs are made up of a verb and the pronoun **sich**. **Sich** means "self" and reflexive verbs often involve doing something to yourself:

sich waschen	to wash oneself
sich setzen	to sit down

The pronoun **sich** changes depending on who is doing the action:

ich wasche mich
du wäscht dich
er/sie/es wäscht sich
wir waschen uns
ihr wascht euch
sie waschen sich
Sie waschen sich

You use **haben** to make the perfect tense of reflexive verbs.

ich habe mich gewaschen

Word order

In a German sentence, the words are in a different order from those in an English sentence. The verb is always the second idea in the sentence with the subject usually first and the object third. Other words or ideas follow in order of time, manner, then place:

Sie liest ein Buch.
She is reading a book.
Sie liest mir das Buch vor.
She is reading the book to me.
Wir fliegen nach Berlin.
We are flying to Berlin.
Wir fahren nächste Woche mit dem Auto nach Berlin. We are going to Berlin by car next week.

In the future and perfect tenses, the infinitive and past participle go right to the end of the sentence:

Ich werde eine Party geben.
I am going to have a party.
Er hat seine Brieftasche gefunden.
He has found his wallet.

Negatives

To make a negative in German, you put **nicht** ("not") after the verb:

Er spricht nicht laut.
He is not speaking loudly.
Ich werde nicht ausgehen.
I will not go out.

In the perfect tense the **nicht** comes just before the past participle:

Ich habe das Eis nicht gegessen.
I did not eat the ice-cream.

The word **kein** ("no" or "not a", see page 97) is used with nouns to make negatives:

Ich habe keine Katze. I do not have a cat./I have no cat.

Questions

To form a question, you put the subject after the verb, as in English:

Hast du ein neues Kleid?
Have you/Do you have a new dress?
Wird deine Schwester auch kommen?
Will your sister come too?

Here are some questions beginning with common question words:

Wer ist das? Who is that?
Was machst du? What are you doing?
Wann ist sie nach Frankfurt gefahren?
When did she go to Frankfurt?
Wie bist du hierher gekommen?
How did you get here?
Wie viel kostet die Fahrkarte?
How much does the ticket cost?
Wie viele Brüder hast du?
How many brothers have you got?
Warum hat sie das gesagt?
Why did she say that?
Wo ist das Kino?
Where is the cinema?
Woher kommst du?
Where do you come from?

Welcher means "which" or "what". It changes like **dieser**, **diese**, **dieses** to agree with the noun which follows:

Welches Buch liest du?
What book are you reading?

Welche Sprachen kennt er?
Which languages does he know?

Irregular verbs

Here are the present tenses of some very useful common irregular verbs.

dürfen to be allowed to

ich darf
du darfst
er/sie/es darf
wir dürfen
ihr dürft
sie dürfen
Sie dürfen

können to be able to

ich kann
du kannst
er/sie/es kann
wir können
ihr könnt
sie können
Sie können

mögen to like

ich mag
du magst
er/sie/es mag
wir mögen
ihr mögt
sie mögen
Sie mögen

müssen to have to

ich muss
du musst
er/sie/es muss
ihr müßt
sie müssen
Sie müssen

sollen to be expected to, to have to

ich soll
du sollst
er/sie/es soll
wir sollen
ihr sollt
sie sollen
Sie sollen

wissen to know

ich weiß
du weißt
er/sie/es weiß
wir wissen
ihr wisst
sie wissen
Sie wissen

wollen to want to, to intend to

ich will
du willst
er/sie/es will
wir wollen
ihr wollt
sie wollen
Sie wollen

These are verbs which make their perfect with **sein**:

ankommen	to arrive
aufstehen	to get up
aufwachen	to wake up
begegnen	to meet
bleiben	to stay
einschlafen	to fall asleep
erscheinen	to appear
erschrecken	to be frightened
fahren	to go (by a means of transport), to drive
fallen	to fall
fliegen	to fly
folgen	to follow
gehen	to go (on foot)
gelingen	to succeed
geschehen	to happen
klettern	to climb
kommen	to come
misslingen	to fail
passieren	to happen
schmelzen	to melt
schwimmen	to swim
segeln	to sail
Ski laufen	to ski
steigen	to climb, to go up
sterben	to die
vergehen	to pass, to go by
wachsen	to grow
werden	to become

Strong verbs

Here is a list of common strong verbs. The parts given are the infinitive and the **er** form of the present and the perfect tenses. Try to learn these three parts for every strong verb.

beginnen	**beginnt**	**hat begonnen**	to begin
bitten	**bittet**	**hat gebeten**	to ask
bleiben	**bleibt**	**ist geblieben**	to stay
essen	**isst**	**hat gegessen**	to eat
fahren	**fährt**	**ist gefahren**	to go, to drive
finden	**findet**	**hat gefunden**	to find
geben	**gibt**	**hat gegeben**	to give
gehen	**geht**	**ist gegangen**	to go
geschehen	**geschieht**	**ist geschehen**	to happen
halten	**hält**	**hat gehalten**	to hold
heißen	**heißt**	**hat geheißen**	to be called
helfen	**hilft**	**hat geholfen**	to help
kommen	**kommt**	**ist gekommen**	to come
lassen	**läßt**	**hat gelassen**	to leave
laufen	**läuft**	**ist gelaufen**	to run
lesen	**liest**	**hat gelesen**	to read
liegen	**liegt**	**hat gelegen**	to lie
nehmen	**nimmt**	**hat genommen**	to take
rufen	**ruft**	**hat gerufen**	to call
scheinen	**scheint**	**hat geschienen**	to seem
schlafen	**schläft**	**hat geschlafen**	to sleep
schließen	**schließt**	**hat geschlossen**	to shut
schreiben	**schreibt**	**hat geschrieben**	to write
schwimmen	**schwimmt**	**ist geschwommen**	to swim
sehen	**sieht**	**hat gesehen**	to see
sein	**ist**	**ist gewesen**	to be
singen	**singt**	**hat gesungen**	to sing
sitzen	**sitzt**	**hat gesessen**	to sit
sprechen	**spricht**	**hat gesprochen**	to speak
stehen	**steht**	**hat gestanden**	to stand
steigen	**steigt**	**ist gestiegen**	to climb, to rise
sterben	**stirbt**	**ist gestorben**	to die
tragen	**trägt**	**hat getragen**	to carry, to wear
treffen	**trifft**	**hat getroffen**	to meet
trinken	**trinkt**	**hat getrunken**	to drink
tun	**tut**	**hat getan**	to do
verlieren	**verliert**	**hat verloren**	to lose
waschen	**wäscht**	**hat gewaschen**	to wash
werden	**wird**	**ist geworden**	to become
werfen	**wirft**	**hat geworfen**	to throw

Phrase explainer

Throughout the illustrated section of this book, there are useful short phrases and everyday expressions. You may find these easier to remember if you understand the different words that make them up.

This section lists the expressions under the page number where they appeared (although those whose word for word meaning is like the English have been left out). After reminding you of the suggested English equivalent, it shows you how they break down and, wherever possible, gives you the literal translations of the words involved*. Any grammatical terms used (e.g. accusative) are explained in the grammar section.

page 4
• **Auf Wiedersehen** Goodbye:
auf=on; **wieder**=again; **sehen**=to see
• **Bis bald**. See you later:
bis=until, **bald**=soon
• **Wie geht's?** How are you?
Wie=how; **geht**=goes; **es**=it (**es** is abbreviated to **'s**).

page 5
• **Das meine ich auch.** I agree:
das=that; **ich meine**=I think; **auch**=also
• **Wie heißt du?** What's your name?
• **Ich heiße...** My name is...
• **Er heißt...** His name is...
wie=how; **heißen**=to be called; **du heißt**=you are called; **ich heiße**=I am called; **er heißt**=he is called.

page 12
• **Ich bin zu Hause.** I'm at home:
ich bin=I am; **zu Hause**=at home (**das Haus**= house).

page 18
• **Vorsicht bissiger Hund!** Beware of the dog!
die Vorsicht=care, caution;
bissig=biting, vicious; **der Hund**=dog.

page 20
• **Guten Morgen** Good morning:
for greetings, you use **gut** with the time of day.

page 25
• **Gute Nacht** Good-night: See above.

page 26
• **Das Essen ist fertig**. It's ready:
das Essen=the meal; **ist fertig**=is ready.
• **Greif zu**. Help yourself:
zugreifen=to dig in, to grab.
• **Guten Appetit.** Enjoy your meal:
gut=good; **der Appetit**=appetite. This is a polite phrase you say to people who are about to eat.

page 36
• **Zugabe!** Encore!
die Zugabe=extra, bonus, addition.

page 37
• **Was hätten Sie gerne?** What would you like?
was=what; **Sie hätten**=you would have (**Sie** is the polite form of "you" singular); **gerne** (or **gern**)=with pleasure, willingly.
• **Mit Bedienung?** Service included?
mit=with; **die Bedienung**=service
• **Ohne Bedienung!** Service not included!
ohne=without.

page 43
• **Wie viel macht das?** How much is that?
wie viel=how much; **machen**=to

*Literal meanings of German words are introduced by the sign =.

make; **das**=that; (**kosten**=to cost, can be used instead of **machen**: **wie viel kostet das?**)
• **Das macht...** That will be...
das macht=that makes, e.g. **Das macht fünf Mark**=That will be five marks; (you could also say **Das kostet...** See below, under page 44).
• **Ein Kilo...** A kilo of...
• **Ein Pfund...** Half a kilo of...
e.g. **Ein Kilo Äpfel, bitte**=A kilo of apples, please. Note that the German word for "pound" means half a kilo.

page 44
• **Das ist preiswert.** It's good value:
das ist=that is; **preiswert**=good value.
• **Womit kann ich dienen?** Can I help you? **womit**=with what; **kann ich**=can I; **dienen**=serve.
• **Ich hätte gern...** I'd like...
(See note above for **Was hätten Sie gerne?** page 37); **ich hätte**=I would have; **gern(e)**=with pleasure, willingly.
• **Welche Größe ist es?** Which size is this?
welche=which; **die Größe**=size; **es ist**=it is
• **Was kostet...?** How much is...?
• **Das kostet...** It costs...
was=what; **kosten**=to cost, e.g. **Was kostet das T-Shirt?** How much is the T-Shirt?

page 47
• **Haben Sie Kleingeld?** Have you any small change?
haben=to have (**Sie**=polite form of "you" singular); **das Kleingeld** derives from **klein**=small and **das Geld** =money.

page 48
• **Hier ist Anke.** It's Anke:
hier=here; **ist**=is.
• **Ich rufe dich zurück.** I'll call you back:
rufen=to call; **ich rufe**=I call (note that the present tense is used); **dich**=you (accusative).
• **Wiederhören** Goodbye:
wieder=again, **hören**=to hear (only used on the telephone).

page 49
• **Sehr geehrte Damen und Herren,** Dear Sir/Madam,
sehr=very; **geehrt**=honoured; **Dame**=lady, Madam; **und**=and; **Herr**=gentleman, sir. This is how you begin a formal letter.
• **Beigefügt finden Sie** I enclose:
beigefügt=enclosed, added; **find**=to find; **Sie**=polite singular "you".
• **Mit freundlichen Grüßen** Yours faithfully: **mit**=with; **freundlich** =friendly; **der Gruß(¨e)**=greeting.
• **Schön, mal wieder von dir zu hören.** It was lovely to hear from you:
schön=lovely, good; **mal wieder**=once again; **von dir**=from you; **zu**=to; **hören**=to hear.
• **Mit getrennter Post erhältst du...** I am sending... separately:
mit=with; **getrennt**=separate; **erhalten**=to receive; **du erhältst**=you receive.
• **Alles Gute...** Love from...
=all that is good; all the best.
• **Es ist ganz toll hier.** Having a lovely time:
es ist=it is; **ganz**=very, really; **toll**=great, good; **hier**=here.

• **Schade, dass du nicht hier bist.** Wish you were here:
schade=a shame, a pity; **dass**=that; **du bist**=you are; **nicht**=not.
• **Dringend stop sofort zu Hause anrufen stop** Urgent message stop

phone home stop:
dringend=urgent; **sofort**=immediately; **zu Hause**=home, at home; **anrufen**=to ring/telephone.

page 50
• **In welcher Richtung ist...?** Which way is...?
in=in; **welcher**=which; **die Richtung** =direction; ist=is.

page 52
• **Parkverbot!** No parking!
parken=to park; **das Verbot**=ban.

page 54
• **Nichtraucher** No smoking:
nicht=not/non; **der Raucher**=smoker.

page 57
• **Bitte anschnallen.** Please fasten your seatbelts:
bitte=please; **anschnallen**= to strap on/up, to clip on. Note how the infinitive is used to give a polite order.

page 58
• **etwas besichtigen** to sightsee:
etwas=something (also=some, any, a little); **besichtigen**=to look at.

page 73
Viel Glück. Good luck:
viel=much; **das Glück**=luck, happiness.

page 78
• **Herzlichen Glückwunsch zum Geburtstag.** Happy birthday:
herzlich=warm, sincere; **der Glückwunsch(¨e)**=congratualtions (from **das Glück**=luck and **der Wunsch**=wish); **zum** (short for **zu dem**) **Geburtstag**=for the birthday.

• **Danke schön.** Thank you very much:
danke=thanks; **schöne**=nice, beautiful, good (here it simply means "very much", similar to "thank you").
• **Glückliches Neues Jahr.** Happy New Year:
glücklich=happy; **neu**=new; **das Jahr**=year.

page 82
• **Es wird hell/dunkel.** It's getting light/dark.
• **Es ist hell/dunkel.** It is light/dark:
es wird=it is becoming (from **werden**=to become); **es ist**=it is; **hell**=light; **dunkel**=dark.

page 83
• **Wie spät ist es?** What is the time?
wie=how; **spät**=late; **ist es**=is it.
• **Es ist ein/drei Uhr.** It is 1/3 o'clock:
die Uhr=clock, watch.
• **Viertel vor zehn** a quarter to 10:
Viertel=quarter; **vor**=before; **zehn**=ten.
• **Viertel/fünf nach zehn** a quarter/ five past 10:
nach=past, after.
• **halb elf** half past 10:
halb=half; **elf**=eleven (Note that this does not mean "half past eleven").
• **acht Uhr morgends/abends**
8 am/pm:
acht Uhr=eight o'clock; **morgens**=in the morning; **abends**=in the evening.

page 85
• **Wie ist das Wetter?** What is the weather like?
=how is the weather?
• **Mir ist warm.** I'm hot:
mir ist=it is to me, I feel; **warm**=warm.

English-German word list

Here you will find all the German words, phrases and expressions from the illustrated section of this book, listed in English alphabetical order. Wherever useful, phrases and expressions are cross-referenced, and the words they are made up from are included in the list. Following each German term, you will find its pronunciation in italics. To pronounce German properly, you need to listen to a German person speaking. This pronunciation guide will give you an idea as to how to pronounce new words and act as reminder to words you have heard spoken. Remember that the German **ß** is like ss, **w** is like an English v, **v** is like an English f, **z** is like ts and **j** is like y in "yawn".

When using the pronunciation hints in italics, read the "words" as if they were English but bear in mind the following points:

- *ah* should be said like the a in "farther"
- *a* like *ah*, but shorter
- *ow* like ow in "now" (not in "crow")
- *ew* is not quike like any English sound. It is like a sharp u. To make it, say "ee", but keep your lips rounded
- *ee* should be said like ee in "week"
- *ay* should be said like in "day", and *oy* like in "boy"; otherwise *y* is like in "try", except before a vowel when it should be said like in "yawn"
- *g* is always hard, as in "garden"
- *kh* should be said like ch in the Scottish word "loch" or h in "huge"
- *r* is made at the back of the mouth and sounds a litte like gargling
- *e(r)* is like e in "the" (not "thee"), and the *r* is not pronounced
- *u(r)* is like the i in "bird", and the *r* is not pronounced.

A

accident	**der Unfall(¨er)**	*derr oonfal*
actor	**der Schauspieler(-)**	*derr shaow-shpeeler*
actress	**die Schauspielerin(nen)**	*dee shaow-shpeelerin*
to add	**zusammenzählen**	*tsoo-zammen-tsehlen*
address	**die Adresse(n)**	*dee addresse(r)*
advertisement	**die Reklame(n)**	*dee reklame(r)*
aeroplane	**das Flugzeug(e)**	*dass floog-tsyok*
Africa	**Afrika**	*Africa*
afternoon	**der Nachmittag(e)**	*der nakh-mittakh*
against	**gegen (acc)**	*gay-gen*
age	**das Alter(-)**	*dass al-ter*
I agree, agreed	**Das meine ich auch.**	*dass meyne(r) ikh owkh*
air hostess	**die Stewardess(en)**	*dee stewardess*
airline ticket	**der Flugschein(e)**	*derr floog-shyne*
airmail	**Luftpost**	*looftpost*
airport	**der Flughafen(¨)**	*derr floog-hahfen*
aisle	**der Gang(¨e)**	*derr gang*
alarm clock	**der Wecker(-)**	*derr vecker*
alone	**allein**	*a-lyne*
alphabet	**das Alphabet(e)**	*dass alphabayt*
ambulance	**der Krankenwagen(-)**	*derr kranken-vahgen*
among	**zwischen (acc or dat)**	*tsvishen*
anchor	**der Anker(-)**	*derr anker*
and	**und**	*oont*
animal	**das Tier(e)**	*dass teer*
ankle	**der Knöchel(-)**	*der knu(r)kh-el*
to answer the telephone	**ans Telefon gehen**	*anss telephone gayen*
apple	**der Apfel(¨)**	*derr apfel*
apple tree	**der Apfelbaum(¨e)**	*derr apfel-bowm*
apricot	**die Aprikose(n)**	*dee aprreekose(r)*
April	**April**	*a-prill*
architect (m)	**der Architekt(en)**	*derr arkhee-tekt*
architect (f)	**die Architektin(nen)**	*dee arkhee-tetkin*
area code	**die Vorwahl(en)**	*dee vor-vahl*
arm	**der Arm(e)**	*derr arm*
armchair	**der Sessel(-)**	*derr zessel*
Arrivals	**Ankunft (f)**	*an-koonft*
art gallery	**die Kunstgalerie(n)**	*dee koonst-galleree*
article (in paper)	**der Artikel(-)**	*derr arteekel*
to ask	**fragen**	*fra-gen*
to ask a question	**etwas fragen**	*etvass fragen*
to ask the way	**nach dem Weg fragen**	*nakh dym veg fra-gen*
to fall asleep	**einschlafen**	*yne-shlaf-en*
at the seaside	**am Meer**	*am mayr*
athletics	**die Leichtathletik**	*dee lykht-etlytik*
Atlantic Ocean	**der Atlantik**	*derr atlantic*
attic	**der Dachboden(¨)**	*derr dakh-boden*
audience	**das Publikum**	*dass pooblikoom*
August	**August**	*ow-goost*
aunt	**die Tante(n)**	*dee tante(r)*
Australia	**Australien**	*owstra-lian*
autumn	**der Herbst**	*derr herpst*
away from	**weg von (dat)**	*veck fon*

B

baby	**das Baby(s)**	*dass baby*
back	**der Rücken**	*derr rewken*
to do back-stroke	**rückenschwimmen**	*rewken-shvimmen*
backwards	**rückwärts**	*rewk-verts*
bait	**der Köder(-)**	*derr koyder*
baker	**der Bäcker**	*derr becker*
balcony	**der Balkon(s)**	*derrr bal-cone*
with balcony	**mit Balkon**	*mit bal-cone*
bald head	**die Glatze(n)**	*dee glatse(r)*
to be bald	**eine Glatze haben**	*yne glatse haben*
ball	**der Ball(¨e)**	*derr bal*
ballet	**das Ballet**	*dass bailett*
ballet dancer (m)	**der Balletttänzer**	*derr bailet-tentser*
ballet dancer (f)	**die Balletttänzerin**	*dee bailet-tentserin*
balloon	**der Luftballon(s)**	*derr looft-ballon*
banana	**die Banane(n)**	*dee banane(r)*
bandage	**der Verband(¨e)**	*derr ferbant*
bank river	**das Ufer(-)**	*dass oofer*
bank	**die Bank(en)**	*dee bank*
bank manager	**der Geschäftsführer(-) der Bank**	*derr geshefts fewrer derr bank*
barefoot	**barfuß**	*barfooss*
bargain	**das Sonderangebot**	*dass zonder angeboat*
to bark	**bellen**	*betten*
barn	**die Scheune(n)**	*dee shoyne(r)*
basement	**das Untergeschoss(e)**	*dass oonter-geshoss*
basket	**der Korb(¨e)**	*derr korp*
basket, shopping	**der Einkaufskorb**	*drr yne-kowfs-korp*
bath	**die Badewanne(n)**	*dee bahde-vanne(r)*
to have a bath	**ein Bad nehmen**	*yne baht naymen*
to run a bath	**das Badewasser einlaufen lassen**	*dass bahde(r)-vasser yne-lowfen lassen*
bathmat	**die Badematte(n)**	*dee bahde-matte(r)*
bath robe	**der Bademantel(¨)**	*derr bahde-mantle*
bathroom	**das Badezimmer(-)**	*dass bahde-tsimmer*
to be	**sein**	*zyne*
to be born	**geboren werden**	*geboren verden*
to be called, to be named	**heißen**	*hyssen*
to be fond of	**lieb haben**	*leep ha-ben*
to be frozen	**halb erfroren sein**	*halp erforen zyne*
to be happy	**glücklich sein**	*glewklikh zyne*
to be hungry	**Hunger haben**	*hoong-er ha-ben*
to be late	**zu spät kommen**	*tsoo shpyt kommen*
to be on time	**pünktlich sein**	*pewnkt-likh zyne*
to be seasick	**seekrank sein**	*zay-krank zyne*
to be sick	**sich übergeben**	*sikh owber-gayben*
to sleepy	**schläfrig sein**	*shlyvrikh zyne*
to be thirsty	**Durst haben**	*doorst ha-ben*
beach	**der Strand(¨e)**	*der shtrand*
beak	**der Schnabel(¨)**	*derr shna-bel*
beans	**die Bohnen (pl)**	*dee bonen*
green bean	**die Schnittbohne(n)**	*dee shnitt-bonen*
beard	**der Bart(¨e)**	*derr bart*
to have a beard	**einen Bart haben**	*ynen bart haben*
bed	**das Bett(en)**	*dass bet*
to go to bed	**ins Bett gehen**	*inss bet gayen*
bedroom	**das Schlafzimmer(-)**	*dass shlahf-tsimmer*
bedside table	**der Nachttisch(e)**	*derr nakht-tish*
bedspread	**die Tagesdecke(n)**	*dee dahgez-decke(r)*
bedtime	**die Schlafenszeit**	*dee shlahfens-tsyte*
bee	**die Biene(n)**	*dee beene(r)*
beer	**das Bier**	*dass beer*
behind	**hinter (acc or dat)**	*hinter*
Belgium	**Belgien**	*belg-yen*
bell, doorbell	**die Klingel(n)**	*dee kling-el*
to belong, to be a member	**Mitglied sein**	*mitgleed zyne*
belt	**der Gürtel(-)**	*derr gewrtel*
safety belt, seatbelt	**der Sicherheitsgurt(e)**	*derr zikher-hytes-goort*
bench	**Bank(¨e)**	*dee bank*
beside	**neben (acc or dat)**	*nayben*
better	**besser**	*besser*
to feel better	**sich besser fühlen**	*zich besser fewlen*
between	**zwischen (acc or dat)**	*tsvishen*
beware of the dog!	**Vorsicht bissiger Hund!**	*farzikht bissiger hoont*
bicycle	**das Fahrrad(¨er)**	*dass far-rat*
big	**groß**	*gross*
bill	**die Rechnung(en)**	*dee rekhnoong*
bin	**der Mülleimer(-)**	*derr mewl-ymer*
biology	**die Biologie**	*dee bee-ologee*
bird	**der Vogel (¨)**	*derr fogel*
birth	**die Geburt(en)**	*dee geboort*
birthday	**der Geburtstag(e)**	*derr geboorts-tag*
birthday card	**die (Geburtstags) Karte(n)**	*dee geboorts-tags-karte(r)*
Happy birthday	**Herzlichen Glückwunsch zum Geburtstag**	*herslikhen glewkvewnsh tsoom geboorts-tag*
biscuit	**der Keks(-)**	*der kecks*
black	**schwarz**	*shwarts*
blackbird	**die Amsel(n)**	*dee amsel*
blackboard	**die Tafel(n)**	*dee tahfel*
block of flats	**der Wohnblock (s)**	*derr vone-block*
blond	**blond**	*blont*
blond hair	**blondes Haar(e)**	*blondes har*
blouse	**die Bluse(n)**	*dee blooze(r)*
blue	**blau**	*blaow*
to board (ship or plane)	**einsteigen**	*yne-shtygen*
board game	**dass Brettspiel(e)**	*dass brett-shpeel*
boarding house	**die Pension(en)**	*dee penzee-oan*
boat	**das Boot(e)**	*dass boat*
to travel by boat	**mit dem Schiff fahren**	*mit dehm shiff far-en*
body	**der Körper(-)**	*derr kewrpe(r)*
bonnet (car)	**die Motorhaube(n)**	*dee motor-howbe(r)*
book	**das Buch(¨er)**	*dass bookh*
picture book	**das Bilderbuch(¨er)**	*dass Bilder-bookh*
booked up, fully booked	**belegt**	*belaygt*
bookshop	**der Buchladen(¨)**	*derr bookh-lahden*
bookshop and stationer's	**der Buchladen(¨) und die Schreibwarhung -handlung(en)**	*derr booklahden oont dee shrypvaren-handloong*

boot (of car)	**der Kofferraum(¨e)**	*derr kowfer-rowm*
boot	**der Stiefel(-)**	*derr shteefel*
wellington boots	**die Gummistiefel (pl)**	*dee-goomee-shteefel*
boring	**langweilig**	*langwyl-ig*
to be born	**geboren werden**	*geboren verden*
boss (m)	**der Chef(s)**	*derr chef*
boss (f)	**die Chefin(nen)**	*dee chefin*
bottle	**die Flasche(n)**	*dee flashe(r)*
bouquet	**der Blumenstrauß(¨e)**	*derr bloomen-shtrows*
boutique	**die Boutique(n)**	*dee boutique*
bowl	**die Suppentasse(n)**	*dee zoopen-tasse(r)*
box office	**die Kasse(n)**	*dee kasse(r)*
boy	**der Junge(n)**	*der yoong-e(r)*
bra	**der BH(s)**	*derr bay-ha*
bracelet	**das Armband(¨er)**	*dass arm-bant*
to brake	**bremsen**	*bremzen*
branch	**der Ast(¨e)**	*derr ast*
brave	**mutig**	*mootig*
Bravo!	**Encore!**	*oncore*
bread	**das Brot**	*dass broat*
break (at school)	**die Pause(n)**	*dee powze(r)*
to break your leg	**sich das Bein brechen**	*zikh dass byne brekhen*
breakdown (vehicle)	**die Panne(n)**	*dee panne(r)*
to have a breakdown (vehicle)	**eine Panne haben**	*yne panne haben*
breakfast	**das Frühstück(e)**	*dass frew-shtewk*
to do breast-stroke	**brustschwimmen**	*broost-shvimmen*
bricklayer	**der Maurer(-)**	*der maowrer*
bride	**die Braut(¨e)**	*dee browt*
bridegroom	**der Bräutigam(e)**	*derr browtigam*
bridge	**die Brücke(n)**	*dee brewke(r)*
bright	**leuchtend**	*loykhtend*
to bring up	**aufziehen**	*owf-tsee-en*
broad	**breit**	*brite*
brooch	**die Brosche(n)**	*dee broshe(r)*
brother	**der Bruder(¨)**	*derr brooder*
brown	**braun**	*brown*
brown hair	**braunes Haar (n)**	*brown-es har*
bruise	**der blaue Fleck(en)**	*derr blaowe fleck*
brush (for painting)	**der Pinsel(-)**	*derr pinzel*
brush	**die Bürste(n)**	*dee bewrste(r)*
hairbrush	**die Haarbürste(n)**	*dee hahr-bewrste(r)*
toothbrush	**die Zahnbürste(n)**	*dee tsahn-bewrste(r)*
to brush your hair	**sich die Haare bürsten**	*zikh dee hahre bewrst-en*
Brussels sprouts	**der Rosenkohl**	*deer rosen-cole*
bucket	**der Eimer(-)**	*derr eye-mer*
budgie	**der Wellensittich(e)**	*derr vellen-zittikh*
buffet car	**der Speisewagen(-)**	*derr shpyez(r)-vahgen*
building	**das Gebäude(-)**	*dass geboyde(r)*
bulb (plant)	**die Blumenzwiebel**	*dee bloomen-tsveebel*
bunch of flowers	**der Blumenstrauß(¨e)**	*derr bloomen-shtrowss*
burn	**die Verbrennung(en)**	*dee fer-brennoong*
to burst out laughing	**in Gelächter ausbrechen**	*in geleichter awssbrekhen*
bus	**der Bus(se)**	*derr booss*
bus stop	**die Bushaltestelle(n)**	*dee boosshalte-stelle*
to take the bus	**mit dem Bus fahren**	*mit daym booss faren*
bush	**der Strauch(¨er)**	*derr shtrowkh*
busy	**beschäftigt**	*bee-sheftikt*
bustling	**belebt**	*be-laybt*
butcher (or butcher's shop)	**der Fleischer (-)**	*derr flysher*
butter	**die Butter**	*dee booter*
buttercup	**die Butterblume(n)**	*dee booter-bloome(r)*
butterfly	**der Schmetterling(e)**	*derr shmetterling*
button	**der Knopf(¨e)**	*derr knopf*
to buy	**kaufen**	*kowfen*
by return of post	**postwendend**	*post-vendend*

C

cabbage	**der Weißkohl**	*derr vyss-cole*
cabin	**die Kabine(n)**	*dee ka-beene(r)*
cage	**der Käfig(e)**	*derr kayfig*
cake	**die Torte(n)**	*dee torte(r)*
cream cake	**die Sahnetorte**	*dee zahne-torte(r)*
cake shop	**die Konditorei(en)**	*dee kondeeto-rye*
to calculate	**rechnen**	*rekhnen*
calendar	**Kalender(-)**	*derr kalender*
calf	**das Kalb(¨r)**	*dass kulp*
camel	**das Kamel(e)**	*dass kamayl*
camera	**die Kamera(s)**	*dee kamera*
to camp, to go camping	**zelten**	*tselten*
campsite	**der Campingplatz(¨e)**	*derr camping-plats*
Can I help you?	**Womit kann ich dienen?**	*vo-mitt kan ikh deenen*
Canada	**Kanada**	*canada*
candle	**die Kerze(n)**	*dee kertse(r)*
canoe	**das Kanu(s)**	*dass kanoo*
cap	**die Mütze(n)**	*dee mewtse(r)*
capital letter	**der Großbuchstabe(n)**	*derr gross-bookh-shtabe(r)*
to capsize	**kentern**	*kentern*
captain	**der Kapitän(e)**	*derr kup-y-tayn*
car	**das Auto(s)**	*dass owto*
car-park	**der Parkplatz(¨e)**	*derr park-plats*
caravan	**der Wohnwagen(-)**	*derr vone-vahgen*
card	**die Karte(n)**	*dee karte(r)*
credit card	**die Kreditkarte(n)**	*dee kredit-karte(r)*
postcard	**die Postkarte(n)**	*dee post-karte(r)*
card (playing cards)	**die Karte(n)**	*dee karte(r)*
to play cards	**Karten spielen**	*karten shpeelen*
cardigan	**die Strickjacke(n)**	*dee shtrick-yacke(r)*
careful	**vorsichtig**	*for-zikhtig*
careless	**unvorsichtig**	*oon-for-zikhtig*
caretaker (m)	**der Hausmeister(-)**	*derr house-myster*
caretaker (f)	**die Hausmeisterin(nen)**	*dee house-mysterin*
cargo	**die Ladung(en)**	*dee la-doong*
carpet	**der Teppich(e)**	*derr teppikh*
fitted carpet	**der Teppichboden(¨)**	*derr teppikh-boden*
carriage	**der Wagen(-)**	*derr va-gen*
carrier-bag	**die Tragetasche(n)**	*dee trahge-tashe*
to carry	**tragen**	*tra-gen*
carrot	**die Karotte(n)**	*dee karotte(r)*
cashier (m)	**der Kassierer(-)**	*derr kasserer*
cashier (f)	**die Kassiererin(nen)**	*dee kasseerin*
cassette	**die Kassette(n)**	*dee kassette(r)*

cassette recorder	**der Kassettenrecorder(-)**	*derr kassetten-recorder*
casualty department	**die Unfallsstation(en)**	*dee oonfal-shtatsion*
cat	**die Katze**	*dee katse(r)*
to catch	**fangen**	*fangen*
to catch a fish	**einen Fisch fangen**	*ybeb fish fangen*
to catch a train	**den Zug erreichen**	*dan tsug er-rykhen*
cathedral	**der Dom(e)**	*derr dome*
cauliflower	**der Blumenkohl**	*derr bloomen-coal*
to celebrate	**feiern**	*fy-ern*
cellar	**der Keller(-)**	*derr keller*
cello	**das Cello(-)**	*dass cello*
to play the cello	**Cello spielen**	*cello shpeelen*
cemetery	**der Friedhof(¨e)**	*freed-hofe*
centimetre	**der Zentimeter(-)**	*tsentimayter*
centre (politics)	**liberal**	*liberal*
chair	**der Stuhl(¨e)**	*derr shdool*
chairlift	**der Sessellift(e)**	*derr zessel-lift*
chalk	**die Kreide(n)**	*dee kryder(r)*
change (money)	**das Kleingeld**	*dass klyn-gelt*
Have you any small change?	**Haben Sie Kleingeld?**	*ha-ben zee klyne-gelt*
to change money	**Geld wechseln**	*gelt vexeln*
channel (TV and radio)	**das Programm(e)**	*dass program*
to chase	**jagen**	*ya-gen*
to chat	**sich unterhalten**	*ziih ootler-halten*
check-in	**der Check-In**	*derr check-in*
cheek	**die Backe(n)**	*dee backe(r)*
cheerful	**fröhlich**	*fru(r)likh*
cheese	**der Käse(-)**	*derr kyze(r)*
checkout	**die Kasse(n)**	*dee kasse(r)*
chemist	**die Drogerie(n)**	*dee drogeree*
chemistry	**die Chemie**	*dee khemee*
cheque	**der Scheck(s)**	*derr sheck*
to write a cheque	**einen Scheck ausstellen**	*ynen sheck owss-shtellen*
cheque-book	**das Scheckbuch(¨er)**	*dass sheck-bookh*
cherry	**die Kirsche(n)**	*dee kirshe(r)*
to play chess	**Schach spielen**	*shakh shpeelen*
chest	**die Brust(¨e)**	*dee broost*
chicken	**das Huhn(¨er)**	*dass hoon*
child	**das Kind(er)**	*dass kint*
childhood	**die Kindheit**	*dee kint-hyt*
chimney	**der Schornstein(e)**	*derr shorn-shtyn*
chin	**das Kinn(e)**	*dass kinn*
China	**China**	*kheena*
chocolate	**die Schokolade**	*dee shokolahde(r)*
choir	**der Chor(¨e)**	*der core*
chop (meat)	**das Kotelett(s)**	*dass kot-let*
Christmas	**Weihnachten**	*vy-nakhten*
Christmas carol	**das Weihnachtlied(er)**	*dass vy-nakhts-leed*
Christmas Day	**der erste Weihnachtstag**	*derr erste(r) vy-nakhts-tag*
Christmas eve	**der Heilige Abend**	*derr hylige(r) ahbend*
Happy Christmas	**Frohe Weihnachten**	*frohe(r) vynakhten*
Christmas tree	**der Weihnachtsbaum(¨e)**	*derr vynakthsbowm*
church	**die Kirche(n)**	*dee kirkhe(r)*
cinema	**das Kino(s)**	*dass keeno*
to go to the cinema	**ins Kino gehen**	*inss keeno gayen*
circle	**der Kreis**	*derr kryss*
city	**die Großstadt(¨e)**	*dee gross-shtat*
to clap	**klatschen**	*klatshen*

classroom	**das Klassenzimmer**	*dass klassentsimmer*
claw	**die Kralle(n)**	*dee kralle(r)*
clean	**sauber**	*zowber*
to clean your teeth	**sich die Zähne putzen**	*zikh dee tsyne(r) pootsen*
climate	**das Klima**	*dass kleema*
to climb	**klettern**	*klettern*
to climb a tree	**auf einen Baum klettern**	*aowf ynen baowm klettern*
climber (m)	**der Bergsteiger(-)**	*derr berg-shtyger*
climber (f)	**die Bergsteigerin(nen)**	*dee ber-shtygerin*
cloakroom	**die Garderobe(n)**	*dee garde(r)-robe(r)*
clock	**die Uhr(en)**	*dee our*
alarm clock	**der Wecker(-)**	derr vecker
to close	**zumachen**	*tsoo-makhen*
clothes, clothing	**die Oberbekleidung**	*dee obar-beklydoonk*
clothes peg	**die Wäscheklammer(n)**	*dee veshe(r)-klammer*
cloud	**die Wolke**	*dee volke(r)*
coach	**der Reisebus(se)**	*derr ryze(r) booss*
coat	**der Mantel(¨)**	*derr mantel*
cock	**der Hahn(¨e)**	*derr hahn*
cob	**der Kabeljau(e)**	*derr kabel-yaow*
coffee	**der Kaffee**	*derr kaffay*
coffee-pot	**die Kaffeekanne(n)**	*dee kaffay-kanne(r)*
coin	**die Münze(n)**	*dee mewntse(r)*
cold	**kalt**	*kalt*
It's cold.	**Es ist kalt.**	*ess ist kalt*
cold water	**kaltes Wasser**	*kaltes vasser*
to have a cold	**eine Erkältung haben**	*yne(r) erkeltoong haben*
to collect	**sammeln**	*zammel*
to collect stamps	**Briefmarken sammeln**	*breef-marken zsammeln*
collection	**die Sammlung(en)**	*dee zamloong*
collection, collection time	**die Leerung(en)**	*dee layroong*
colour	**die Farbe(n)**	*dee farbe(r)*
colourful	**bunt**	*boont*
comb	**der Kamm(¨e)**	*derr kamm*
to comb your hair	**sich die Haar kämmen**	*zikh dee hahre(r) kemmen*
comic (book)	**das Comic-Heft(e)**	*dass comic-heft*
complexion	**der Teint**	*derr te(n)*
computer	**der Computer(-)**	*derr computer*
computer studies	**die Informatik**	*dee informatik*
conductor (orchestra) (m)	**der Dirigent(en)**	*derr dirigent*
conductor (f)	**die Dirigentin(nen)**	*dee dirigentin*
cone	**der Kegel(n)**	*derr kaygel*
to congratulate	**gratulieren**	*gratoo-leeren*
continent	**der Erdteil**	*derr erd-tile*
to cook	**kochen**	*kokhen*
corner	**die Ecke(n)**	*dee ecke(r)*
to cost	**kosten**	*kosten*
It costs...	**Das kostet...**	*dass kostet*
cot	**das Kinderbett(en)**	*dass kinder-bet*
cotton (made of cotton)	**aus Baumwolle**	*owss bowm-volle(r)*
counter	**die Theke(n)**	*dee taeke(r)*
country	**das Land(¨er)**	*dass lant (dee lender)*
countryside	**das Land**	*dass lant*
cousin (m)	**der Vetter(n)**	*derr fetter*
cousin (f)	**die Kusine(n)**	*dee koozeene(r)*

cow	**die Kuh(¨e)**	*dee koo*
cowshed	**der Kuhstall(¨e)**	*derr koo-shtal*
crab	**der Krebs(e)**	*derr krayps*
to crawl, to do the crawl	**kraueln**	*krow-len*
crayon	**der Buntstift(e)**	*derr boont-shtift*
cream	**die Sahne**	*dee zahne(r)*
cream cake	**die Sahnetorte(n)**	*dee zahne(r)-tort(e)*
credit card	**die Kreditkarte**	*dee kredit-karte(r)*
crew	**die Besatzung(en)**	*dee bezatsoong*
cross, angry	**böse**	*bu(r)ze(r)*
to cross the street	**die Straße überqueren**	*dee shtrasse(r) ewberkveren*
crossing (sea)	**die Überfahrt(en)**	*dee ewber-fart*
crowd	**die Menge**	*dee meng-e(r)*
to cry	**weinen**	*vynen*
cup	**die Tasse(n)**	*dee tasse(r)*
cupboard	**der Küchenschrank(¨e)**	*derr kewkhen-shrank*
to cure	**heilen**	*hylen*
curly hair	**Locken (pl)**	*locken*
curtain	**der Vorhang(¨e)**	*derr for-hang*
customer (m)	**der Kunde(m)**	*derr derr koonde(r)*
customer (f)	**die Kundin(nen)**	*dee koondin*
customs	**der Zoll**	*derr tsoll*
customs officer (m)	**der Zollbeamte(n)**	*derr tsoll-be(r)-amte(r)*
customs officer (f)	**die Zollbeamtin(nen)**	*dee tsoll-be(r)-amtin*
cut (wound)	**die Schnittwunde(n)**	*dee shnitt-voonde(r)*

D

daffodil	**die Osterglocke(n)**	*dee oaster-glocke(r)*
dahlia	**die Dahlie(n)**	*dee dal-ye(r)*
daisy	**das Gänseblümchen(-)**	*dass genze(r) blewmkhen*
to dance	**tanzen**	*tantsen*
dance floor	**die Tanzfläche(n)**	*dee tants-flekhe(r)*
dark	**dunkel**	*doornkel*
dark (complexion)	**braun**	*brown*
It is dark.	**Es ist dunkel.**	*ess ist doonkel*
It is getting dark.	**Es wird dunkel.**	*ess veerrt doonkel*
date	**das Datum (pl: die Daten**	*dass datoom (pl: dee da-ten)*
daughter	**die Tochter(¨)**	*dee tokhter*
only daughter	**die einzige Tochter**	*dee eyntsige(r) tokhter*
dawn	**das Morgengrauen(-)**	*dass morgen-graowen*
day, daytime, in the daytime	**der Tag(e)**	*derr tahg*
the day after tomorrow	**übermorgen**	*ewbermorgen*
the day before yesterday	**vorgestern**	*forgestern*
Dear...	**Lieber (m)/Liebe (f)**	*leeber/leebe(r)*
Dear Sir/Madam	**Sehr geehrte Damen und Herren**	*zayr ge(r)-rte(r) da-men oont herren*
death	**der Tod**	*der tot*
December	**Dezember**	*day-tzember*
deck	**das Deck(s)**	*das deck*
deep	**tief**	*teef*
delicatessen	**das Feinkostgeschäft(e)**	*das fine-kost-gesheft*
delicious	**lecker**	*lecker*
to deliver	**austeilen**	*owss-tylen*
democratic	**demokratisch**	*demokratish*
dentist (m)	**der Zahrnaszt(¨e)**	*derr tsahn-artst*
dentist (f)	**die Zahnärztin(en)**	*dee tsahn-ertstin*
department (in shop)	**die Abteilung(en)**	*dee ap-tyloong*
department store	**das Kaufhaus (¨er)**	*dass kauf-house*
Departures (in airport)	**Abflug(¨e)**	*ap-floog*
desert	**die Wüste(n)**	*dee wowste(r)*
designer (m)	**der Designer(-)**	*derr designer*
designer (f)	**die Designerin(nen)**	*dee designer-in*
dessert, pudding	**die Nachspeise(n)/ das Dessert(s)**	*dee nakh-shpyze(r)/dass dessert*
diary	**der Kalender(-)**	*derr ka-lender*
to die	**sterben**	*shtarben*
different	**unterschiedlich**	*oonter-sheedlikh*
difficult	**schwierig**	*shveerig*
to dig	**graben**	*gra-ben*
dining room	**das Esszimmer(-)**	*dass ess-tsimmer*
dirty	**schmutzig**	*shmootsig*
disc jockey	**der Diskjockey(s)**	*derr disc-jockey*
discotheque	**die Disko**	*dee Disko*
to go to a discotheque	**in die Disko gehen**	*in dee disco gayen*
district	**der Stadtteil(e)**	*derr shtat-tile*
to dive	**tauchen**	*taowkhen*
to divide	**teilen**	*tylen*
divided by (maths)	**geteilt durch**	*getylt doorkh*
diving board	**das Sprungbrett(er)**	*dass shproong-brett*
to do	**tun**	*toon*
to do, to make	**machen**	*makhen*
to do back-stroke	**rückenschwimmen**	*rewken-shvimmen*
to do breast-stroke	**brustschwimmen**	*broost-shvimmen*
to do the gardening	**im Garten arbeiten**	*im garten arbyten*
docks, quay	**der Kai(s)**	*derr kye*
doctor (m)	**der Arzt(¨e)**	*der artst*
doctor (f)	**die Ärztin(nen)**	*dee ertstin*
dog	**der Hund(e)**	*derr hoont*
donkey	**der Esel(-)**	*derr ayzel*
door	**die Tür(en)**	*dee tewr*
front door	**die Wohnungstür(en)**	*dee vo-noongs-tewr*
doorbell	**die Klingel(n)**	*dee kling-el*
doormat	**die Fußmatte(n)**	*dee foos-matte(r)*
double room	**das Doppelzimmer(-)**	*dass dopple-tsimmer*
doughnut	**der Berliner Pfannkuchen(-)**	*derr berliner pfann-kookhen*
down	**hinunter**	*hinoonter*
downstairs	**unten**	*oonten*
to go downstairs	**nach unten gehen**	*nakh oonten gayen*
dragonfly	**die Libelle(n)**	*dee libelle(r)*
to play draughts	**Dame spielen**	*da-me(r) shpeeln*
to dream	**träumen**	*troymen*
dress	**das Kleid(er)**	*dass klyde (dee klyde(r)*
to get dressed	**sich anziehen**	*sikh antsee-en*
dressing gown	**der Morgenmantel(¨)**	*derr morgen-mantle*
to drink	**trinken**	*trinken*
to drive	**fahren**	*fahren*
driver (m)	**der Fahrer(-)**	*derr fahrer*
driver (f)	**die Fahrerin(nen)**	*dee fahrerin*
to drop	**fallen lassen**	*fa-len lassen*
drums	**das Schlagzeug(e)**	*dass shlag-tsoig*

to play drums	**Schlagzeug spielen**	*shlag-tsoig shpeelen*
to dry, to wipe	**abtrocknen**	*ap-trocknen*
to dry your hair	**sich die Haare fönen**	*zickh dee ha-re(r) fu(r)-nen*
to dry yourself	**sich abtrocknen**	*zich ap-trocknen*
duck	**die Ente(n)**	*dee ente(r)*
dull	**trüb**	*trewb*
dungarees	**die Latzhose(n)**	*dee lats-hoze(r)*
dustman	**der Müllmann(¨er)**	*derr mewl-man*
duty-free shop	**der Duty-free-Shop**	*der duty-free-shop*
duvet	**das Federbett(en)**	*dass fayder-bet*

E

eagle	**der Adler(-)**	*derr ahdler*
ear	**das Ohr(en)**	*dass ore*
earring	**der Ohrring(e)**	*derr ore-ring*
east	**der Osten**	*derr ost-en*
Easter	**Ostern**	*oastern*
easy	**einfach**	*yne-fakh*
to eat	**essen**	*essen*
to have eaten well	**gut gegessen haben**	*goot gegessen ha-ben*
egg	**das Ei(er)**	*das eye*
eight	**acht**	*akht*
8 in the morning, 8 a.m.	**acht Uhr morgens**	*akht oor morgens*
8 in the evening, 8 p.m.	**acht Uhr abends**	*akth oor ahbends*
eighteen	**achtzehn**	*akht-tsayn*
eighty	**achtzig**	*akht-tsig*
elbow	**der Ellbogen(-)**	*der ellbogen*
election	**die Wahl(en)**	*dee vahl*
electricity	**der Strom**	*derr shtrome*
elephant	**der Elefant(en)**	*derr ele-phant*
eleven	**elf**	*elf*
emergency	**der Notfall(¨e)**	*derr note-fal*
to employ someone	**jemanden einstellen**	*yaymanden yne-shtellen*
employee (m)	**der Angestellte(n)**	*derr an-ge(r)-shtellte(r)*
employee (f)	**die Angestellte(n)**	*dee an-ge(r)-shtellte(r)*
empty	**leer**	*layr*
to empty	**leeren**	*layren*
Encore!	**Zugabe!**	*tsoo-gahbe(r)*
to get engaged	**sich verloben**	*zsikh ferlohben*
engine	**die Lokomotive(n)**	*dee lokomoteeve(r)*
English (language or subject)	**Englisch**	*english*
Enjoy your meal	**Guten Appetit!**	*gooten appeteet*
to enjoy yourself	**sich gut unterhalten**	*zikh goot oonterhalten*
to enjoy yourself, to have fun	**Spaß haben**	*shpass ha-ben*
enormous	**riesig**	*reezig*
entrance	**der Eingang(¨e)**	*derr yne-gang*
no entry (road)	**keine Einfahrt**	*kyne yne-fart*
envelope	**der Umschlag(¨e)**	*derr oomshlag*
Equator	**der Äquator**	*derr ay-quator*
escalator	**die Rolltreppe(n)**	*dee roll-treppe(r)*
Europe	**Europa**	*oy-ropa*
evening	**der Abend(e)**	*derr ahbend*
this evening	**heute Abend**	*hoyte(r) ahbend*
exam	**die Prüfung(en)**	*dee prewfoong*
to fail an exam	**durchfallen**	*doorkh-fa-len*
to pass an exam	**bestehen**	*beshtyen*
to sit an exam	**eine Prüfung machen**	*eyne(r) prew-foong makhen*
exchange rate	**der Umtauschkurs(e)**	*derr oomtaowh-koors*
to exercise	**trainieren**	*tren-eeren*
exercise book	**das Heft(e)**	*dass heft*
exhibition	**die Ausstellung(en)**	*dee owss-shtelloong*
exit	**der Ausgang(¨e)**	*derr owss-gang*
expensive	**teuer**	*toyer*
It's expensive.	**Das ist teuer.**	*dass ist toyer*
eye	**das Auge(n)**	*dass owge(r)*

F

fabric	**der Stoff(e)**	*derr stoff*
face	**das Gesicht(er)**	*dass gzikht*
factory	**die Fabrik(en)**	*dee fabreek*
to fail an exam	**durchfallen**	*doorkh-fa-len*
to faint	**in Ohnmacht fallen**	*in oan-makht fa-len*
fair	**hellhäutig**	*hell-hoytig*
to fall asleep	**einschlafen**	*eyne-shlafen*
false	**falsch**	*falsh*
family	**die Familie(n)**	*dee fameel-ye(r)*
famous	**berühmt**	*berewmt*
far	**weit**	*vyte*
far away from	**weit weg von (dat)**	*vyte veck von*
How far is...?	**Wie weit ist...?**	*vee vyte ist*
fare	**der Fahrpreis(e)**	*derr fahr-price*
farm	**der Bauernhof(¨e)**	*derr baowern-hofe*
farmer (m)	**der Bauer(n)**	*derr baower*
farmer (f), farmer's wife	**die Bäuerin(nen)**	*dee boyerin*
farmhouse	**das Bauernhaus(¨er)**	*dass baowern-house*
farmyard	**der Hof(¨e)**	*derr hofe*
fashionable	**modisch**	*mo-dish*
fast	**schnell**	*shnell*
fasten your seatbelts	**bitte anschnallen**	*bette(r) an-shnal-en*
fat	**dick**	*dick*
father	**der Vater(¨)**	*derr fahter*
feather	**die Feder(n)**	*dee favder*
February	**Februar**	*febroo-ar*
to feed	**füttern**	*fewtern*
to feel better	**sich besser fühlen**	*zikh besser fewlen*
to feel ill	**sich krank fühlen**	*zikh krank fewlen*
ferry	**die Fähre(n)**	*dee feh-re(r)*
to fetch	**bringen**	*bringen*
field	**das Feld(en)**	*dass felt*
fifteen	**fünfzehn**	*fewnf-tsehn*
the fifth (for dates only)	**der, die, das fünfte**	*derr, dee, dass fewnfte(r)*
fifty	**fünfzig**	*fewnf-tsig*
to fill	**füllen**	*fewlen*
to fill up with petrol	**volltanken**	*foll-tanken*
to have a filling	**sich einen Zahn plombieren**	*zikh eynen tsahn plombeeren*
film	**der Film(e)**	*der feelm*
It's fine.	**Es ist schön.**	*Ess ist shu(r)n*
finger	**der Finger(-)**	*derr fing-er*
fire	**das Feuer**	*dass foy-er*
fire engine	**das Feuerwehrauto(s)**	*dass foy-erfyr-owto*
to fire someone	**jemanden entlassen**	*yaymanden entlassen*
fire station	**die Feuerwache(n)**	*dee foyer vakhe(r)*

fireman	**der Feuerwehrmann(¨er)**	*derr foy-er-vyr-man*
fireplace	**der Kamin(e)**	*derr kameen*
the first	**der, die, das erste**	*derr, dee, dass erst(r)*
first class	**die erste Klasse**	*dee erste(r) klase(r)*
first floor	**der erste Stock**	*derr erste(r)stock*
first name	**der Vorname(n)**	*derr for-nahme(r)*
fish	**der Fisch(e)**	*derr fish*
to go fishing	**zum Angeln gehen**	*tsoom ang-eln gayen*
fishing boat	**das Fischerboot(e)**	*dass fisher-boat*
fishing red	**die Angelrute(n)**	*dee ang-el-roote(r)*
fishmonger	**der Fischhändler**	*derr fish-hendler*
to keep fit	**fit halten**	*fit halten*
fitted carpet	**der Teppichboden**	*derr teppich-boden*
five	**fünf**	*fewnf*
five past 10	**fünf nach zehn**	*fewnf nakh tsyn*
flag	**die Flagge(n)**	*dee flagge(r)*
flannel	**der Waschlappen(-)**	*der vash-lappen*
flat	**die Wohnung(en)**	*dee vonoong*
block of flats	**der Wohnblock(¨e)**	*derr vone-block*
flat tyre	**der Platte**	*derr platte(r)*
flavour, taste	**der Geschmack**	*derr geshmak*
to float	**treiben**	*try-ben*
flock	**die Herde(n)**	*dee herde(r)*
flood	**die Überschwem-mung(en)**	*dee ewbersh-vemmoong*
floor	**der Fußboden(¨)**	*derr fooss-boden*
ground floor	**das Erdgeschoss(e)**	*dass erd-geshoss*
second floor	**der zweite Stock**	*derr zsvyte(r) shtock*
florist	**das Blumengeschäft(e)**	*dass bloomen-gesheft*
flour	**das Mehl**	*dass mayl*
flower	**die Blume(n)**	*dee Bloome(r)*
bunch of flowers	**der Blumenstrauß(¨e)**	*derr bloomen-shtrows*
flowerbed	**das Blumenbeet(e)**	*dass bloomen-bayt*
flowered (with flower pattern)	**geblümt**	*geblewmt*
fly	**die Fliege(n)**	*die fleege(r)*
to fly	**fliegen**	*fleegen*
fog	**der Nebel**	*derr naybel*
It's foggy.	**Es ist neblig.**	*ess ist nayblig*
to follow	**verfolgen**	*ferfolgen*
to be fond of	**lieb haben**	*leep ha-ben*
foot	**der Fuß(¨e)**	*derr fooss*
football, ball	**der Fußball(¨e)**	*derr fooss-bal*
to play football	**Fußball spielen**	*fooss-bal shpeelen*
forget-me-not	**das Vergissmeinnicht(-)**	*dass fergiss-mine-nikht*
fork	**die Gabel(n)**	*dee gahbel*
form	**das Formular(e)**	*dass formulahr*
forty	**vierzig**	*feertsig*
forward	**vorwärts**	*for-verts*
foundation cream	**das Make-up(s)**	*dass make-up*
four	**vier**	*feer*
the fourth (for dates only)	**der, die, das vierte**	*derr, dee, dass feerte(r)*
fourteen	**vierzehn**	*feer-tsayn*
fox	**der Fuchs(¨e)**	*derr fooks*
fraction	**der Bruch(¨e)**	*derr brookh*
France	**Frankreich**	*frank-rykh*
freckles	**die Sommersprossen (pl)**	*dee zommer-shprossen*
French (language or subject)	**Französisch**	*fran-tseu(r)z-ish*
fresh	**frisch**	*frish*
Friday	**Freitag(m)**	*fry-tahg*
fridge	**der Kühlschrank(¨e)**	*derr kewl-shrank*
friend (m)	**der Freund(e)**	*derr froynt*
friend (f)	**die Freundin(nen)**	*dee fronydin*
friendly	**freundlich**	*froynt-likh*
frightened	**ängstlich**	*engst-likh*
fringe	**das Pony(s)**	*dass pony*
frog	**der Frosch(¨e)**	*derr frosh*
front door	**die Wohnungstür(en)**	*dee vo-noongs-tewr*
to frown	**die Stirn runzeln**	*dee shteern roontseln*
frost	**der Frost**	*derr frost*
frozen food	**die Tiefkühlkost**	*dee teef-kewl-kost*
to be frozen	**halb erfroren sein**	*halp erforen zyne*
fruit	**das Obst**	*dass ohpst*
fruit juice	**der Fruchtsaft**	*derr frookht-zaft*
full	**voll**	*foll*
full stop	**der Punkt(e)**	*derr poonkt*
fully booked	**belegt**	*belaygt*
fun	**der Spaß**	*derr shpass*
to have fun	**Spaß haben**	*shpass ha-ben*
funeral	**die Beerdigung(en)**	*be(r)-erdigoong*
funnel (ship)	**der Schornstein(e)**	*derr shorn-shtyne*
funny	**komisch**	*ko-mish*
fur	**das Fell**	*dass fell*
furniture	**die Möbel(pl)**	*dee mu(r)-bel*
future	**die Zukunft**	*dee tsookoonft*
in the future	**in der Zukunft**	*in derr tsookoonft*

G

galaxy	**die Milchstraße(n)**	*dee milk-shtrasse(r)*
art gallery	**die Kunstgalerie(n)**	*dee koonst-galleree*
game	**das Spiel(e)**	*dass shpeel*
gangway	**die Landungsbrücke(n)**	*dee landoongs-brewke*
garage	**die Garage(n)**	*dee ga-rahshe(r)*
garden	**der Garten(¨)**	*derr garten*
garden shed	**das Gartenhäuschen**	*dass garten-hors-khen*
gardener (m)	**der Gärtner(-)**	*derr gertner*
gardener (f)	**die Gärtnerin(nen)**	*dee gertnerin*
to do the gardening	**im Garten arbeiten**	*im garrten arbyten*
garlic	**der Knoblauch**	*derr k-no-blaowkh*
gas	**das Gas**	*dass gas*
gate	**das Tor(e)**	*dass tore*
to gather speed	**schneller werden**	*shneller verden*
generous	**großzügig**	*gross-tsewgig*
geography	**die Erdkunde**	*dee erd-koonde(r)*
geranium	**die Geranie(n)**	*dee gerannee-ye*
German (language or subject)	**Deutsch**	*doytsh*
Germany	**Deutschland**	*doytsh-lant*
to get dressed	**sich anziehen**	*zich an-tsee-en*
to get engaged	**sich verloben**	*zich ferloben*
to get married	**heiraten**	*hye-raten*
to get off (a bus or a train)	**aussteigen**	*owss-shtygen*
to get on	**einsteigen**	*yne-shtygen*

to get undressed	**sich ausziehen**	*sikh owss-tsee-en*
to get up	**aufstehen**	*owf-stay-en*
giraffe	**die Giraffe(n)**	*dee giraffe(r)*
girl	**das Mädchen(-)**	*dass med-chen*
to give	**geben**	*gayben*
to give (a present)	**schenken**	*shenken*
glass	**das Glas(¨er)**	*dass glahss*
glasses, pair of glasses	**die Brille(n)**	*dee brille(r)*
sunglasses	**die Sonnenbrille(n)**	*dee zonnen-brille(r)*
to wear glasses	**eine Brille tragen**	*yne(r) brille(r) trahgen*
glove	**der Handschuh(e)**	*derr hant-shoe*
to go	**gehen**	*gay-en*
to go to bed	**ins Bett gehen**	*inss bet gay-en*
to go to the cinema	**ins Kino gehen**	*inss keeno gay-en*
to go downstairs	**nach unten gehen**	*nakh oonten gay-en*
to go fishing	**zum Angeln gehen**	*tsoom ang-eln gay-en*
to go on holiday	**in Urlaub fahren**	*in oorlaowp fa-ren*
to go mountaineering	**zum Bergsteigen gehen**	*tsoom berg-shtygen gay-en*
to go upstairs	**nach oben gehen**	*nakh oben gay-en*
to go for a walk	**spazieren gehen**	shpatseeren *gay-en*
to go window-shopping	**einen Schaufenster-bummel machen**	*eynen shaowf-fenster boomel makhen*
to go to work	**zur Arbeit gehen**	*tsoor arbyte gay-en*
goal	**das Tor(e)**	*dass tore*
goalkeeper	**der Torwart(e)**	*derr tore-vart*
goat	**die Ziege(n)**	*dee tseege(r)*
gold	**das Gold**	*dass golt*
made of gold	**aus Gold**	*owss golt*
goldfish	**der Goldfisch(e)**	*derr golt-fish*
goldfish bowl	**das Goldfischglas(¨er)**	*dass golt-fish-glahss*
golf club	**der Golfschläger(-)**	*derr golf-shlager*
to play golf	**Golf spielen**	*golf speelen*
good	**gut**	*goot*
Good luck!	**Viel Glück.**	*feel glewk*
Good morning	**Guten Morgen**	*gooten morgen*
good value	**preiswert**	*price-vert*
It's good value.	**Das ist preiswert.**	*dass ist price-vert*
It tastes good.	**Das schmeckt gut.**	*dass shmeckt goot*
Goodbye	**Auf Wiedersehen**	*owf veeder-zay-en*
Goodbye (on telephone)	**Wiederhören**	*veeder-huren*
Good night	**Gute Nacht**	*goote nakhd*
goods train	**der Güterzug(¨e)**	*derr gewter-tsoog*
goose	**die Gans(¨e)**	*dee ganss*
gorilla	**der Gorilla(s)**	*derr gorila*
government	**die Regierung(en)**	*dee regeeroong*
grain	**das Getreide**	*dass getryde(r)*
grammar	**die Grammatik**	*dee gram-atik*
granddaughter	**die Enkelin(nen)**	*dee eknelin*
grandfather	**der Großvater(¨)**	*derr gross-fahter*
grandmother	**die Großmutter(¨)**	*dee gross-mooter*
grandson	**der Enkel(-)**	*derr enkel*
grape	**die Weintraube(n)**	*dee vine-trowbe(r)*
grass	**das Gras**	*dass grahss*
Great Britain	**Großbritannien**	*gross britannien*
green	**grün**	*grewn*
greenhouse	**das Gewächshaus(¨er)**	*dass gevecks-house*
grey	**grau**	*graow*
grocery shop	**das Lebensmittel geschäft(e)**	*dass laybens-mittel-gesheft*
ground floor	**das Erdgeschoss(e)**	*dass erd-geshoss*
to growl	**knurren**	*knooren*
guard	**der Schaffner**	*derr shaffner*
guest (m)	**der Gast(¨e)**	*der gast*
guest house, boarding house	**die Pension(en)**	*dee penz-ion*
guinea pig	**das Meerschweinchen(-)**	*dass mayr-shvine-khen*
guitar	**die Gitarre(n)**	*dee gitarre(r)*
to play the guitar	**Gitarre spielen**	*gitarre(r) shpeelen*
gymnastics	**die Gymnastik**	*dee gem-nastik*
gym shoes	**die Turnschuhe (pl)**	*dee toorn-sho-e(r)*

H

hail	**der Hagel**	*derr hahgel*
to hail a taxi	**ein Taxi rufen**	*yne taxi roofen*
hair	**das Haar(e)**	*dass har*
to have (...) colour hair	**(...) Haar haben**	*... har ha-ben*
hairdresser (m), hairdresser's	**der Friseur(e)**	*derr frizz-er*
hairdresser (f), hairdresser's	**die Friseurin(nen)**	*dee frizz-ewrin*
hair-drier	**der Fön(s)**	*derr fo(r)n*
a half	**die Hälfte(n)**	*dee helfte(r)*
half a kilo	**ein Pfund(e)**	*yne pfoont*
half a litre	**ein halber Liter(-)**	*yne halber litre*
half past 10	**halb elf**	*halp elf*
ham	**der Schinken(-)**	*derr shinken*
hammer	**der Hammer(¨)**	*derr hammer*
hamster	**der Hamster(-)**	*derr hamster*
hand	**die Hand(¨e)**	*dee hant*
handbag	**die Handtasche(n)**	*dee hant-tashe(r)*
hand luggage	**das Handgepäck**	*dass hant-gepeck*
handsome	**gutaussehend**	*goot ows-zayend*
to hang on to	**sich festhalten an**	*zikh fest hal-ten an*
to hang up (telephone)	**auflegen**	*owf-laygen*
happy	**glücklich**	*glewk-likh*
to be happy	**glücklich sein**	*glewk-likh zyne*
Happy birthday	**Herzlichen Glückwunsch zum Geburtstag**	*hertszlikhen glewk-voonsh tsoom geboorts-tahg*
Happy New Year	**Glückliches Neues Jahr**	*glewklikhes noyes yar*
hard	**hart**	*hart*
hard-working	**fleißig**	*fly-sig*
to harvest	**ernten**	*ernten*
hat	**der Hut(¨e)**	*derr hoot*
Have you any small change?	**Haben Sie Kleingeld?**	*ha-ben zee klyne-gelt*
to have	**haben**	*ha-ben*
to have a bath	**ein Bad nehmen**	*yne baht naymen*
to have a break-down (vehicle)	**eine Panne haben**	*yne panne(r) ha-ben*

to have a cold	**eine Erkältung haben**	*yne erkeltoong ha-ben*
to have a filling	**sich einen Zahn plombieren lassen**	*zickh ynen tsahn plom-bieeeren lassen*
to have a flat tyre	**einen Platten haben**	*ynen platen ha-ben*
to have fun	**Spaß haben**	*shpass ha-ben*
to have a showder	**duschen**	*dooshen*
to have stomach ache	**Bauchweh haben**	*baowkh-vay ha-ben*
to have a temperature	**Fieber haben**	*feeber ha-ben*
to have toothache	**Zahnschmerzen haben**	*tsahn shmert-sen ha-ben*
Having a lovely time.	**Es ist ganz toll hier.**	*ess ist gants toll here*
hay	**das Heu**	*dass hoy*
haystack	**der Hauhaufen(-)**	*derr hoy-howfen*
head	**der Kopf(¨e)**	*derr kopf*
to have a headache	**Kopfschmerzen haben**	*kopf-shmertsen ha-ben*
headband	**das Stirnbank(¨er)**	*dass shteeri-bant*
headlight	**der Scheinwerfer(-)**	*derr shine-verfer*
headline	**die Schlagzeile(n)**	*dee shlag-tsyle(r)*
headmaster	**der Direktor(en)**	*derr direkt-or*
headmistress	**die Direktorin(nen)**	*dee direkt-orin*
headphones	**die Köpfhörer (pl)**	*dee kuhpf-hu)r)-rer*
healthy	**gesund**	*gezoont*
heavy	**schwer**	*shver*
to be heavy	**schwer sein**	*shver zyne*
hedgehog	**der Igel(-)**	*derr eegel*
heel	**die Ferse(n)**	*dee ferze(r)*
height	**die Größe**	*dee gru(r)sse(r)*
Hello	**Hallo**	*hallo*
to help	**helfen**	*helfen*
Help yourself!	**Greif zu.**	*grife tsoo*
Can I help you?	**Womit kann ich dienen?**	*vo-mit kan ikh deenen*
henhouse	**der Hühnerstall(¨e)**	*derr hewner-shtal*
herbs	**die Kräuter (pl)**	*dee kryter*
hero	**der Held(en)**	*derr helt*
heroine	**die Heldin(nen)**	*dee heldin*
herring	**der Hering(e)**	*derr hayring*
to hide	**sich verstecken**	*zikh verstecken*
hill	**der Hügel(-)**	*derr hewgel*
hippopotamus	**das Nilpferd(e)**	*dass neel-pfert*
His name is...	**Er heißt...**	*er hysst*
history	**die Geschichte**	*dee geshikhte(r)*
hold (ships)	**der Laderaum(¨e)**	*derr lahde(r)-raowm*
to hold	**halten**	*hal-ten*
holiday	**der Ulaub(e)**	*der oorlaowp*
to go on holiday	**in Urlaub fahren**	*in ooralaowp fa-ren*
honey	**der Honig**	*derr ho-nig*
honeymoon	**die Flitterwochen (pl)**	*dee flitter-vokhen*
hook (for fishing)	**der Angelhaken(-)**	*derr ang-el haken*
horn	**die Hupe(n)**	*dee hoope(r)*
horse	**das Pferd(e)**	*dass pfert*
horse racing	**das Pferderennen(-)**	*dass pferde(r)-rennen*
hospital	**das Krankenhaus(¨er)**	*dass kranken-house*
hot	**heiß**	*hyss*
hot water	**heißes Wasser**	hysses vasser
I'm hot.	**Mir ist warm.**	*meer ist varm*

hotel	**das Hotel(s)**	*dass hotel*
to stay in a hotel	**im Hotel wohnen**	*im hotel vo-nen*
hour	**die Stunde(n)**	*dee stoonde(r)*
house	**das Haus(¨er)**	*dass hows*
How are you?	**Wie geht's?**	*vee gayts*
How far is...?	**Wie weit ist...?**	*vee vyte ist*
how much..?	**wie viel..?**	*vee feel*
How much is...?	**Was kostet...?**	*vass kostet*
How much is that?	**Wie viel macht das?**	*vee feel makht das*
How old are you?	**Wie alt bist du?**	*vee alt bist doo*
hump (camel's)	**der Höcker(-)**	*derr hu(r)ker*
hundred	**hundert**	*hoondert*
to be hungry	**Hunger haben**	*hoong-er ha-ben*
husband	**der Ehemann(¨er)**	*derr aye(r)-man*

I

I agree.	**Das meine ich auch.**	*dass myne(r) ikh owkh*
I am sending ... separately	**Mit getrennter Post erhältst du...**	*mit getrennter post erhelst doo*
I enclose (...)	**Beigefügt finden Sie (...)**	*by-gefu(r)gt finden zee*
I'll call you back. (on telephone)	**Ich rufe dich zurück.**	*ikh roofe(r) dikh zoorewk*
I would like...	**Ich hätte gern...**	*ikh hette gern*
I'm nineteen.	**Ich bin neunzehn.**	*ikh bin noyn-tsayn*
ice-cream	**das Eis**	*dass ice*
icicle	**der Eiszapfen**	*derr ice-tsapfen*
ill	**krank**	*krank*
to feel ill	**sich krank fühlen**	*zikh krankh fewlen*
important	**wichtig**	*vikh-tig*
in (for sports)	**nicht aus**	*nikht ows*
in	**in (dat)**	*in*
in focus	**scharf**	*sharf*
in front of	**vor (dat or acc)**	*for*
in the future	**in der Zukunft**	*in derr tsookoonft*
India	**Indien**	*indien*
indicator	**der Blinker(-)**	*derr blinker*
ingredient	**die Zutat(en)**	*dee tsoo-tat*
injection	**die Spritze(n)**	*dee shpritse(r)*
instrument	**das Instrument(e)**	*das instru-ment*
inter-city-train	**der Intercity**	*derr intercity*
interesting	**interessant**	*interess-ant*
to interview	**interviewen**	*interviewen*
into	**in (acc)**	*in*
to introduce	**vorstellen**	*for-shtellen*
to invite	**einladen**	*yne-laden*
to iron	**bügeln**	*bewgeln*
Is service included?	**Mit Bedienung?**	*mit bedeenoong*
It costs...	**Das kostet...**	*dass kostet*
It is getting light.	**Es wird hell.**	*ess veert hell*
It is light.	**Es ist hell.**	*es ist hell*
It is 1 o'clock.	**Es ist ein Uhr.**	*ess ist yne oor*
It is 3 o'clock.	**Es ist drei Uhr.**	*ess ist drye oor*
It's... (on phone)	**Hier ist...**	*here ist*
It's cold.	**Es ist kalt.**	*ess ist kalt*
It's fine.	**Es ist schön.**	*ess ist shawn*
It's foggy.	**Es ist neblig.**	*ess ist nayblig*
It's good value.	**Es ist preiswert.**	*ess ist price-vert*
It's raining.	**Es regnet.**	*ess raygnet*
It's ready. (for meal)	**Das Essen ist fertig.**	*dass essen ist fertig*
It's snowing.	**Es schneit.**	*ess schnyte*
It's windy.	**Es ist windig.**	*ess ist vindig*

It was lovely to hear from you.	**Schön, mal wieder von dir zu hören.**	*sho(r)n, mal veeder fon deer tsoo ho(r)-ren*
Italy	**Italien**	*italien*

J

jacket	**die Jacke(n)**	*dee yacke(r)*
jam	**die Marmelade(n)**	*dee marme(r)-lade(r)*
Japan	**Japan**	*yapan*
jeans	**die Jeans (pl)**	*dee jeans*
jewellery	**der Schmuck**	*derr shmook*
job, profession	**der Beruf(e)**	*derr beroof*
to jog	**joggen**	*yoggen*
to join	**Mitglied werden**	*mit-gleed verden*
joint, roast	**der Braten**	*derr brahten*
journalist (m)	**der Journalist(en)**	*derr journaleest*
journalist (f)	**die Journalistin(nen)**	*dee jounrna-leestin*
judge (m)	**der Richter(-)**	*derr rikhter*
judge (f)	**die Richterin(en)**	*dee rikhterin*
juice	**der Safte(¨e)**	*derr zaft*
fruit juice	**der Fruchtsaft(¨e)**	*derr frookht-zaft*
jug	**der Krug(¨e)**	*derr kroog*
July	**Juli**	*yulee*
jumper	**der Pullover(-)**	*derr pulover*
June	**Juni**	*yunee*
jungle	**der Dschungel(-)**	*derr djoongel*

K

kangaroo	**das Känguruh(s)**	*dass kengooroo*
to keep an eye on	**aufpassen auf**	*owf-pasen owf*
to keep fit	**fit halten**	*fit halten*
kennel	**die Hundehütte(n)**	*dee hoonde(r)-hewte(r)*
keyboard	**die Tastatur(en)**	*dee tass-ta-toor*
kilo	**das Kilo(-)**	*dass keelo*
A kilo of...	**Ein Kilo...**	*yne keelo*
Half a kilo of...	**Ein Pfund...**	*yne pfoont*
to kiss	**küssen**	*kewsen*
kitchen	**die Küche(n)**	*dee kewkhe(r)*
kitten	**das Kätzchen(-)**	*dass ktes-khen*
knee	**das Knie(-)**	*dass k-nee*
to kneel down	**sich hinknien**	*sikh hin k noo en*
to be kneeling	**knien**	*k-nee-en*
knife	**das Messer(-)**	*dass messer*
to knit	**stricken**	*shtricken*
knitting needles	**die Stricknadeln (pl)**	*dee shtrick-nadeln*
to knock over	**umwerfen**	*oom-verfen*

L

label	**ein Anhänger(-)**	*yne an-hen-ger*
ladder	**die Leiter(-)**	*dee lyter*
lake	**der See(n)**	*derr zay*
lamb	**das Lamm(¨er)**	*dass lamb*
lamp	**die Lampe(n)**	*dee lampe(r)*
to land	**landen**	*landen*
landlady	**die Eigentümerin(nen)**	*dee eygen-tewmerin*
landlord	**der Eigentümer(-)**	*derr eygen-tewmer*
landscape	**die Landschaft(en)**	*dee lantshaft*
large (clothes size)	**groß**	*gross*
last	**letzte**	*letste(r)*
late	**verspätet**	*fer-shpaytet*
to be late	**zu spät kommen**	*tsoo shpayt kommen*
to laugh	**lachen**	*lakhen*
to burst out laughing	**in Gelächter ausbrechen**	*in glekhder ows-brekhen*
lawn	**der Rasen(-)**	*derr rahzen*
lawnmower	**der Rasenmäher(-)**	*derr rahzen-mayer*
lawyer (m)	**der Rechtsanwalt(¨e)**	*derr rekhts-anvalt*
lawyer (f)	**die Rechtsanwältin(nen)**	*dee rekhts-anvaltin*
to lay eggs	**Eier legen**	*eyer legen*
to lay the table	**den Tisch decken**	*den tishdekcen*
lazy	**faul**	*fowl*
leader (m/f)	**der/die Vorsitzende(n)**	*derr/dee for-zitsende(r)*
leaf	**das Blatt(¨er)**	*das blatt*
to lean on	**lehnen an**	*laynen an*
to learn	**lernen**	*lernen*
left luggage office	**die Gepäckaufbewahrung**	*dee gepeck-owfbevahroon*
left, left side	**die linke Seite**	*dee linke(r) zyte(r)*
on the left, left wing	**links**	*links*
leg	**das Bein(e)**	*dass bine*
lemon	**die Zitrone(en)**	*dee tsitrone(r)*
lentils	**die Linsen (pl)**	*dee linzen*
length	**die Länge(n)**	*dee lenge(r)*
lesson	**die Unterrichtsstunde(n)**	*dee oonter-rikhts-shtoonde(r)*
letter	**der Brief(e)**	*derr brief*
letter of alphabet	**der Buchstabe(n)**	*derr bookh-shtahbe*
letter box	**der Briefkasten(¨)**	*derr brief-kasten*
library	**die Bücherei(en)**	*dee bewkher-eye*
to lie down	**sich hinlegen**	*zikh hin-laygen*
life	**das Leben**	*dass layben*
lifeguard	**der Rettungs-schwimmer(-)**	*derr rettoongs-shvimmer*
lift	**der Aufzug(¨e)**	*derr owf-tsoog*
light (weight)	**leicht**	*lykht*
to be light (weight)	**leicht sein**	*lykht zine*
light (lamp)	**die Lampe(n)**	*dee lampe(r)*
It is light.	**Es ist hell.**	*ess ist hell*
It is getting light.	**Es wird hell.**	*ess veert hell*
lightning	**der Blitz(e)**	*derr blitz*
liner	**das Passagierschiff(e)**	*dass passageer-shiff*
lion	**der Löwe(n)**	*derr lo(r)ve(r)*
lip	**die Lippe(n)**	*dee lippe(r)*
lipstick	**der Lippenstift(e)**	*derr lippen-shtift*
list	**die Liste**	*dee liste(r)*
to make a list	**eine Liste machen**	*yne(r) liste(r) makhen*
to listen	**hören**	*ho(r)-en*
to listen to music	**Musik hören**	*moozeek ho(r)-en*
to listen to radio	**Radio hören**	*ra-dio ho(r)-en*
litre	**der Liter(-)**	*derr leeter*
half a litre	**ein halber Liter(-)**	*yne halber leeter*
litter bin	**der Papierkorb(¨e)**	*derr papeer-korp*
to live	**wohnen**	*vo-nen*
to live in a house	**in einem Haus wohnen**	*in ynem house vo-nen*
lively	**lebhaft**	*layb-haft*
living room	**das Wohnzimmer(-)**	*dass vone-tsimmer*
to load	**laden**	*la-den*
loaf	**der Laib(e)**	*derr lybe*

long	**lang**	*lang*
to look for	**suchen**	*zukhen*
loose	**weit**	*vyte*
lorry	**der Lastwagen(-)**	*derr last-vagen*
lorry driver	**der Lastenwagenfahrer(-)**	*derr lastvagen-fahrer*
to lose	**verlieren**	*fer-leeren*
loudspeaker	**der Lautsprecher(-)**	*derr laowt-shprekher*
Love from... (end of letter)	**Alles Gute...**	*al-ez goote(r)*
to love	**lieben**	*leeben*
luck	**das Glück**	*dass glewk*
Good luck	**Viel Glück**	*feel glewk*
luggage-rack	**die Gepäckablage(n)**	*dee gepeck-ap-lahge(r)*
lullaby	**das Schlaflied(er)**	*dass shlahf-leet*
lunch	**das Mittagessen(n)**	*dass mittag-essen*
lunch hour	**die Mittagspause(n)**	*dee mittags-powze(r)*
to be lying down	**liegen**	*leegen*

M

made of metal	**aus Metall**	*owss metall*
made of plastic	**aus Plastik**	*owss pla-stick*
magazine	**die Zeitschrift(en)**	*dee tsyte-shrift*
airmail	**Luftpost**	*looft-post*
main course	**das Hauptgericht(e)**	*dass howpt-gerikht*
main road	**die Hauptstraße(n)**	*dee howpt-strasse(r)*
to make	**machen**	*makhen*
to make a list	**eine Listen machen**	*yne(r) liste makhen*
to make a phonecall	**telefonieren**	*telephoneeren*
to make, to build	**bauen**	*bow-en*
to put on make-up	**sich schminken**	*zikh shminken*
man	**der Mann(¨er)**	*der man*
map	**die Karte(n)**	*dee karte(r)*
March	**März**	*merts*
margarine	**die Margarine**	*dee mar-ga-reene(r)*
market	**der Markt(¨e)**	*derr markrt*
market place	**der Marktplatz(¨e)**	*derr markt-plats*
to shop at the market	**auf dem Markt einkaufen**	*owf daym markt yne-kowfen*
market stall	**der Marktstand(¨e)**	*derr markt-stant*
marriage	**die Ehe(n)**	*dee aye(r)*
to get married	**heiraten**	*hye-raten*
mascara	**die Wimperntusche(n)**	*dee vimpern-tooshe(r)*
maths	**Mathematik**	*matema-tick*
May	**Mai**	*mey*
meadow	**die Wiese(n)**	*dee veese(r)*
measure	**messen**	*messen*
meat	**das Fleisch**	*dass flysh*
mechanic (m)	**der Automechaniker(-)**	*derr owto-mekhaniker*
the media	**die Medien (pl)**	*dee maydien*
medium (clothes size)	**mittel**	*mittell*
to meet	**treffen**	*treffen*
melon	**die Melone(n)**	*dee melone(r)*
member (m/f)	**das Mitglied (er)**	*dass mit-gleet*
member of parliament (m/f)	**der/die Abgeordnete(n)**	*derr/dee apge(r)ordnete(r)*
to mend	**reparieren**	*repareeren*
to mend (clothing)	**flicken**	*flicken*
menu	**die Speisekarte(n)**	*dee shpyze-kart(r)*
metal	**das Metall(e)**	*dass metall*
made of metal	**aus Metall**	*ows metall*
metre	**der Meter(-)**	*derr mayter*
to mew	**miauen**	*miaw-en*
midday	**Mittag**	*mitag*
midnight	**Mitternacht**	*mitter-nakht*
milk	**die Milch**	*dee milkh*
to milk	**melken**	*melken*
a million	**eine Million**	*yne(r) mill-yon*
mineral water	**das Mineralwasser**	*dass miner-al-vasser*
minus (maths)	**weniger**	*vayniger*
mirror	**der Spiegel(-)**	*derr shpeegel*
miserable	**schlecht gelaunt**	*shlekht gelaownt*
to miss the train	**den Zug verpassen**	*dayn tsoog fer-passen*
to mix	**rühren**	*rewren*
model (m/f)	**das Mannequin(s)**	*dass manay-kin*
mole	**der Maulwurf(¨e)**	*derr mowl-worf*
Monday	**Montag(e)**	*mon-tag*
money	**das Geld**	*dass gelt*
to change money	**Geld wechseln**	*gelt veckseln*
to put money in the bank, to pay money in	**Geld einzahlen**	*gelt yne-tsahlen*
to take money out	**Geld abheben**	*gelt ap-hayben*
monkey	**der Affe(n)**	*derr affe(r)*
month	**der Monat(e)**	*derr mo-nat*
moon	**der Mond**	*derr moant*
moped	**das Moped(s)**	*dass moped*
morning	**der Morgen(-)**	*derr morgen*
8 in the morning, 8 a.m.	**acht Uhr morgens**	*akht oor morgens*
this morning	**heute Morgen**	*hoyte(r) morgen*
mosquito	**die Mücke(n)**	*dee mewke(r)*
mother	**die Mutter(¨)**	*dee mooter*
motor racing	**das Autorennen(-)**	*dass owto-rennen*
motorbike	**das Motorrad(¨er)**	*dass mo-to-rad*
mountain	**der Berg(e)**	*derr berg*
mountaineering	**das Bergsteigen**	*dass berg-shtygen*
to go mountaineering	**zum Bergsteigen gehen**	*tsoom berg-stygen gay-en*
mouse	**die Maus(¨e)**	*dee mouse*
moustache	**der Schnurrbart(¨e)**	*derr shnoorbart*
to have a moustache	**einen Schnurrbart haben**	*ynen shnoorbart ha-ben*
mouth	**der Mund(¨er)**	*derr moont*
to move in	**einziehen**	*yne-tsee-en*
to move out	**ausziehen**	*owss-tsee-en*
to mow the lawn	**den Rasen mähen**	*dayn ra-zen mayen*
to multiply	**malnehmen**	*mal-naymen*
music	**die Musik(en)**	*dee moozeek*
classical music	**die klassische Musik**	*dee klassishe(r) moozeek*
pop music	**die Popmusik**	*dee pop-moozeek*
musician (m)	**der Musiker(-)**	*derr mooziker*
musician (f)	**die Musikerin(nen)**	*dee moozikerin*
mussel	**die Muscheln (pl)**	*deemossheln*
mustard	**der Senf**	*derr zenf*
My name is...	**Ich heiße...**	*ikh hysse(r)*

N

naked	**nackt**	*nackt*
name	**der Name(n)**	*derr na-me(r)*
first name	**der Vorname(n)**	*derr for-na-me(r)*
surname	**der Nachname(n)**	*derr nakh-na-me(r)*
His name is...	**Er heißt...**	*er hysst*

My name is...	**Ich heiße...**	*ikh kysse*
What's your name?	**Wie heißt du?**	*vee hysst doo*
napkin	**die Serviette(n)**	*dee serv-iette(r)*
narrow	**schmal**	*shmal*
naughty	**frech**	*frekh*
navy blue	**marineblau**	*marine(r)-blaow*
near	**nahe an (dat)**	*nahe(r) an*
neck	**der Hals(¨e)**	*derr halss*
necklace	**die Halskette(n)**	*dee halss-kette(n)*
needle	**die Nadel(n)**	*dee na-del*
needlework and wool shop	**das Handarbeits-geschäft(e)**	*dass hant-arbyts-gesheft*
neighbour (m)	**der Nachbar(n)**	*derr nakhbar*
neighbour (f)	**die Nachbarin(nen)**	*dee nakhbarin*
nephew	**der Neffe(n)**	*derr neffe(r)*
nest	**das Nest(er)**	*dass nest*
net (tennis court)	**dass Netz(e)**	*dass nets*
net (fishing)	**das Netz(e)**	*dass nets*
Netherlands	**die Niederlande (pl)**	*dee needer-lande(r)*
new	**neu**	*noy*
New Year's Day	**Neujahr**	*noy-yar*
New Year's Eve	**Silvester**	*zilvester*
Happy New Year	**Glückliches Neues Jahr**	*glewk-likhes noyez yar*
New Zealand	**Neuseeland**	*noy-zaylant*
news	**die Nachrichten (pl)**	*dee nakh-rikhten*
newspaper	**die Zeitung(en)**	*dee tsyte-oong*
newspaper stand	**der Kiosk(e)**	*derr kiosk*
next	**nächste**	*nexte(r)*
the next day	**am nächsten Tag**	*am nexten tahg*
next Monday	**nächsten Montag**	*nexten moan-tahg*
next week	**nächste Woche**	*nexte(r) vokhe(r)*
niece	**die Nichte(n)**	*dee nikhte(r)*
night	**die Nacht(¨e)**	*dee nakht*
nightdress	**das Nachthemd(en)**	*dass nakht-hemt*
nine	**neun**	*noyn*
999 call	**der Notruf(e)**	*derr note-roof*
nineteen	**neunzehn**	*noyn-tsayn*
ninety	**neunzig**	*noyn-tsig*
no	**nein**	*nine*
no entry (road sign)	**keine Einfahrt**	*kyne yne-fart*
no parking	**Parkverbot**	*park ferboat*
no smoking	**Nichtraucher**	*nikht-rowkher*
noise	**laut**	*lauwt*
noodles	**die Nudeln (pl)**	*dee noodeln*
north	**der Norden**	*derr norden*
North Pole	**der Nordpol**	*derr nord-pole*
nose	**die Nase(n)**	*dee naze(r)*
note (money)	**die Banknote(n)**	*dee banknote(r)*
nothing	**nichts**	*nikhts*
Nothing to declare	**Nicht zu verzollen**	*nikhts tsoo fer-tsollen*
novel	**der Roman(e)**	*derr ro-man*
November	**November**	*november*
now, nowadays	**jetzt**	*jetst*
number plate	**das Nummernschild(er)**	*dass noomern-shilt*
nurse (m)	**der Krankenpfleger**	*derr kranken-pflayger*
nurse (f)	**die Krankenschwester**	*dee kranken-shvester*

O

oak tree	**die Eiche(n)**	*dee ykhe(r)*
oar	**das Ruder**	*dass rooder*
obedient	**gehorsam**	*gehorzam*
It is one o'clock.	**Es ist ein Uhr.**	*ess ist yne oor*
It is 3 o'clock.	**Es ist drei Uhr.**	*ess ist dry oor*
October	**Oktober**	*october*
odd jobs	**das Heimwerken**	*dass hyme-verken*
office	**das Büro(s)**	*dass bewro*
offices, office block	**das Bürogebäude**	*dass bewro-geboyde(r)*
oil (engine food)	**das Öl**	*dass o(r)l*
old	**alt**	*alt*
old-fashioned	**altmodisch**	*alt-modish*
old age	**das Alter**	*dass alt-er*
older than	**älter als**	*elter alss*
on	**auf (acc or dat)**	*aowf*
on time	**pünktlich**	*pewnkt-likh*
one	**eins**	*ynss*
onion	**die Zwiebel(n)**	*dee tsveebel*
open	**offen**	*offen*
to open	**öffnen**	*o(r)fnen*
to open a letter	**einen Brief öffnen**	*ynen brief o(r)fnen*
to open the curtains	**die Vorhänge aufziehen**	*dee foreheng(r) owf-tsee-en*
opera	**die Oper(n)**	*dee o-per*
operating theatre	**der Operationssaal**	*derr operatsee-onz-zahl*
operation	**die Operation(en)**	*dee operatsee-oan*
orange (colour)	**orange**	*o-range(r)*
orange (fruit)	**die Apfelsine(n)**	*dee apfel-zeene(r)*
orchard	**der Obstgarten(¨)**	*derr oapst-garten*
orchestra	**das Orchester(-)**	*dass orkester*
to order	**bestellen**	*be-shtellen*
ostrich	**der Strauß**	*derr shtrowss*
out (for sports)	**aus**	*owss*
out of	**aus (dat)**	*owss*
out of focus	**unscharf**	*oon-sharf*
oven	**der Backofen(¨)**	*derr back-oafen*
over	**über (acc or dat)**	*ewber*
to overtake	**überholen**	*ewber-holen*
overtime	**Überstunden (pl)**	*ewber-shtoonden*
owl	**die Eule(n)**	*dee oyle(r)*

P

Pacific Ocean	**der Pazifik**	*derr pa-tsifeek*
to pack	**packen**	*packen*
packet	**das Päckchen**	*dass peck-khen*
to paddle	**planschen**	*plan-shen*
paint	**die Farbe(n)**	*dee farbe(r)*
to paint	**malen**	*ma-len*
painter (m)	**der Künstler(-)**	*derr kewnstler*
painter (f)	**die Künstlerin(nen)**	*dee kewnstlereen*
painting	**das Gemälde(-)**	*dass gemelde(r)*
pale	**blass**	*blass*
paper	**das Papier**	*dass papeer*
paperback	**das Taschenbuch(¨)**	*dass tashen-bookh*
parcel	**das Paket(e)**	*das pa-keyt*
parents	**die Eltern (pl)**	*dee eltern*
park	**der Park(s)**	*derr park*
park keeper	**der Parkwächter(-)**	*der park-vekhter*
to park	**parken**	*parken*
no parking	**Parkverbot**	*park-ferbote*
parliament	**das Parlament(e)**	*dass parlament*
party (celebration)	**die Party(s)**	*dee party*
party (political)	**die Partei(en)**	*dee part-eye*
to pass an exam	**bestehen**	*be(r)-shtayen*
passenger (m/f)	**der Pasagier(e)**	*derr passajeer*

passport	**der Pass(¨e)**	*derr pass/dee pesse(r)*
past	**die Vergangenheit**	*dee fer-gangenhyte*
pastry, Danish pastry	**der Hefekuchen(-)**	*derr hayfe(r)-ko(e)-khen*
path	**der Weg(e)**	*derr vayg*
path, country lane	**der Pfad(e)**	*derr pfaht*
patient (m)	**der Patient(en)**	*derr pats-yent*
patient (f)	**die Patientin(nen)**	*dee pats-yentin*
pattern	**das Muster(-)**	*das mooster*
pavement	**der Bürgersteig(e)**	*derr bewrg-er-shtyge*
paw	**die Pfote(n)**	*dee pfote(r)*
PE	**der Sport**	*derr shport*
pea	**die Erbse(n)**	*dee erpse(r)*
peaceful	**friedlich**	*freed-likh*
peach	**die Pfirsich(e)**	*dee pfirzikh*
pear	**die Birne(n)**	*dee beerne(r)*
pedestrian (m)	**der Fußgänger(-)**	*derr fooss-genger*
pedestrian (f)	**die Fußgängerin(nen)**	*dee fooss-gengereen*
pedestrian crossing	**der Zebrastreifen(-)**	*derr zebra-shtryfen*
pen	**der Füller(-)**	*derr fewler*
ball-point	**der Kugelschreiber(-)**	*derr koogel-shryber*
pencil	**der Bleistift**	*derr bly-shtift*
pencilcase	**das Etui(s)**	*dass ay-twee*
penguin	**der Pinguin(e)**	*derr pingooin*
pepper	**der Pfeffer**	*derr pfeffer*
to perch	**hocken**	*hocken*
to perform, to appear on stage	**auftreten**	*owf-trayten*
perfume	**das Parfüm(s)**	*dass parfume*
petrol	**das Benzin**	*dass benzeen*
petrol station	**die Tankstelle(n)**	*dee tank-shtelle(r)*
to full up with petrol	**volltanken**	*foll-tanken*
petticoat, slip	**der Unterrock(¨e)**	*derr oonter-rock*
photograph	**das Foto(s)**	*dass photo*
to take a photo	**ein Foto machen**	*yne photo makhen*
photographer (m)	**der Fotograf(en)**	*derr photograph*
photographer (f)	**die Fotografin(nen)**	*dee photographin*
photography	**die Fotografie(n)**	*dee photographee*
physics	**die Physik**	*dee phewzick*
piano	**das Klavier(e)**	*dass klaveer*
to play the piano	**Klavier spielen**	*klaveer shpeelen*
to pick	**pflücken**	*pflewken*
to pick flowers	**Blumen pflücken**	*bloomen pflewken*
to pick up	**aufheben**	*owf-hayben*
to pick up the receiver	**den Telefonhörer abheben**	*den telephon-ho(r)er apnaymen*
picnic	**das Picknick**	*dass picnic*
pig	**das Schwein(e)**	*dass shvine*
pigeon	**die Taube(n)**	*dee taowebe(r)*
pill	**die Tablett(en)**	*dee tablette(r)*
pillow	**das Kopfkissen**	*dass kopf-kissen*
pilot (m)	**der Pilot(en)**	*derr pee-lote*
pilot (f)	**die Pilotin(nen)**	*dee pee-lotin*
pin	**die Stecknadel(n)**	*dee shteck-nahdel*
pine tree	**die Tanne(n)**	*dee tanne(r)*
pink	**rosa**	*roza*
pitch (for sports)	**der Sportplatz(¨e)**	*derr shport-plats*

to pitch a tent	**ein Zelt aufbauen**	*yne tselt owf-bowen*
plaice	**die Scholle(n)**	*dee sholle(r)*
to plant	**pflanzen**	*pflantsen*
plastic	**das Plastik**	*dass plastic*
made of plastic	**aus Plastik**	*ows plastic*
plate	**der Teller**	*derr teller*
platform	**der Bahnsteig(e)**	*derr bahn-shteyk*
platform ticket	**die Bahnsteigkarte(n)**	*dee bahn-shtyk-karte(r)*
play (theatre)	**das Stück(e)**	*dass shtewk*
to play (to play an instrument)	**spielen**	*shpeelen*
to play cards	**Karten spielen**	*karten shpeelen*
to play chess	**Schach spielen**	*shakh shpeelen*
to play draughts	**Dame spielen**	*dahme(r) shpeelen*
to play golf	**Golf spielen**	*golf shpeelen*
to play squash	**Squash spielen**	*sqash shpeelen*
to play tennis	**Tennis spielen**	*tennis shpeelen*
player (m)	**der Spieler(-)**	*derr shpeeler*
player (f)	**die Spielerin(nen)**	*dee shpeelerin*
playful	**verspielt**	*fer-shpeelt*
playground	**der Schulhof(¨e)**	*derr shool-hofe*
pleased with	**zufrieden mit**	*tsoofreeden mit*
to plough	**pflügen**	*pflewgen*
plug (electric)	**der Stecker(-)**	*derr shtecker*
plug (bath or sink)	**der Stöpsel**	*derr shto(r)psel*
plum	**die Pflaume(n)**	*dee pflaowme(r)*
plumber	**der Klempner(-)**	*derr klempner*
plus (maths)	**und**	*oont*
pocket	**die Tasche(n)**	*dee tashe(r)*
poem	**das Gedicht(e)**	*dass gedikht*
poetry	**Gedichte (pl)**	*gedikhte(r)*
polar bear	**der Eisbär(en)**	*derr ice-bear*
police	**die Polizei**	*dee politsye*
police car	**das Polizeiauto(s)**	*dass politsye-owto*
police station	**die Polizeiwache(n)**	*dee politsye-vakhe(r)*
policeman	**der Polizist(en)**	*derr politsist*
policewoman	**die Polizistin(nen)**	*dee politsistin*
polite	**höflich**	*ho(r)flikh*
politics	**die Politik**	*dee politik*
pond	**der Teich(e)**	*derr tykh*
popular	**beliebt**	*beleebt*
port	**der Hafen(¨)**	*derr ha-fen*
porter (in hotel)	**der Portier(s)**	*derr port-yay*
porter (in airport, station...)	**der Gepäckträger(-)**	*derr gepeck-trayger*
porthole	**das Bullauge(n)**	*dass boll-owge(r)*
to post	**einwerfen**	*yne-verfen*
post office	**das Postamt(¨er)**	*dass post-amt*
postal code	**die Postleitzahl**	*dee ost-lyt-tsahl*
post-box	**der Briefkasten(¨)**	*derr brief-kasten*
postcard	**die Postkarte(n)**	*dee post-karte(r)*
postman	**der Briefträger(-)**	*derr brief-trayger*
postwoman	**die Briefträgerin(nen)**	*dee brief-traygerin*
potato	**die Kartoffel(n)**	*dee kartoffel*
to pour	**gießen**	*geess-en*
powerboat	**das Motorboot(e)**	*dass motor-boat*
prescription	**das Rezept(e)**	*dass re-tsept*
present (now)	**die Gegenwart**	*dee gaygen-vart*
present (gift)	**das Geschenk(e)**	*dass geshenk*
president (m)	**der Präsident(en)**	*derr president*
president (f)	**die Präsidentin(nen)**	*dee presidentin*
pretty	**hübsch**	*hewbsh*
price	**der Preis(e)**	*derr price*

prime minister (m)	**der Bundeskanzler(-)**	*derr boondes-kantsler*
prime minister (f)	**die Bundeskanzlerin(nen)**	*dee boondes-kantslerin*
programme	**die Sendung(en)**	*dee zendoong*
pudding	**das Dessert(s)**	*das dessert*
puddle	**die Pfütze(n)**	*dee pfewtse(r)*
to take someone's pulse	**den Puls fühlen**	*dayn poolss fewlen*
to pull	**ziehen**	*tsee-en*
pupil (m)	**der Schüler(-)**	*derr shewler*
pupil (f)	**die Schülerin(nen)**	*dee shewlerin*
puppy	**der junge Hunde**	*derr yoonge(r) hoont*
purple	**lila**	*leela*
purr	**schnurren**	*shnoorren*
purse	**die Geldbörse(n)**	*dee gelt-bo(r)se(r)*
to push	**drücken**	*drewken*
pushchair	**der Sportwagen(-)**	*derr shport-vahgen*
to put down	**hinstellen**	*hin-shtellen*
to put money in, to pay money in	**Geld einzahlen**	*gelt yne-tsahlen*
pyjamas	**der Schlafanzug(¨e)**	*derr shlaf-antsoog*

Q

a quarter	**das Viertel(-)**	*das feertel*
a quarter past 10	**Viertel nach zehn**	*feertel nakh tsayn*
a quarter to 10	**Viertel vor zehn**	*feertel for tsayn*
to ask a question	**etwas fragen**	*etvass fra-gen*
to queue	**anstehen**	*an-shtayen*
quiet, calm	**ruhig**	*roo-ig*

R

race, racing	**das Rennen(n)**	*dass rennen*
rabbit	**das Kaninchen(-)**	*dass kaneen-khen*
racket	**der Schläger(-)**	*der shlayger*
radiator	**der Heizkörper(-)**	*derr hyts-ko(r)per*
railway	**die Eisenbahn**	*dee yzen-bahn*
rain	**der Regen**	*der raygen*
rainbow	**der Regenbogen(-)**	*derr raygen-bogen*
raincoat	**der Regenmantel(¨)**	*derr raygen-mantel*
raindrop	**der Regentropfen(-)**	*derr raygen-tropfen*
to rain	**regnen**	raygnen
It's raining.	**Es regnet.**	*ess raygnet*
rake	**die Harke(n)**	*dee harke(r)*
raspberry	**die Himbeere(n)**	*dee heembayre(r)*
raw	**roh**	*ro*
razor	**der Rasierapparat(e)**	*derr razeer-apparat*
to read	**lesen**	*layzen*
to read a book	**ein Buch lesen**	*yne bookh layzen*
to read a story	**eine Geschichte vorlesen**	*yne(r) geshikhte(r) forlayzen*
It's ready. (meat)	**Das Essen ist fertig.**	*dass essen ist fertig*
receipt	**die Quittung(en)**	*dee kveetoong*
to receive	**bekommen**	*bekommen*
receiver	**der Telefonhörer(-)**	*derr telephone-ho(r)-rer*
reception	**der Empfang**	*derr empfang*
recipe	**das Rezept(e)**	*dass retsept*
record	**die Platte(n)**	*dee platte(r)*
record player	**der Plattenspieler(-)**	*derr platten-shpeeler*
record shop	**das Schallplattengeschäft(e)**	*dass shallplatten-gesheft*
rectangle	**das Rechteck**	*dass rekht-eck*
red	**rot**	*rote*
red hair	**rotes Haar**	*rot-ez har*
reed	**das Schilf**	*dass shilf*
referee	**der Schiedsrichter(-)**	*derr sheeds-rikhter*
to be related to	**verwandt sein mit**	*fervant zyne mit*
to reserve	**reservieren**	*reserveeren*
to reserve a room	**ein Zimmer reservieren**	*yne tsimmer reserveeren*
to reserve a seat	**einen Platz reservieren**	*ynen plats reserveeren*
reserved seat	**der reservierte Platz**	*derr reserveerte plats*
to rest	**sich ausruhen**	*zikh ows-roohen*
restaurant	**das Restaurant(s)**	*dass restaurant*
to retire	**aufhören zu arbeiten**	*owf-hu(e)-en tsoo arbytten*
by return of post	**postwendend**	*post-vendend*
return ticket	**die Rückfahrkarte(n)**	*dee rewk-far-karte(r)*
rice	**der Reis**	*derr rice*
to ride a bicycle	**mit dem Rad fahren**	*mit daym far-rat fa-ren*
on the right	**rechts**	*rekhts*
right side	**die rechte Seite**	*dee rekhte zyte(r)*
right wing	**konservativ**	*konservateef*
ring	**der Ring(e)**	*derr ring*
to ring	**läuten**	*loyten*
to ring the bell	**klingeln**	*klin-geln*
ripe	**reif**	*rife*
river	**der Fluss(¨e)**	*derr flooss*
to roar	**brüllen**	*brewlen*
rock	**der Felsen(-)**	*derr felzen*
roll	**das Brötchen(-)**	*dass bro(e)t-khen*
roof	**das Dach(¨er)**	*dass dakh*
room	**das Zimmer(-)**	*dass tsimmer*
double-room	**das Doppelzimmer(-)**	*dass dopple-tsimmer*
single room	**das Einzelzimmer(-)**	*das eynzel-tsimmer*
rose	**die Rose(n)**	*dee rose(r)*
roundabout	**das Karussell(e)**	*dass caroosel*
to row	**rudern**	*roodern*
rowing boat	**dass Ruderboot(e)**	*dass rooder-boat*
to rub your eyes	**sich die Augen reiben**	*zikh dee owgen rypen*
rubber	**der Radiergummi(s)**	*derr radeer-goomee*
rucksack, backpack	**der Rucksack(¨e)**	*derr rook-zack*
rude	**unhöflich**	*oon-ho(e)flikh*
ruler	**das Lineal(e)**	*dass lin-e-ahl*
to run	**laufen**	*lowfen*
to run a bath	**das Badewasser einlaufen lassen**	*dass bahde(r)-vasser yne-lowfen lassen*
to run away	**weglaufen**	*veck-lowfen*
runway	**die Landebahn(en)**	*dee lande(r)-bahn*
Russia	**Russland**	*rooss-lant*

S

safety belt	**der Sicherheitsgurt(e)**	*derr zikher-hytes-goort*
sailor	**der Seemann (die Seeleute)**	*dee zeeloyte(r)*
salad	**der Salat(e)**	*derr zalat*
salami	**die Salami**	*dee zalami*
sale (in shop)	**der Schlussverkauf(¨e)**	*derr shloossferkowf*
sales representative (m)	**der Vertreter(-)**	*derr fertrayter*
sales representative (f)	**die Vertreterin(ne)**	*dee fertrayterin*
salt	**das Salz**	*dass zalts*
same	**gleich**	*glykh*
the same age as	**genauso alt wie**	*genow zo alt vee*
sand	**der Sand**	*derr zant*
sandal	**die Sandale(n)**	*dee zandale(r)*
sandcastle	**die Sandburg(en)**	*dee zant-boorg*
satchel	**die Schultasche(n)**	*dee shooltashe(r)*
Saturday	**Samstag**	*zamstahg*
saucepan	**der Kochtopf(¨e)**	*derr kokh-topf*
saucer	**die Untertasse(n)**	*dee oontertasse(r)*
sausage	**die Wurst(¨e)**	*dee voorst*
saw	**die Säge(n)**	*dee zayge(r)*
to say	**sagen**	*zahgen*
scales	**die Waage(n)**	*dee vahge(r)*
Scandinavia	**Skandinavien**	*scandinah-vien*
scarecrow	**die Vogelscheuche(n)**	*dee fogelshoykhe(r)*
scarf	**der Schal(s)**	*derr shahl*
scenery	**das Bühnebild(er)**	*dass bewnenbilt*
school	**die Schule(n)**	*dee shoole(r)*
at school	**in der Schule**	*in derr shoole(r)*
nursery school	**der Kindergarten(¨)**	*derr kindergarten*
at nursery school	**im Kindergarten**	*im kindergarten*
primary school	**die Grundschule(n)**	*dee groontshoole(r)*
secondary school	**das Gymnasium (die Gymnasien)**	*dass gewmnazium*
scissors	**die Schere(n)**	*dee shayre(r)*
to score a goal	**ein Tor schießen**	*yne tore sheesen*
screwdriver	**der Schraubenzieher(-)**	*derr shraowbentsee-er*
sea	**das Meer(e)**	*dass mayr*
seagull	**die Möwe(n)**	*dee mo(r)ve(r)*
to be seasick	**seekrank sein**	*zeh-krank zyne*
at the seaside	**am Meer**	*am mayr*
season	**die Jahreszeit(en)**	*dee yahreztsyte*
season ticket	**die Zeitkarte(n)**	*dee tsytekarte(r)*
seat	**der Platz(¨e)**	*derr plats*
reserved seat	**der reservierte Platz**	*derr reserveerte(r) plats*
seaweed	**der Seetang**	*derr zay-tang*
second (unit of time)	**die Sekunde(n)**	*dee zekoonde(r)*
second	**zweite**	*tsvyte(r)*
the second	**der, die, das zweite**	*derr, dee, das tsvyte(r)*
second class	**die zweite Klasse**	*dee tsvyte(r) klasse(r)*
second floor	**der zweite Stock**	*derr tsvyte(r) shtock*
secretary (m)	**der Sekretär(e)**	*derr zekreter*
secretary (f)	**die Sekretärin(nen)**	*dee zekreterin*
to see	**sehen**	*zayen*
See you later.	**Bis bald.**	*biss balt*
seed	**der Blumensamen(-)**	*derr bloomenzahmen*
to sell	**verkaufen**	*fer-kkowfen*
to send	**schicken**	*shicken*
I am sending (...) separately.	**Mit getrennter Post erhältst du...**	*mit getrennter post erhelst doo*
to send a postcard	**eine Ansichtskarte schicken**	*yne(r) anzikhtskarte(r) shicken*
to send a telegram	**ein Telegramm schicken**	*yne telegram shicken*
sentence	**der Satz(¨e)**	*derr zats*
September	**September**	*september*
to serve (a meal)	**servieren**	*zerveeren*
to serve (in a sport)	**aufschlagen**	*owf-shlahgen*
service	**die Bedienung**	*dee bedeenoong*
Is service included?	**Mit Bedienung?**	*mit bedeenoong*
Service is not included.	**Ohne Bedienung.**	*ohne(r) bedeenoong*
seven	**sieben**	*zeeben*
seventeen	**siebzehn**	*zeeb-tsyn*
seventy	**siebzig**	*zeeb-tsig*
to sew	**nähen**	*nay-en*
shade	**der Schatten(-)**	*derr shatten*
to shake hands with	**die Hand schütteln**	*dee hant shewteln*
shallow	**flach**	*flakh*
shampoo	**das Shampoo(s)**	*dass shampoo*
shape	**die Form(en)**	*dee form*
to shave	**sich rasieren**	*zikh razeeren*
electric shaver	**der elektrische Rasierapparat**	*derr elektrishe(r) razeer-apparat*
shaving foam	**der Rasierschaum**	*derr razeershaowm*
sheep	**das Schaf(e)**	*dass shahf*
sheepdog	**der Hütehund(e)**	*derr hewte(r)hoont*
sheet	**das Bettlaken(-)**	*dass bet-lahken*
shell	**die Muscheln(n)**	*dee mooshel*
to shine	**scheinen**	*shynen*
ship	**das Schiff(e)**	*dass shiff*
shirt	**das Hemd(en)**	*dass hemt*
shoe	**der Schuh(e)**	*derr shoe*
gym shoe	**Die Turnschuhe (pl)**	*dee toorn-shoe-e(r)*
shop	**das Geschäft(e)**	*dass gesheft*
shop assistant (m)	**der Verkäufer(-)**	*derr ferkoy-fer*
shop assistant (f)	**die Verkäuferin(nen)**	*dee ferkoy-ferin*
shopkeeper (m)	**der Ladenbesitzer(-)**	*derr lahdenbezitser*
shopkeeper (f)	**die Ladenbesitzerin(nen)**	*dee lahdenbezitserin*
shop window	**das Schaufenster(-)**	*dass shaowfenster*
to shop at the market	**auf dem Markt einkaufen**	*owf daym markt yne-kowfen*
to go shopping	**einkaufen gehen**	*yne-kowfen gay-en*
shopping bag	**die Einkaufstausche(n)**	*dee yne-kowfstashe(r)*
to be short	**klein sein**	*klyne zyne*
shoulder	**die Schulter(n)**	*dee shoolter*
to shout	**rufen**	*roofen*
shower	**die Dusche(n)**	*dee doosher(r)*
to have a shower	**duschen**	*dooshen*
with shower	**mit Dusche**	*mit dooshe*
shut	**geschlossen**	*geshlossen*
shy	**schüchtern**	*skewkhtern*
to be sick	**sich übergeben**	*zikh ewbergayben*
side	**die Seite(n)**	*dee zyte(r)*
to sightsee	**etwas besichtigen**	*etvass*

		bezikhtigen
signpost	**das Hinweisschild(er)**	*dass hin-vyss-shilt*
silly	**albern**	*al-bern*
silver	**das Silber**	*dass zilber*
made of silver	**aus Silber**	*owss zilber*
to sing	**singen**	*zingen*
to sing out of tune	**falsch singen**	*falsh zingen*
singer (m)	**der Sänger(-)**	*derr zenger*
singer (f)	**die Sängerin(nen)**	*dee zengerin*
single room	**das Einzelzimmer(-)**	*dass yntsel-tsimmer*
sink	**die Spüle**	*dee shpewle(r)*
sister	**die Schwester(n)**	*dee shwester*
to sit an exam	**eine Prüfung machen**	*yn(e) prwfong makhen*
to sit by the fire	**am Kamin sitzen**	*am kameen zitsen*
to sit down	**sich setzen**	*zikh zetsen*
to be sitting down	**sitzen**	*zitsen*
six	**sechs**	*zex*
sixteen	**sechzehn**	*zekh-tsayn*
sixty	**sechzig**	*zekh-tsig*
size	**die Größe(n)**	*dee gru(e)sse(r)*
What size is this?	**Welche Größe ist es?**	*velkhe gru(r)sse(r) ist es*
skis	**die Skier (pl)**	*dee shee-er*
ski boots	**die Skistiefel (pl)**	*dee shee-shteefel*
ski instructor (m)	**der Skilehrer(-)**	*derr shee-layrer*
ski instructor (f)	**die Skilehrerin(nen)**	*dee shee-layrerin*
ski pole	**der Skistock(¨e)**	*derr shee-shtock*
ski resort	**der Skiort(e)**	*derr shee-ort*
ski slope, ski run	**der Hang(¨e)**	*derr hang*
to go skiing	**zum Skilaufen gehen**	*tsoom shee-lawfen gayen*
skilled, good with your hands	**geschickt**	*geshickt*
skin	**die Haut**	*dee howt*
skirt	**der Rock(¨e)**	*derr rock*
sky	**der Himmel**	*derr himmel*
skyscraper	**der Wolkenkratzer**	*derr volken-kratser*
sledge	**der Schlitten(en)**	*derr shlitten*
to sleep	**schlafen**	*shlahfen*
Sleep well.	**Schlaf gut.**	*shlahf goot*
sleeping-car	**der Schlafwagen(-)**	*derr shlahf-vahgen*
sleeping ag	**der Schlafsack(¨e)**	*derr shlahf-zakc*
to be sleepy	**schläfrig sein**	*shlayfrig zyne*
slide	**die Rutschbahn(en)**	*dee rootsh-bahn*
slim	**schlank**	*shlank*
to slip	**ausrutschen**	*owss-rootshen*
slippers	**die Hausschuhe (pl)**	*dee house-shoe-e(r)*
slope	**der Hang(¨e)**	*derr hang*
slow	**langsam**	*langzam*
small	**klein**	*klyne*
small (clothes size)	**klein**	*klyne*
to smile	**lächeln**	*lekheln*
smoke	**der Rauch**	*derr rowkh*
snake	**die Schlange(n)**	*dee shlange(r)*
to sneeze	**niesen**	*neezen*
to snore	**schnarchen**	*shnarkhen*
snow	**der Schnee**	*der shnay*
It's snowing.	**Es schneit.**	*ess shnyte*
snowman	**der Schneemann(¨er)**	*derr shnay-man*
soaked to the skin	**klatschnass**	*klatsh-nass*
soap	**die Seife(n)**	*dee zyfe(r)*
society	**die Gesellschaft**	*dee gezell-shaft*
sock	**die Socke(n)**	*dee zocke(r)*
sofa	**das Sofa(s)**	*dass zofa*

soft	**weich**	*vykh*
soil	**die Erde**	*dee erde(r)*
soldier	**der Soldat(en)**	*derr zoldat*
someone	**jemand**	*yaymant*
son	**der Sohn(¨e)**	*derr zone*
only son	**der einzige Sohn**	*derr yntsige(r) zone*
to sort, to sort out, to arrange	**sortieren**	*zorteeren*
soup	**die Suppe(n)**	*dee zoope(r)*
sour, sharp	**sauer**	*zaower*
south	**der Süden**	*derr zewden*
South America	**Südamerika**	*zewd-america*
South Pole	**der Südpol**	*derr zewd-pole*
to sow	**säen**	*zey-en*
space	**der Weltraum**	*derr velt-raowm*
spaceship	**das Raumschiff(e)**	*dass raowm-shif*
spade	**der Spaten(-)**	*der shpahten*
spade (shovel or child's spade)	**die Schaufel(n)**	*dee shaowfel*
Spain	**Spanien**	*shpahnien*
Spanish (language or subject)	**Spanisch**	*spahnish*
sparrow	**der Spatz(en)**	*derr shpats*
spelling	**die Rechtschreibung**	*dee rekht-shryboong*
to spend money	**Geld ausgeben**	*glet owss-gayben*
spice	**das Gewürz**	*dass gewewrts*
spider	**die Spinne(n)**	*dee shpeenne(r)*
spinach	**der Spinat**	*derr shpinat*
to splash	**spritzen**	*shpritsen*
spoon	**der Löffel(-)**	*derr lo(r)ffel*
sport	**der Sport**	*derr shport*
sports equipment (section in shop)	**die Sportabteilung(en)**	*dee shport-aptyloong*
spotlight	**der Scheinwerfer(-)**	*derr shine-verfer*
spotted	**gepunktet**	*gepoonktet*
to sprain your wrist	**sich die Hand verstauchen**	*zikh dee hant-fershtaowkhen*
spring	**der Frühling**	*derr frewling*
square (shape)	**das Quadrat(e)**	*das kvadrat*
square (in a town)	**der Platz(¨e)**	*der plats*
to play squash	**Squash spielen**	*squash shpeelen*
squirrel	**das Eichhörnchen**	*dass ykh-ho(r)n-khen*
stable	**der Pferdestall(¨e)**	*derr pferde(r)-shtal*
stage (theatre)	**die Bühne(n)**	*dee bewne(r)*
staircase (stairs)	**die Treppen(n)**	*dee treppe(r)*
stamp	**die Briefmarke(n)**	*dee brief-marke(r)*
to stand up	**aufstehen**	*owf-shta-yen*
to be standing	**stehen**	*shtay-en*
star	**der Stern(e)**	*derr shtern*
to start off (a vehicle)	**losfahren**	*loss-fahren*
starter (meal)	**die Vorspeise(n)**	*dee fore-shpyze(r)*
statue	**die Statue(n)**	*dee shtatoo-e(r)*
to stay in a hotel	**im Hotel wohnen**	*im hotel vo-nen*
steak	**das Steak(s)**	*dass steak*
to steal	**stehlen**	*shtaylen*
steep	**steil**	*shtyle*
steering wheel	**das Lenkrad(¨er)**	*dass lenk-rat*
to stick	**einkleben**	*yne-klayben*
sticking plaster	**das Heftpflaster(-)**	*das heft-pflaster*
to sting	**stechen**	*shtekhen*
stomach	**der Bauch(¨e)**	*der bowkh*
to have stomach-ache	**Bauchweh haben**	*bowkh-vay haben*
storm	**der Sturm(¨e)**	*derr shtoorm*
story	**die Geschichte(n)**	*dee geshikhte(r)*
stove	**der Kocher(-)**	*derr kokher*

straight (for hair)	**glatt**	*glatt*
straight hair	**glattes Haar**	*glatt-ez hahr*
to go straight on	**geradeaus weiterfahren**	*ge-rade(r)-owss vyter-fahren*
strawberry	**die Erdbeere(n)**	*dee ert-bayre(r)*
stream	**der Bach(¨e)**	*der bakh*
street	**die Straße(n)**	*dee shtrasse(r)*
street light	**die Straßenlaterne(n)**	*dee shtrassen-laterne(r)*
side-street	**die Seitenstraße(n)**	*dee zyten-shtrasse(r)*
one way street	**die Einbahnstraße(n)**	*dee yne-bahn-shtrasse(r)*
stretch	**sich strecken**	*zikh shtrecken*
stretcher	**die Bahre(n)**	*dee bahre(r)*
striped	**gestreift**	*ge-stryft*
strong	**stark**	*shtark*
student (m)	**der Student(en)**	*derr shtudent*
student (f)	**die Studentin(nnen)**	*dee shtudentin*
to study	**studieren**	*shtoodeeren*
subject (of study)	**das Fach(¨er)**	*dass fakh*
suburb	**der Vorort(e)**	*derr for-ort*
subway	**die Unterführung(en)**	*dee oonter-fewroong*
sugar	**der Zucker**	*der tsooker*
suitcase	**der Koffer(-)**	*derr koffer*
summer	**der Sommer**	*derr zommer*
summit	**der Gipfel(-)**	*derr gipfel*
sun	**die Sonne**	*dee zonne(r)*
The sun is shining.	**Die Sonne scheint.**	*dee zonne(r) shynt*
to sunbathe	**sonnenbaden**	*zonnen-bahden*
Sunday	**Sonntag (m)**	*zonn-tahg*
sunglasses	**die Sonnenbrille(n)**	*dee zonnen-brille(r)*
sunrise	**der Sonnenaufgang(¨e)**	*derr zonnen-owf-gang*
sunset	**der Sonnenuntergang(¨e)**	*derr zonnen-oonter-gang*
sunshade	**der Sonnenschirm(e)**	*der zonnen-sheerm*
sun lotion	**das Sonnenschutz mittel(-)**	*dass zonnen-shoots-mittel*
supermarket	**der Supermarkt(¨e)**	*derr zupermarkt*
to go to the supermarket	**in den Supermarkt gehen**	*in dayn zuper-markt gay-en*
supper	**das Abendessen(-)**	*dass ahbend-essen*
surgeon (m)	**der Chirurg(en)**	*der sheeroorg*
surgeon (f)	**die Chirurgin(nen)**	*dee sheeroorgin*
surname	**der Nachname(n)**	*derr nakh-nahme(r)*
to sweat	**schwitzen**	*shvitsen*
sweet, charming	**süß**	*zewss*
sweet (sugar)	**süß**	*zewss*
sweet (smelling)	**duftend**	*dooftend*
to swim	**schwimmen**	*shvimmen*
to have a swim, to go in	**ins Wasser gehen**	*ins vasser gay-en*
swimming pool	**das Schwimmbad(¨er)**	*dass shvimm-baht*
swing	**die Schaukel(n)**	*dee showkel*
to switch off	**ausschalten**	*owss-shalten*
to switch the light on	**das Licht anmachen**	*das likht an-makhen*
Switzerland	**die Schweiz**	*dee shvyts*

T

table	**der Tisch(e)**	*derr tish*
beside table	**der Nachttisch(e)**	*derr nakht-tish*
to lay the table	**den Tisch decken**	*den tish decken*
tablecloth	**die Tischdeck(en)**	*dee tish-decke(r)*
tail	**der Schwanz(¨e)**	*derr shvants*
to take	**nehmen**	*naymen*
to take the bus	**mit dem Bus fahren**	*mit daym booss fa-ren*
to take a photograph	**ein Foto machen**	*yne photo makhen*
to take someone's pulse	**den Puls fühlen**	*dayn pools fewlen*
to take someone's temperature	**die Temperatur messen**	*dee temeratoor messen*
to take off	**starten**	*shtarten*
to take out, to draw	**abheben**	*ap-hayben*
to take money out	**Geld abheben**	*gelt ap-hyben*
to be tall	**groß sein**	*gross zyne*
tame	**zahm**	*tsahm*
tanned	**braun**	*brawn*
tap	**der Wasserhahn(e)**	*derr vasser-hahn*
to tap your feet	**den Takt mitklopfen**	*dayn takt mit-klopfen*
tart, flan (small)	**das Obsttörtchen**	*dass opst-to(r)rt-khen*
taste, flavour	**der Geschmack**	*derr geshmack*
to taste, to try	**probieren**	*probeeren*
It tastes good.	**Das schmeckt gut.**	*das shmeckt goot*
tax	**die Steuer(n)**	*dee shtoyer*
taxi	**das Taxi(s)**	*dass taxi*
to hail a taxi	**ein Taxi rufen**	*yne taxi roofen*
tea	**der Tee**	*derr tay*
tea towel	**das Geschirrtuch(¨er)**	*dass gesheer-tookh*
to teach	**lehren**	*layren*
teacher (m)	**der Lehrer(-)**	*derr layrer*
teacher (f)	**die Lehrerin(nen)**	*dee layrerin*
team	**die Mannschaft(en)**	*dee man-shaft*
teapot	**die Teekanne(n)**	*dee tay-kanne(r)*
to tear	**zerreißen**	*tser-ryssen*
telegram	**das Telegramm(e)**	*dass telegram*
telephone	**das Telefon(e)**	*dass telephone*
telephone area code	**die Vorwahl**	*dee vor-vahl*
telephone box	**die Telefonzelle(n)**	*dee telephone-tselle(r)*
telephone directory	**das Telefonbuch(¨er)**	*dass telephone-bookh*
telephone number	**die Telefonnummer(n)**	*dee telephone-noomer*
to answer the telephone	**ans Telefon gehen**	*anss telephone gay-en*
to make a telephone call	**telefonieren**	*telephoneeren*
telescope	**das Fernrohr**	*dass fern-raor*
television	**der Fernseher(-)**	*der fern-zayer*
to have a temperature	**Fieber haben**	*feeber ha-ben*
to take someone's temperature	**die Temperatur messen**	*dee temartoor messen*
ten	**zehn**	*tseyn*
tenant (m)	**der Mieter(-)**	*derr meeter*
tenant (f)	**die Mieterin(nen)**	*dee meeterin*
tennis	**das Tennis**	*dass tennis*
tennis court	**der Tennisplatz(¨e)**	*derr tennis-plats*
to play tennis	**Tennis spielen**	*tennis shpeelen*
tent	**das Zelt(e)**	*dass tselt*
term	**das Schulhalbjahr**	*dass shool-hlap-yahr*
to thank	**sich bedanken**	*zikh bedanken*
Thank your for your letter of...	**Vielen Dank für ihren Brief vom...**	*feelen dank fewr eeren brief fom*
Thank you very much.	**Danke schön.**	*danke(r) sho(r)n*
That will be/cost...	**Das macht...**	*dass makht*
to thaw	**tauen**	*taowen*
theatre	**das Theater(-)**	*dass tay-ahter*
then	**damals**	*da-mals*

thermometer	**das Thermometer(-)**	*dass termo-mayter*
thin	**dünn**	*dewn*
a third	**das Drittel(-)**	*dass drittel*
the third	**der, die, das dritte**	*derr, dee, dass dritte(r)*
thirteen	**dreizehn**	*dry-tsayn*
thirty	**dreißig**	*dry-sig*
to be thirsty	**Durst haben**	*doorst ha-ben*
this evening	**heute Abend**	*hoyte(r) ahbend*
this morning	**heute Morgen**	*hoyte(r) morgen*
a thousand	**tausend**	*toawzend*
thread	**der Faden(¨)**	*derr fa-den*
three	**drei**	*dry*
three quarters	**Dreiviertel**	*dry-feertel*
through	**durch (acc)**	*doorkh*
to throw	**werfen**	*verfen*
thrush	**die Drossel(n)**	*dee drossel*
thumb	**der Daumen(-)**	*derr dowmen*
thunder	**der Donner**	*derr donner*
Thursday	**Donnerstag (m)**	*donners-tahg*
ticket	**die Fahrkarte(n)**	*dee fahr-karte(r)*
airline ticket	**der Flugschein(e)**	*derr floog-shine*
platform ticket	**die Bahnsteigkarte(n)**	*dee bahn-shtyg-karte(r)*
return ticket	**die Rückfahrkarte(n)**	*dee rewk-fahr-karte(r)*
ticket collector	**der Fahrkarten-automat(en)**	*derr fahr-karten-owtomat*
ticket office	**der Fahrkartenschalter(-)**	*derr fahr-karten-shalter*
to tidy up	**aufräumen**	*owf-roymen*
tie	**die Krawatte(n)**	*dee kravatte(r)*
tiger	**der Tiger(-)**	*derr teeger*
tight	**eng**	*eng*
tights	**die Strumpfhose(n)**	*dee shtroompf-hoze(r)*
time	**die Zeit**	*dee tsyte*
on time	**pünktlich**	*pewnkt-likh*
to be on time	**pünktlich sein**	*pewnkt-likh zyne*
What time is it?	**Wie spät ist es?**	*vee shpayt ist ess*
times (maths)	**mal**	*mal*
timetable for students)	**der Stundenplan(¨e)**	*derr shtooden-plan*
timetable (for transport)	**der Fahrplan(¨e)**	*derr fahr-plan*
tin	**die Dose(n)**	*dee doze(r)*
tinned food	**die Konserve(n)**	*dee conserve(r)*
tiny	**winzig**	*vintsig*
tip	**das Trinkgeld(er)**	*dass trink-gelt*
to, towards	**auf ... (acc) zu**	*owf ... tsoo*
today	**heute**	*hoyte(r)*
toe	**der Zeh(en)**	*derr tsay*
together	**zusammen**	*tsoo-zammen*
toilet	**die Toilette(n)**	*dee twalette(r)*
tomato	**die Tomate(n)**	*dee tomate(r)*
tomorrow	**morgen**	*morgen*
tomorrow evening	**morgen Abend**	*morgen ahbend*
tomorrow morning	**morgen früh**	*morgen frew*
tongue	**die Zunge(n)**	*dee tsoonge(r)*
tooth	**der Zahn(¨e)**	*derr tsahn*
to have toothache	**Zahnschmerzen haben**	*tsahn-shmersten haben*
toothpaste	**die Zahnpasta**	*dee tsahn-pasta*
to touch	**berühren**	*berewren*
tourist (m)	**der Tourist(en)**	*derr too-rist*
tourist (f)	**die Touristin(nen)**	*dee too-ristin*
towel	**das Handtuch(¨er)**	*das hant-tookh*
town	**die Stadt(¨e)**	*dee shtat*
town centre	**die Innenstadt(¨e)**	*dee innen-shtat*
town hall	**das Rathaus(¨er)**	*dass rat-house*
toy, toys	**das Spielzeug**	*das shpeel-tsoyg*
toys (section in shop)	**Spielwaren**	*shpeel-va-ren*
track	**die Gleise (pl)**	*dee glyze(r)*
tracksuit	**der Trainingsanzug(¨e)**	*derr trainings-antsoog*
tractor	**der Trecker(-)**	*derr trecker*
trade union	**die Gewerkschaft(en)**	*dee geverk-shaft*
traffic	**der Verkehr**	*derr fer-kehr*
traffic jam	**der Stau(s)**	*derr staow*
traffic lights	**die Ampel(n)**	*dee ampel*
train	**der Zug(¨e)**	*derr tsoog*
The train from...	**Der Zug aus...**	*derr tsoog owss*
The train to...	**Der Zug nach...**	*derr tsooh nakh*
intercity train	**der Intercity**	*der intercity*
goods train	**der Güterzug(¨e)**	*derr gewter-tsoog*
to travel by boat	**mit dem Schiff fahren**	*mit daym shiff fa-ren*
traveller (m/f)	**der/die Reisende(n)**	*derr/dee ryzende(r)*
tray	**das Tablett(s)**	*dass ta-peltt*
tree	**der Baum(¨e)**	*derr baowm*
triangle	**das Dreieck(e)**	*dass dry-eck*
trolley (for luggage)	**der Gepäckwagen(-)**	*derr gepeck-vahgen*
trolley (for shopping)	**der Einkaufswagen(-)**	*derr yne-kowfss-vahgen*
trousers	**die Hose(n)**	*dee hoze(r)*
trowel	**die Schaufel(n)**	*dee showfel*
true	**wahr**	*var*
trumpet	**die Trompete(n)**	*dee trompayte(r)*
to play the trumpet	**Trompete spielen**	*trompayte(r) shpeelen*
trunk (elephant's)	**der Rüssel(-)**	*derr rewssel*
T-Shirt	**das T-Shirt(s)**	*dass t-shirt*
Tuesday	**Dienstag (m)**	*deens-tahg*
Tuesday, the second of June	**Dienstag, der zweite Juni**	*deens-tahg, derr tsvyte(r) joonee*
tulip	**die Tulpe(n)**	*dee toolpe(n)*
tune	**die Melodie(n)**	*dee meload-ee*
to turn	**abbiegen**	*ap-beegen*
to turn left	**links abbiegen**	*links ap-beegen*
to turn right	**rechts abbiegen**	*rekhts ap-beegen*
turtle	**die Schildkröte**	*dee shilt-kro(r)te(r)*
tusk	**der Stoßzahn(¨e)**	*derr shtoass-tsahn*
twelve	**zwölf**	*tsvo(r)lf*
twenty	**zwanzig**	*tsvantsig*
twin (brother or sister)	**der Zwilling(e)**	*derr tsvilling*
two	**zwei**	*tsvye*
tyre	**der Reifen**	*der ryfen*
to have a flat tyre	**einen Platten haben**	*ynen platten haben*

U

umbrella	**der Regenschirm(e)**	*derr raygen-sheerm*
uncle	**der Onkel(-)**	*der onkel*
under	**unter (acc or dat)**	*oonter*
underground	**die U-Bahn(en)**	*dee oo-bahn*
underground station	**die U-Bahnstation(en)**	*dee oo-bahn-shtats-yoan*
underpants	**die Unterhose(n)**	*dee oonter-houze(r)*
to get undressed	**sich ausziehen**	*zikh owss-tsee-en*
unemployment	**die Arbeitslosigkeit**	*dee arbyts-lozig-kyte*

United States	**die USA (pl)**	*dee oo-ess-ah*
universe	**das Universum**	*dass ooniversoom*
to unload	**ausladen**	*owss-lahden*
up	**hinauf (acc)**	*hin-owf*
to get up	**aufstehen**	*ofw-shty-en*
upstairs	**oben**	*o-ben*
to go upstairs	**nach oben gehen**	*nakh o-ben gay-en*
Urgent message	**Dringend stop sofort zu**	*dringned shtop zofort tsoo howse(r)*
stop phone	**Hause anrufen stop**	*anroofen shtop*
home stop		
useful	**nützlich**	*newtslikh*
usherette	**die Platzanweiserin(nen)**	*dee plats-anvyzerin*

V

to vacuum	**staubsaugen**	*shtowb-zowgen*
valley	**das Tal(¨er)**	*dass tahl*
van	**der Lieferwagen(-)**	*derr leefer-vahgen*
veal	**das Kalbfleisch**	*dass kalp-flysh*
vegetable patch	**das Gemüsebeet(e)**	*dass gemewze(r) beyt*
vegetables	**das Gemüse(-)**	*dass gemewze(r)*
Very well, thank you. (Answer to "How are you?")	**Danke, gut.**	*danke(r), goot*
vest	**das Unterhemd(en)**	*dass oonter-hemt*
vicar	**der Pfarrer(-)**	*derr pfarrer*
video	**der Videorecorder(-)**	*derr video recorder*
video camera	**die Videokamera**	*dee video camera*
view	**die Aussicht**	*dee owss-zikht*
village	**das Dorf(¨er)**	*dass dorf*
vine	**die Rebe(n)**	*dee reybe(r)*
vinegar	**der Essig**	*derr esig*
vineyard	**der Weinberg(e)**	*derr vine-berg*
violin	**die Geige(n)**	*dee gyge(r)*
to play the violin	**Geige spielen**	*gyge(r) shpeeln*
volume	**der Inhalt(e)**	*derr inhalt*
to vote	**wählen**	*vaylen*

W

to wag its tail	**mit dem Schwanz wedeln**	*mit daym shvants veydeln*
wages	**der Lohn(¨e)**	*derr loan*
waist slip	**der Halbunterrock(¨e)**	*derr halp-unter rock*
to wait for	**warten auf**	*varten owf*
waiter	**der Ober(-)**	*derr o-ber*
waiting room	**der Wartesaal(¨e)**	*der varte(r)-zahl*
to wake up	**aufwachen**	*owf-vakhen*
to go for a walk	**spazieren gehen**	*shpatseeren gay-en*
to walk	**gehen**	*gay-en*
to walk barefoot	**barfuß gehen**	*barfooss gay-en*
to take the dog for a walk	**den Hund ausführen**	*dayn hoont owss-fewren*
wall	**die Wand(¨e)**	*dee vant*
wallet	**die Brieftasche(n)**	*dee brief-tashe(r)*
to wash, to have a wash	**sich waschen**	*zikh vashen*
to wash up	**abwaschen**	*ap-vashen*
to wash your hair	**sich die Haare waschen**	*zikh dee hahre(r) vashen*
washing line	**die Wäscheleine(n)**	*dee veshe(r) line(r)*
washing machine	**die Waschmaschine(n)**	*die vash-masheene*
wasp	**die Wespe**	*dee vespe(r)*
to watch television	**fernsehen**	*fern-zay-en*
watch	**die Armbanduhr**	*dee armbant-oor*
mineral water	**das Mineralwasser**	*dass miner-al-vasser*
watering can	**die Gießkanne(n)**	*dee geess-kanne(r)*
to waterski	**Wasserski laufen**	*vasser-shee-laowfen*
wave	**die Welle(n)**	*dee velle(r)*
to ask the way	**nach dem Weg fragen**	*nakh daym vayg fra-gen*
Which way is...?	**In welcher Richtung ist...?**	*in velkher rikhtoong ist*
weak	**schwach**	*shvakh*
to wear	**tragen**	*trahgen*
to wear glasses	**eine Brille tragen**	*yne(r) brille(r) trahgen*
weather	**das Wetter**	*das vetter*
weather forecast	**die Wettervorhersage(n)**	*dee vetter-fore-her-zahge(r)*
What is the weather like?	**Wie ist das Wetter?**	*vee ist dass vetter*
wedding	**die Hochzeit(en)**	*dee hokh-tsyte*
wedding ring	**der Ehering(e)**	*derr aye(r)-ring*
Wednesday	**Mittwoch (m)**	*mit-wokh*
weed	**das Unkraut(¨er)**	*dass oonkraowt*
to weed	**das Unkraut jäten**	*dass oonkraowt yay-ten*
week	**die Woche(n)**	*dee vokhe(r)*
week-end	**das Wochenende(n)**	*dass vokhen-ende(r)*
weeping willow	**die Trauerweide(n)**	*dee traower-vyde(r)*
to weigh	**wiegen**	*veegen*
to weigh yourself	**sich wiegen**	*zikh veegen*
weight	**das Gewicht(e)**	*dass gevikht*
well	**gut**	*goot*
to have eaten well	**gut gegessen haben**	*goot gegessen ha-ben*
Very well, thank you. (answer to "How are you")	**Danke, gut.**	*danke(r), goot*
wellington boots	**die Gummistiefel (pl)**	*dee goomee-shteefel*
west	**der Westen**	*derr vesten*
What is the weather like?	**Wie ist das Wetter?**	*vee ist dass vetter*
What size is this?	**Welche Größe es?**	*velkhe(r) gru(r)sse(r) ist ess*
What time is it?	**Wie spät ist es?**	*vee shpayt ist ess*
What's your name?	**Wie heißt du?**	*vee hysst doo*
What would you like?	**Was hätten Sie gerne?**	*vass hetten zee gerne(r)*
wheel	**das Rad(¨er)**	*dass raht*
wheelbarrow	**die Schubkarre(n)**	*dee shoob-karre(r)*
Which way is...?	**in welcher Richtung ist...?**	*in velkher rikhtoong ist*
to whisper	**flüstern**	*flewstern*
white	**weiß**	*vyss*
width	**die Breite(n)**	*dee bryte)r)*
wife	**die Ehefrau(en)**	*dee aye(r)-fraow*
wild	**wild**	*vilt*
wild flowers	**die Wiesenblumen (pl)**	*dee veezen-bloomen*
to win	**gewinnen**	*gevinnen*
wind	**der Wind**	*derr vint*

window	**das Fenster**	*dass fenster*
to go window-shopping	**einen Schaufenster-bummel machen**	*ynen shaow-fenster-boomel makhen*
window display, shop window	**das Schaufenster(-)**	*dass shaow-fenster*
windscreen	**die Windschutzscheibe(n)**	*dee vint-shoots-shybe(r)*
to windsurf	**windsurfen**	*vint-surfen*
It's windy.	**Es ist windig.**	*ess ist vindig*
wine	**der Wein(e)**	*der vine*
wing	**der Flügel(-)**	*derr flewgel*
winter	**der Winter**	*derr vinter*
to wipe	**abtrocknen**	*ap-trocknen*
Wish you were here.	**Schade, dass du nicht hier bist.**	*shahde(r), dass doo nikht here bist*
with	**mit (dat)**	*mit*
with balcony	**mit Balkon**	*mit balcone*
with shower	**mit Dusche**	*mit dooshe(r)*
without	**ohne (acc)**	*ohne(r)*
woman	**die Frau(en)**	*dee fraow*
wood	**der Wald(¨er)**	*der valt*
wooden, made of wood	**aus Holz**	*ows holts*
woodwork	**das Tischlern**	*dass tishlern*
wool	**die Wolle**	*dee volle(r)*
woollen	**aus Wolle**	*owss volle(r)*
word	**das Wort(¨er)**	*dass vort*
to work	**arbeiten**	*arbyten*
to go to work	**zur Arbeit gehen**	*tsoor arbyte gay-en*
world	**die Welt(en)**	*dee velt*
I would like...	**Ich hätte gern...**	*ikh hette(r) gern*
wrapping	**die Verpackung(en)**	*dee ferpackoong*
to write	**schreiben**	*shryben*
to write a cheque	**einen Scheck ausstellen**	*ynen sheck owss-stellen*
to write a letter	**einen Brief schreiben**	*ynen brief shryben*
wrist	**das Handgelenk(e)**	*dass hant-gelenk*
writing paper	**das Schreibpapier**	*dass shrybe-papeer*

Y

to yawn	**gähnen**	*gaynen*
year	**das Jahr(e)**	*dass yar*
yellow	**gelb**	*gelp*
yes	**ja**	*ya*
yesterday	**gestern**	*gestern*
yesterday evening	**gestern Abend**	*gestern ahbend*
yesterday morning	**gestern Morgen**	*gestern morgen*
yoghurt	**das Joghurt(s)**	*dass yo-goort*
young	**jung**	*yoong*
younger than	**jünger als**	*yewnger alss*
Yours faithfully	**Mit freundlichen Grüßen**	*mit froyntlikhen grewssen*

Z

zebra	**das Zebra(s)**	*dass tsayr-bra*
zero	**null**	*nool*
zip	**der Reißverschluss**	*der rice-fershlooss*
zoo	**der Zoo(s)**	*derr tso*
zoo keeper	**der Wärter(-)**	*derr verter*

Usborne Publishing is not responsible and does not accept liability for the availability or content of any Web site other than its own, or for any exposure to harmful, offensive, or inaccurate material which may appear on the Web. Usborne Publishing will have no liability for any damage or loss caused by viruses that may be downloaded as a result of browsing the sites it recommends.

Usborne downloadable puzzles and sounds are the copyright of Usborne Publishing Ltd and may not be reproduced in print or in electronic form for any commercial or profit-related purpose.

First published in 1988 by Usborne Publishing Ltd
Usborne House, 83-85 Saffron Hill,
London EC1N 8RT, England. www.usborne.com
Copyright © 2002, 1988 Usborne Publishing Ltd.

The name Usborne and the devices are Trade Marks of Usborne Publishing Ltd.
All rights reserved. No part of this publication may be reproduced, stored in a retrieval system or transmitted by any form or by any means mechanical, electronic, photocopying, recording or otherwise, without the prior permission of the publisher.

Printed in Great Britain.